Cracks in the Glass

Lynette Creswell

Published in 2016 by Createspace
Copyright © Lynette E. Creswell

First Edition
The author Lynette Creswell has asserted their moral right
under the Copyright, Designs and Patents Act, 1988, to be
identified as the author of this work.

Other Stories by Lynette E. Creswell

Fantasy:
Sinners of Magic
Betrayers of Magic
Defenders of Magic
Clump A Changeling's Story

Romance:
The Witching Hour (Short Story)

For my dad, because blood is thicker than water.

Acknowledgements

No book writes itself, and no author is published without the help of others. I have many to thank for this book seeing the light of day, too many to mention them all here. My thanks, though, must go to Sandra Fraser, my wee Scottish friend who has always shown such enthusiasm about my writing, given me useful suggestions and spurred me on even after suffering personal tragedy.

Also to Valerie Hemlin for her spirit and drive, her honesty and ultimate friendship. To my daughters-in-law Vanessa and Hannah who are up to their eyeballs in baby sick but who still insist on giving me wonderful comments on the text, with the sort of messages that keep me connected to my mobile for hours, to the point where my husband often objects with "Get off the 'phone! You've had your book time, now it's my time!" To the rest of my family for putting up with a mum who always has her eyes on her laptop. A special thanks to Alex, who's name I used in the book and who is going to make the most enthralling book trailer for Cracks in the Glass (although he doesn't know it yet).

To Joy wood, author and dear friend, who has been by my side from the very beginning, critically reading and helping to thrash out the plot and shape my characters. To my colleagues Sally Brockbank, Helen Cutting, Jill Payne, Cherisse Pymm, Gayle Gibson, Sandra Shephard, Helen Robinson, Jane Davis, Carolyn Watson, Tracey Emerson, Carolyn Hopper, Pauline Griffiths, Courtney Farrell, Jo Revill and many others for being enthusiastic, providing interesting discussion and for being in awe of the story in all the right places. To Sophie Andrews for falling in love with Ethan the first time she heard his name. To Jacqui Barwell for reading the manuscript in its final stage and for her dedication to the story that went way beyond the call of duty.

Of course, last but by no means least, my thanks must go to my editor, Clive Johnson, who polished my manuscript until it shone like gold.

Prologue

Mia closed her eyes and prayed her worst nightmare would soon be at an end. White-faced and terrified, she dug her fingernails deeper into the plastic mattress of the hospital bed.

A voice, someone calling her name, forced her to open her eyes. Through the glimmer of early morning light, she recognised the soft rounded face of the midwife. The woman was perched on a stool, half-hidden between her legs. She looked to be in her mid-forties, wore a plastic apron and a warm, encouraging smile.

"Just a few more pushes," she urged, her eyes bright and hopeful. "That's all we need to get your baby out."

Mia chewed her bottom lip, scared of what was yet to come. She tried hard not to push when the time came, but the excruciating pain which tightened her abdomen won out over her desire to keep the child inside. Her body betrayed her, for she bore down, Mother Nature clearly determined to force the child out into this world.

"Come on, love, you can do it, I can almost see the head."

"No, I don't want to… Ahhhh, the pain, I can't stand it, make it stop, please!"

"Puuuussssssh."

"I… I… can't."

"Yes you can; you must."

"No, I've nothing left to give."

Mia began to weep, but the midwife's voice grew firmer.

"I know you're tired, but you can do this. Draw the last of your energy so you can get this baby out. Do you hear me? Yes, that's it… come on. Good girl." Within minutes the cry of a newborn babe filled the air and a sob of despair escaped Mia's throat.

"Congratulations, it's a—"

"I don't want to know," Mia said. "I simply can't bear to look." The midwife hesitated but then lifted the baby a little closer to Mia.

"See, you have a—"

"Are you deaf? Can't you hear me? It doesn't matter whether it's a boy or a girl, it'll always remind me of...*him*."

Clearly stunned, the nurse continued to offer her the infant, but Mia turned her face away and simply stared at the wall. A stream of tears rolled from her eyelashes. In silence they slid down her face as she refused to take hold of the child.

"Now listen to me," said the midwife. "I understand you're emotional, and you're probably frightened too, but this child needs its mother." She pressed the crying infant to Mia's breast and then took a step back.

Mia stared at the nurse whose lips were drawn into a tight, thin line. She flicked her gaze down towards the child lying in the crook of her arm, *their* child. She cradled her baby, and felt her cheeks burn with shame.

After a few minutes, the midwife took the child over to a set of weighing scales, leaving Mia with only her thoughts for company.

Out of the corner of her eye, Mia spotted her mobile 'phone. Her fingers scrambled along the top of the bedside locker to retrieve it. Without hesitation, she grabbed the 'phone and pressed a quick-dial number.

Mia decided she would give him one last chance.

There was a moment's silence whilst the line connected, and then a voice answered, one she knew all too well.

"Mia, is that you?" She took a deep breath, her body shaking from the exertions of having just given birth, and brushed the tears away with the back of her hand, wiping her nose on the short sleeve of her gown. This was the moment she'd dreaded most.

4

It took what little strength she had left to speak to him. In her mind's eye, she could now see his face so vividly: his piercing green eyes, his cute boyish grin… She screwed up her eyes and tried to push his image to the back of her mind.

The voice spoke again, this time with genuine concern.

"Mia, speak to me, are you okay? Has something happened to the baby?"

Ignoring the little flutter in her stomach, Mia pulled herself together.

"I'm in the hospital, the delivery room to be exact," she croaked, no louder than a whisper. "I… I… just gave birth a few minutes ago, to the child you said you never wanted to see."

There was a long pause.

"I know, I'm sorry, especially after everything… Please believe me, it was never my intention to hurt you."

Mia laughed unexpectedly.

"It's a bit late for that," she said down the line. "You broke my heart and threw the fragments to the four winds. You knew what I'd gone through, how I felt about you. You said we'd be together forever, proclaimed your love for me. I understand you weren't ready to be a dad. I know that. But I really believe this baby will help bring us closer together."

She heard him let out a deep sigh.

"I've already told you, I'm too young. I've tried to explain a thousand times that I'm just not ready for such a huge commitment."

Mia dropped her head, biting back more tears. It was at that very moment she realised her last hope of them ever being a family had cracked like glass before her eyes.

"Okay, yes, I get it. I hear you loud and clear, and if I'm honest, it's only what I expected. However, there will be consequences for your actions."

"What do you mean? It was your choice to keep the baby."

A pain, sharper than any blade, pierced straight through her heart. Stung, Mia caught her breath. It was true, it had been her decision to keep the child, but what he didn't know was that she couldn't cope alone and had secretly hoped for a reconciliation.

Wounded by his words, a swell of revenge reared its ugly head. He'd said he loved her and she'd believed him, thought he was the one, convinced herself he'd change his mind once the child was born.

"You bastard," she spat, "you're nothing more than a natural-born liar. But I promise you this: no matter what happens, and whilst I still have breath in my body, I swear I will do everything in my power to make sure you never lay eyes on your son."

At the end of the line, she heard him gasp out loud.

"I... I... have a son?"

Mia took another deep breath, her nerves about to explode.

"No, that's just it, you don't. Well, not anymore. I gave you one last chance to redeem yourself, to make things right, to be a part of his life, but you've betrayed him—betrayed us both."

Filled with despair, Mia threw the 'phone across the room, full force. It bounced against the wall, dropped to the floor and smashed to pieces.

She stared at the scattered parts, as though they exposed her own tattered life. Crashing against her ribs, a wave of desolation rose up from within her, and made her heart contract. In desperation, she wrapped her arms around herself, rocking to contain the misery that now engulfed her. Grief slipped through her fingers, and she threw back her head and let out a bloodcurdling scream, her own torment rising from the very depth of her soul. A cry the midwife would later tell her, sounded feral, animalistic—like a banshee escaping the hounds of Hell.

Chapter 1

Eighteen months earlier…

"I don't understand. What do you mean: you're getting married?"

Mia stared at her mother as though she'd gone mad. "Are you serious? Why, you hardly know the man!"

Sandra glared back at her youngest daughter. "I knew you'd be difficult," she pouted. "Only last night I said to Jack you'd try and put the mockers on our wedding plans."

"Oh, I see, you're going to blame me for the fact you're rushing into a long term relationship? Dad's barely cold in his grave and already you're marrying someone else."

She thought of Tegan, her older sister, and how hurt she'd be at the news.

Mia and Sandra were arguing in the living room of their family home. Sandra was by the tall mantle fireplace, a large crystal glass of Bordeaux in her hand. Mia heard her click her tongue against the roof of her mouth, a sign of her discontent.

"Mia, why can't you just be happy for me?"

"Because I'll be the one who picks up the pieces when it all goes tits up."

"It's not like that this time."

"Mum, it's always like that."

Mia watched her mother roll her eyes.

"Right, well, if that's how you feel, then there's no point discussing the matter further."

"Fine, suit yourself," Mia said with a shrug, and turned to leave.

"Oh, and by the way," Sandra called after her. "Jack and the boys are moving in… tonight."

The bullet hit its target and caught Mia right between the eyes.

"What did you say?" she gasped, spinning on her heels. Her brain whirled in disbelief; surely her mother wasn't serious.

"You heard me," Sandra replied, tartly. "You may as well come to terms with the fact that we're going to be one big, happy family."

"Are you crazy? Both his sons are criminals," Mia cried. "Daniel's done time for grievous bodily harm and causing an affray and Jacob's been accused of sexual harassment. If they move in here then you're putting me in danger."

Sandra's eyes flashed with fury.

"Oh, so now we're seeing the truth of the matter. This isn't about me at all, or my happiness, it's all about how my decision affects you. Well, I think it's time you came to realise that the world doesn't revolve around you, young lady. I've already spoken to Jack and he's assured me the boys won't be home much. Besides, he says Jacob simply came on too strong with a French student and that Daniel was trying to protect the family name."

"And you believed him?" Mia cried, incredulously.

Sandra shrugged.

"Yes, of course. He's told me they're both innocent and that's good enough for me. Besides, if it's true about Jacob, the silly girl probably deserved it."

Mia stood frozen to the spot. Did her mother really just say that?

"You're despicable!" she openly gasped. She stared at the woman she was supposed to respect: a calculating, self-centred individual who only ever thought of one person, and that was herself. Sandra suffered from depression and could be thoughtless at times, but this level of maliciousness was new, even to Mia.

Sandra's eyes appeared to glint.

"It's no good looking at me like that. I've seen for myself how girls flaunt themselves whenever Jacob and

8

Daniel are in town. I'm not surprised, either. They're both good looking boys, and girls are always throwing themselves at their feet."

"But, Mum, what if everything we've heard *is* true, and they have done those terrible crimes? Surely you can't be serious about letting them stay here... with us?"

For the first time, Sandra's face appeared pinched.

"It's no use, I've made my decision and it's final. After all, this is my house, and my life. If you don't like it, then you know where the door is."

Mia simply glared at her mother in disbelief. Her features were hard, unrelenting and her eyes appeared to mock Mia.

"You've sold me out for a man," Mia declared, backing away. "After everything we've been through, how could you?"

"Oh, spare me the amateur dramatics," Sandra said. Her lips curled into a cold smile. "At my time of life, I can't pick and choose and Jack's a good man, regardless of his sons' reputations."

"I hate you," Mia said, and without a backward glance, turned and fled to her room.

"Oh, well, it won't be the first time," Sandra shouted up the stairs after her. Mia dashed straight to her bedside table and grabbed her mobile and purse. She stuffed them into an old rucksack then made her way back downstairs. Her eyes stared ahead, the silence shattered when Mia slammed the front door behind her.

Mia headed across town and straight for Tegan's studio flat. She'd had the sense to pack a few belongings before storming out of the house. In her heart she believed she'd never go back, not at least while Jack and his disgusting sons lived there. She cursed herself for not having seen the signs earlier. Damn it, it wasn't like her to walk away from a fight, but she'd seen her mother's temper teetering on a knife edge. Her mother had been primed for an argument and she always played dirty.

She let herself in with the spare key Tegan left under a pot of fake geraniums. Inside the apartment, she dumped her backpack onto the kitchen table and headed straight for the large Galaxy bar her sister kept stashed in the bottom of the fridge. She soon soothed her ruffled feathers, demolishing the chocolate in record time.

Bitch, the scheming bitch, getting me all riled up like that, secretly hoping I would accept her stupid proposal. Her thoughts played the scene over and over again, unable to comprehend. She tried not to mope, and once she'd thrown the wrapper away and hidden all evidence of having eaten her sister's guilty pleasure, she grabbed a diet Coke from the fridge and settled on the sofa, to wait for Tegan to return home.

Her sister worked as a staff nurse at the local hospital and had bought the flat only a few months previously. Tegan and Sandra never saw eye to eye and so it had been a blessing when Tegan moved out. Mia then had somewhere to escape to, a place where her mother couldn't get at her.

It was late when Tegan walked in through the door. She didn't bat an eye when she saw she had company. "God, I'm starving. Have you had the sense to get any food on the go?" She hung up her coat and dashed over to the kettle, grabbing two mugs, pulling a face at her sister when she realised there was nothing ready.

"The ward was so damn busy today," she explained, spooning coffee into the mugs. "Staffing was an all-time low and there was only myself, another nurse and two carers to help with twenty-six patients. I've had no lunch break, and my feet feel as though they're about to fall off."

Mia jumped from the sofa, a wave of guilt washing over her as she headed for the kitchen cupboards. "I remember seeing some cans of meaty soup in here the other day," she said, trying to redeem herself. "Shall I heat some up in the microwave?"

Tegan nodded and gave a light smile. She was a pretty young woman with long dark hair tied up in an untidy bun.

Her light blue uniform accentuated her eyes, which were the colour of jade.

"Sure, why not, but when are you going to tell me why you're here?"

"Huh, no reason, I just thought I'd swing by and see how you're doing." She reached for the tin opener, trying not to make eye contact with her sister.

"Don't bullshit me. I can see you're upset. Have you had a fight with mum again?" She leaned over and placed her hand over Mia's, giving it a light squeeze. "Come on, out with it."

Mia felt tears sting the back of her eyes, but she refused to let them fall.

"You're going to go ballistic when I tell you," she sniffed, pushing a can of Chunky Chicken and Vegetable soup out of the way. Tegan forced her to turn and face her.

"So, spill."

Reluctantly, Mia stared into her sister's green eyes.

"Mum's marrying Jack." There, she'd said it, and the minute the words were out of her mouth, she wished she'd kept her lips firmly closed. Mia had been right, Tegan was furious.

"Why the stupid, selfish cow," she declared, releasing Mia's hand as though she'd just suffered an electric shock. "Tell me, is that woman actually right in the head? I mean, of all the men she's had of late, she chooses Jack Dallison for a husband."

She yanked open a cupboard door then pulled out a bottle of cheap vodka. "Get me some ice," she ordered, and Mia leapt over to the fridge-freezer. The ice cubes clinked as they hit the bottom of a tumbler and Mia watched Tegan fill the glass with more vodka than Coke.

"I think our mother is mentally unstable," Mia's sister announced, draining her glass. "I simply cannot believe she's willing to marry Jack so soon after Dad's death."

Mia felt her pain, her distress. Their father had died just a year before from Leukaemia, yet her mother had dated an old flame the same week he had been laid to rest.

When Mia and Tegan confronted her, Sandra had simply gone all-defensive.

"Your dad told me to get on with my life," she'd insisted, but both daughters were well aware that there had been a constant stream of men and affairs throughout Sandra's married life.

"What are we going to do?" asked Mia, bleakly.

"We're not going to the bloody wedding," Tegan replied. She poured herself another stiff drink, then offered the bottle to Mia, who only shook her head. She wasn't that keen on alcohol. She'd seen how drink had turned her mother into a spiteful, bitter woman and didn't wish to end up the same way.

"She'll never forgive us if we don't go."

"Tough shit. It's shameful what she's doing, and we won't be a part of it."

Mia nodded.

"It gets worse, Jack and his sons are moving in with her tonight," she said. "That's why we had a row."

Tegan halted the glass at her lips. "So, she's rubbing salt into the wound. Strange, that's so not like her," but Mia could see the hurt deepening.

"Well, you're not going back there if she's decided to have those two goons staying with her. I've seen Daniel in A&E at least a dozen times, his fists cut up and bleeding and his eye smashed to a pulp. It's a shame no one has managed to knock some sense into him, and as for Jacob... He's the sleaziest guy I've ever met. The first time I saw him, he made my skin crawl. I've had several run ins with him in the past, but I'm not scared of him. He's a bully and likes to manipulate women but I'm too independent, too headstrong. He likes women he can break... like a twig."

Mia let out a nervous chuckle. Tegan never held back on her opinions of people; it was one of the traits she loved about her.

The atmosphere lightened and Tegan appeared a little less tetchy.

"Right, that said, I'm off for a shower." She popped her empty glass into the sink. "Once I'm clean, we can eat and then sit and watch re-runs of 'The Vampire Diaries'. That'll take your mind off mum's stupid plan for a while."

Mia watched her sister head over to the door to the bathroom, then glanced at the sofa, which folded out into a bed, aware that no amount of re-runs would take her mind off the current situation at home. Her sister now out of the room, Mia's mind wandered. One thing she was sure about was that she wasn't going to back down from her mother's demands, and with that in mind, she headed for the airing cupboard where she knew she'd find spare pillows and a blanket.

Chapter 2

Mia loved books. Since early childhood she'd always had her nose in a novel, so when she'd seen a vacancy in a small book shop in town, she'd been that enthusiastic about getting the job, the owner had been unable to turn her away.

Mia was young and vibrant and oozed life. Her eyes were bright, her face radiated warmth and anyone who ever met her said there was something wholesome about her.

At the end of her shift, she tidied away bits of rubbish left by customers, checked to see the windows were secure and then locked the door behind her. For six months she'd been helping Mrs Craig build up her business and there'd been talk of making her assistant manager. She hoped she'd get the job and was already thinking of how the owner could extend the business, like adding a coffee shop in the frontage to entice in even more customers.

With everything that had happened at home, she now needed this job more than ever, and especially a pay rise. She hadn't been back to the house since the row with her mother a few weeks before, and was now ready to make a fresh start, plan a new life for herself. Staying with Tegan had only ever been temporary and the flat really wasn't big enough for two. Although they rarely had a cross word, Mia sensed her sister missed having her own space. Not to mention the sofa bed was uncomfortable as hell and the hot water barely a trickle. She tried to pay her way in food and gave her sister a small amount of rent but the strain was beginning to show and Mia didn't wish to outstay her welcome.

She crossed the street and was met by the rich aroma of coffee from a nearby Costa. The smell made her nostrils flare and she hoped she could find somewhere to live within an easy walk of Tegan's flat. The streets were lined with tall leafy trees, most having turned a rich bronze colour. Autumn had touched the shrubs too and the cold chill in the air made her pull her collar a little closer. It was five o'clock and already dark. The streets appeared deserted, and for the first time since starting work at the bookshop, Mia quickened her step.

Her head down, she hurried between two tall buildings, relieved she was almost at the flat. She heard a noise, sensed someone behind her and quickly looked back. A shiver crept down her spine when she saw no one was there. Then footsteps, coming up behind her, made her heart skip a beat. This was a good neighbourhood, yet she was unable to shake off the feeling of trepidation. She strode on more urgently and turned a corner, the flat almost in sight, but to her horror she felt a tug on her sleeve and her arm was grabbed. Crying out, she tried to shake off her assailant, assuming she was being mugged, but was forced to turn around and face them.

"What the—"

There before her, under the light of a nearby streetlamp, towered the dark and sombre face of Jacob Dallison. He glared down at her, his wide eyes full of menace. Shockwaves coursed through her entire body.

She took a deep breath and tried to stay calm. She snatched her arm away.

"Don't you dare touch me," she hissed, but inside all she felt was the stab of cold, dark fear. Jacob took a step closer and she automatically backed away. His nostrils flared and his top lip curled.

"Listen, you jumped up little bitch, we need to talk."

"I've nothing to say to you," and she thrust her nose in the air before turning on her heels, ready to make a run for it.

"Not so fast. I haven't finished." Jacob again grabbed her, his hand clenching the muscles at the top of her arm like a vice. She cried out in pain.

"Oh, stop snivelling and listen," he said, close to her ear. "The sooner I say my piece, the better for everyone involved." Mia flinched, unable to stop a shiver of repulsion. Amazingly, other women found him extremely attractive, handsome even, but all she saw was a monster, a violator of women.

"What do you want?"

"Nothing much, just a little communication." He glanced around, refusing to relax his grip, and dragged her further around the corner, into total darkness. Mia didn't know whether to scream or try to kick him in the balls, but a part of her was too terrified.

Stay Calm, she told herself. *Don't panic and you'll be okay.*

Jacob leaned in closer, his warm breath on her skin.

"Let me start with all this nonsense about you and Tegan not going to the wedding."

"Oh, you've heard? Well, that's right, we're not."

"I think you'll change your mind if you know what's good for you. I couldn't care less one way or another whether our parents get hitched, but it appears that once they tie the knot Dad's giving me and Danny our own bachelor pad. He says he wants us to have our own space now he's settled, and I'm sure you'd like nothing more than to see the back of us. This is our chance to get out of this godforsaken town, so you'll do as I say and end these silly schoolgirl antics right now, d'ya hear?" In the darkness, Mia sensed his mood darken further. "If not, you'll receive a pre-wedding present you didn't expect."

Her confusion was further compounded when he grabbed both her arms, and before she realised what was happening, his knee had forced her legs apart. Filled with panic, she tried to push him away, but he just crushed her against the wall. She cried out in distress when something hard pressed against her thigh.

"Oh, my God, what are you doing? Get off me." She let out a shriek, horrified, and tried to break free, her fists raised, pummelling his chest.

Jacob covered her mouth with his hand, gagging her pitiful cries. "This is nothing compared to what I will do to you if you and Tegan don't go to the wedding. Do I make myself clear?"

Mia nodded, terrified. Tears of sheer panic stung her eyes.

"That's a good girl," Jacob said, and, with the tip of his tongue, licked away a stray tear that had rolled down her cheek. Mia recoiled, fretting she was going to wet herself out of fear.

A car rounded the bend, beeped its horn and Jacob shielded his eyes against its headlights.

He relaxed his grip, a little, but didn't let her go...not straight away.

"Now I've got my message across, I think it's time you went shopping for that fabulous new outfit you're intended wearing to the wedding, sis." He stood back and finally released her, but the moment she was free she bolted like a horse whipped. "That's it, run along home, little girl," Jacob called after her, but Mia wasn't listening. Blind with terror, she ran, her brain already processing different ways to protect herself in the future from that animal. It was different for Tegan, she wasn't afraid of Jacob and he knew it, but since her dad's death, Mia had become an emotional wreck and her vulnerability clearly made her an easy target. There was only one way to stay clear of her new tormenter: she must get out of town, and fast. She knew he would be true to his word, and there was no way she was going to attend her mother's wedding, no matter what he said, or what he threatened. She crossed the street to the safety of the flat, convinced that if he ever found her he'd no doubt torture her in ways she couldn't even begin to imagine.

*

She was calmer, at least on the surface, when she let herself into Tegan's flat. Her sister's shift wouldn't finish for another couple of hours, so by the time she returned home Mia would be long gone. She packed her rucksack with the few clothes she owned, helped herself to a bottle of water from the fridge and grabbed her purse. She headed towards the lounge, debating whether she should leave a note, some kind of explanation. She wanted to make it clear why she'd left so suddenly, but Tegan was no fool. If she found out what Jacob had done she would confront him and Mia was scared of the consequences, his retribution. The thought of him touching her like that again was enough to panic her into running.

The whole episode had left her stomach unsettled, so she rubbed her hand over it as she studied the flat. On a small table by the window was a photograph taken a few years previously, long before her father had become ill. She moved closer and couldn't stop a light smile from raising the corners of her mouth.

Tegan looked rather pretty in the new bikini she'd bought especially for the occasion. Mia was by her side, both arms draped around her sister's shoulders, grinning broadly. She'd been a fourteen-year-old kid having a good time, yet the holiday turned out to be the last they would share as a family. She stared down at the image and stroked the glass. How she wished her father was here to hold her right now, to help keep her safe from harm, but his wayward brother would have to do instead.

A rogue tear rolled down her cheek and dripped onto the glass. It smeared her father's smiling face and so she quickly wiped it away, drying her eyes with the back of her sleeve. She bit her lip in an attempt to hold onto her emotions. *Enough self-pity, pathetic cow*, she scalded, and scrambled inside her bag for a tissue. She found a clean Kleenex, screwed up and forgotten inside a small pocket, her mobile 'phone beside it. She blew her nose and then made the call to her uncle. She needed time away, to let the dust settle, and within minutes, everything was arranged for her to stay. Relieved, she took one last look around the flat. A stab of regret made her grit her teeth. She would miss this place, her sister…her job, but she couldn't let Jacob touch her like that ever again. She snapped out of her misery, grabbed her bag and focused on getting out of there, before anyone could witness her leaving.

Mia slept on the train, her arms wrapped protectively around her rucksack. The seat next to her had been vacant so she'd curled her legs onto it, snuggled into a somewhat uncomfortable ball and fallen asleep. The train juddered into life, crawled out of the station and towards open countryside. The wheels clacked over the points, lulling her into a deep sleep. The dreams that followed had been somewhat disturbing, her subconscious creating vivid images of Jacob and what he'd threatened to do if she didn't go to the wedding. They became mixed with the memories of that last holiday she'd shared with her father and Tegan. In her sleep she moaned out loud, distressed, but there was no one else in the compartment to hear her pitiful whimpers.

A couple of hours later, she was startled awake when a passenger slammed the carriage door as they left the train. Confused, she bolted upright and grabbed her rucksack. Mia let out a deep sigh and tried to relax. It was late, cold and outside the rain poured. She focused her eyes on the curtain of condensation across the window, then threw her bag onto the empty seat and leaned forward to wipe it away with the back of her cuff. She peered out in the hope of seeing a sign, something to tell her how far she'd travelled, but saw nothing. Taking her ticket from her bag, she squinted at the small piece of orange and yellow card, checking the time of arrival. She'd caught the 9.35pm to London and should reach her final destination just before midnight. She glanced at her watch: '11.15pm', so not much longer before she arrived.

She was bone weary by the time she reached King's Cross. She headed out of the station and straight for the taxi rank. The line of black cabs' bright yellow lights reminded her of a trail of fat bumble bees. She smirked to herself despite being dog-tired and headed over, pulling open a cab door and throwing her belongings inside.

"Where to?" the driver asked, folding his newspaper.

"Caledonian Road," Mia replied, and slammed the door behind her.

The driver flicked off the vacant sign and slid into a line of traffic. It didn't take them long to reach her final destination but during that time Mia thought only of escaping Jacob's grasp.

"Where do you want dropping off?" the taxi driver mumbled less than ten minutes later, glancing at her in his rear-view mirror.

Mia pulled away from her dark thoughts, recognised a quaint row of shops.

"Oh, just here will do."

The cab slowed to a halt and Mia jumped out and headed for the driver's window. He stretched out his hand and she glanced at the meter before stuffing a few crumpled notes into his palm. He smiled when she told him to keep the change and tipped his cap as he drove away. Mia stared after him. She was standing on a street known favourably by the locals as 'The Cally'. Indeed, Caledonian road ran for about a mile and a half north to south through the London Borough of Islington. The road was mainly residential with a few shops and cafes, including several Ethiopian restaurants. Mia loved it and all it had to offer.

She threw her rucksack over her shoulder and walked the few yards to her uncle's antique shop. Although it was after midnight, the lights were still on. The peeling lead windows revealed old curiosities and an unusual assortment of antiques. Mia felt a flutter of nostalgia. It had been years since she'd last visited her uncle's shop, although they had texted and chatted on the 'phone quite often since her father had died.

She hesitated at the door, taking deep breaths as she plucked up the courage to go inside. What would she do if her uncle had changed his mind and decided she couldn't stay? The mere thought made her tremble with anxiety, her mind's eye conjuring frightening images of Jacob Dallison leering over her body.

She shuddered, the thought of him touching her again, enough for her to push the door open.

As she entered, a small bell jangled overhead.

The shop was lit by a half-dozen tall oil lamps. She had to admit that nothing had changed. The room was warm and welcoming in its sunny yellow light. Displays of pottery, a mixture of old and new, sat on highly polished shelves, some a rich mahogany, others deep oak. Handcrafted jewellery dangled in colourful clusters and breath-taking pieces of art hung on the walls. The smell of bee's wax mixed with wood polish made her inhale deeply and she instantly felt at home.

"Hey, sweet pea, is that you?" A familiar voice called out from behind a curtain, but before she could reply, the red velvet drape shot back to reveal her Uncle Sam.

Mia gave him a warm smile. He looked well, still in his early forties with dark brown hair and bright blue eyes. He'd been the older of the two brothers, but, unlike his sibling, he'd always been young at heart.

"I thought you'd never get here," he said, rushing over, and the mere sight of him made Mia burst into floods of tears. "Hey, what's up? Are you alright?" He opened his arms and Mia flung herself into his embrace.

"Whoa, Mia, this isn't like you. I knew something was wrong when you said you were jumping on the first train down here." Mia screwed up her eyes and refused to speak, somehow managing to stop the flow of tears that threatened to soak her uncle's jumper. She felt warm and safe in his arms and he smelt like…her dad.

Gently, he eased her grip from around his waist.

"Come on, lass, let's go into the back and I'll make some tea. Then you can tell me what's upset you so much." Mia nodded and followed him into a small room that he used as both his kitchen and his office.

He pointed to a small sofa, draped with a moth eaten chenille throw.

"Go on, sit yourself down whilst I get the kettle on."

Mia wiped the last of her tears away and slid her small frame onto the settee. She felt herself sink into the old battered cushions and she dropped her bag and kicked off her shoes.

Sam was soon back, two steaming mugs of tea in his hands. He plonked himself beside her and handed her one: chipped and with the words "Too hot to handle" embossed in black on both sides.

He tugged at her hair, a playful gesture he used to do when she was a small child.

She smiled, warmed by his familiarity.

"Okay, I'm listening."

Mia squirmed under his watchful gaze. It wasn't that she was afraid to re-live the moment with Jacob. It was more she didn't want to drag her uncle into her sordid affairs.

"Is it Sandra?" he probed, his tone clipped.

Mia nodded, fighting with her conscience. *Tell him the truth…*

She frowned, knowing she couldn't.

"Come on, what's the big secret? What's she done now?"

Mia let out a gasp of breath.

"She's getting married again."

"She's what?" Sam sat bolt upright, his eyes wide in alarm.

"It's all arranged. She's marrying Jack Dallison."

Sam's jaw dropped, and he gawped.

"You're not serious?"

Mia nodded.

"So you're telling me she's getting hitched to that bald-headed creep, the guy she once met at karaoke?"

Mia couldn't help but laugh out loud.

"Yep, that's the one."

Sam pushed his fingers through his thick mop of hair.

"Well, for what it's worth, I think she's scraping the barrel."

"Huh, I pretty much said the same, but she doesn't appear to think so."

"No, she wouldn't. Is he loaded?"

Mia nodded again.

"Ah, enough said… She always was a gold digger."

Mia hung her head. What Sam had said was true. It was common knowledge she'd married her late father for his money.

Sam patted her leg, as if he'd read her mind.

"Let the bitch reap what she sows. She may be your mother, but she'll get her just deserts, you wait and see."

Somehow Mia doubted it. No matter what, Sandra always seemed to come up smelling of roses no matter how deep the shite.

"Anyway, let's forget about her for a while," he insisted. "I know it's late, but I've got something I want to share with you, an item that's far more interesting than your mother's marital affairs." Before she could protest, Sam put down his mug and grabbed hers out of her hand.

"Hey, I haven't finished yet."

"Come on, leave it," he urged, dragging her to her feet. "I'll make a fresh cup later."

"Okay, okay, what's so interesting that I can't even have a drink in peace?"

He gave her a light smirk. "Well, if you follow me, I'll show you."

He shot back into the shop and Mia followed, close on his heels. Sam headed over to a small oak veneered glass cabinet. It was filled with golden trinkets and quaint porcelain antiques. Sam dug out a small golden key from down the front of his shirt, dangling on a long chain around his neck.

"You're the first person I've showed this to," he announced, twisting the key in the lock and lifting the lid.

Mia found she was holding her breath. Sam was renowned for collecting rare artefacts, ones often steeped in history. She adored history of any kind, a passion she clearly shared with her uncle. With great care, he pulled out a tatty old letter and placed it gently in the palm of her hand. It was tied with a burgundy ribbon and she noticed the edges of the parchment were tinged yellow.

"Has this been written by someone famous?" she asked, excitedly.

Sam nodded, a smile lifting the corners of his mouth.

"I believe it's from Napoleon to Josephine, after they were divorced."

"Oh, wow, that's so cool. Fancy getting your hands on a letter from Napoleon Bonaparte. Didn't he divorce Josephine, though, when he found out she couldn't produce an heir?"

Sam nodded once again, his eyes bright with excitement.

"Go on then, read it." With dainty fingers, Mia untied the ribbon and opened the letter.

She slowly read each sentence, the script and language hard to follow, but her eyes finally devoured every word.

When she'd finished, she glanced up and stared at Sam in disbelief. "If this letter is authentic, then it means that Josephine gave Napoleon a son."

Sam pursed his lips.

"I know, isn't it fascinating?"

Mia read the letter again, once more staring, opened mouthed, at her uncle.

"But if this really is true, then why keep the child a secret?"

Sam shrugged, "I have no idea, but I reckon this parchment clearly holds the key to something dark."

Mia grinned as she handed the letter back.

"I find it all enthralling. Where did you get it?"

"Inside an old book a friend once gave me. It was a gift. There were other letters inside, none of which held any great value, but then I came across this tatty piece of velum, pressed between the pages. It's strange, but it was my friend's recent passing that made me think of this book."

"So, what's your next step?"

"That's simple. I'm going to check it out, see if it's a fake."

"And if it's not?"

"Then we're about to re-write history."

Chapter 3

The next morning, at breakfast, all Sam missed was the frilly apron. Mia came downstairs to find he'd already set the table and the smell of cooked bacon filled the air.

Mia stared down at her mobile and saw she'd three missed calls from her sister. She'd sent a quick text, late last night, saying something urgent had cropped up and not to worry, that she'd arrived at an undisclosed destination and would be in contact soon. She'd not found the courage to ring her yet. Tegan simply wouldn't understand why she'd run, believing she could protect her. She'd most likely be angry and Mia couldn't face her reprisal, not right now. As she stood in the doorway, she glanced at her uncle, stirring eggs, a soggy tea towel draped over his shoulder. His face looked relaxed almost carefree, and if she stared really hard, she could almost see her father standing there by the cooker instead. They were the same build and pretty much the same height, the only difference being that her dad's hair had been full of curls. Sadly, though, he'd lost most of them soon after the first bout of chemotherapy.

Mia slunk towards a small wooden table. There were two three-legged stools tucked away underneath it.

"Come on, sit down," Sam said, letting go of the eggs long enough to shake the frying pan. "If this bacon gets cooked any longer, we'll be able to use it for shoe leather."

Mia helped herself to juice whilst Sam scrambled about, getting the breakfast into some kind of order.

"Ta-dah." A sizzling plate of fried food slid under her nose. "That'll keep the wolves at bay for a while." He gave her a wink and grabbed the spare chair.

"So, what's your plans for today, sweet pea?"

Mia turned thoughtful, reaching for a slice of buttered toast.

"I hadn't really thought about it. Maybe I'll just laze around here, catch up on Facebook?"

"Really, well, I've got a better idea. How about you come with me to visit a friend of mine who's a dealer in historical manuscripts?"

Mia was confused. "Why would you want me to accompany you?"

Sam sprinkled a fine dusting of pepper over two bright yellow yolks.

"Well, it's more interesting than hanging around here and she'll know whether the letter's genuine."

Mia stopped munching, mid bite.

"Oh, yes, the letter from Napoleon. I thought it was just a dream I'd had last night." She licked her lips, "So, this friend of yours, she can do that?"

Sam nodded and grabbed a carton of juice.

"Yep, it's what she does. Bell deals in historical items such as wax portraits, manuscripts and miniatures."

"Wow, that sounds so cool."

"I know, and if it turns out the letter is authentic, I could be a very rich man."

Mia threw back her head and scoffed, "That's a big fat 'If'."

"O ye of little faith," Sam said, biting down into a succulent pork and leek sausage. "Let's wait and see shall we."

*

Later that morning, they headed into the city. After having taken the tube, Mia then found herself winding through the bustling streets of London. She adored the city with its famous landmarks and breath-taking architecture. It was another world, one where rich people wined and dined and celebrities got the chance to rub shoulders with royalty. How she envied those people the most. Secretly, she had a huge crush on Prince Harry—well, didn't everyone? she thought to herself.

Mia linked her arm through her uncle's as she dreamt about being swept off her feet by a handsome prince.

"So, where exactly are we going?" she asked, her head still in the clouds.

Sam patted her hand with affection.

"We're off to an auction house where Isabel…where Bell works."

"Oh, yes, your friend; has she worked there long?"

"Yes, since leaving university, back in the nineties."

Mia stared up into her uncle's eyes, trying to keep a straight face. "Oh, I didn't realise she was that old."

Sam's crow's feet deepened.

"Hey, less of that you cheeky mare." He raised a mocking eyebrow. "I'll have you know, she's pretty much my age."

"Oh, so she's practically prehistoric then?"

Sam gasped, lunged forward, tried to cuff her around the back of the head, but she quickly dived out of the way. "I bet she'll soon be put out to pasture," she further teased, keeping a safe distance.

"And you'll be on the first train home if you don't zip it, young lady." He smiled, gesturing his hand across her lips.

Mia grinned and dared to link arms once again, pulling him closer. She'd forgotten how much she missed his company. They'd always had a special bond, mostly because he was a big kid himself and that he enjoyed her stupid sense of humour.

They arrived at the auction house and made their way through a large oak and steel door. A flight of stairs stood before them which Sam took two at a time as Mia chased after him. They stepped onto a dark carpeted landing. Electric lights buzzed overhead, revealing several rooms, each having a large picture window and a glass fronted door. Mia thought the offices appeared a little modern considering the age of the building.

It was clear Sam had been here many times before because he rushed to the last door, knocked, but didn't wait to be invited in. Mia dashed after his shadow.

Inside, the room was much larger than she'd expected, the glass fronted office clearly only a reception area.

"I won't be a minute," a woman's voice shouted from behind a slightly ajar door. Sam turned and grinned, making it clear that the voice belonged to Bell. That and the fact Sam's neck was now turning a light shade of pink. *Hmm, interesting... So that's why he'd drowned himself in Aramis cologne this morning.* Mia's eyes narrowed.

As if on cue, the door was thrust open and a pretty blonde, late thirties, rushed towards them.

"So sorry, I meant to be here when you arrived, but I've been working on a complicated piece of art and lost track of time."

Sam greeted Bell with a kiss on both cheeks. "Don't worry, we've only just got here," he reassured her. He turned towards Mia, a nervous smile dancing across his lips. "Bell, I'd like you to meet my niece, Mia. She's come to stay with me for a few days." Bell dashed over and gave her a warm hug. Mia liked her immediately.

"It's lovely to meet you at last. Sam's told me all about you and your sister."

Mia raised a questioning brow.

"He has? That's news to me."

Bell's dimples flashed. "Er, yes, quite a bit actually. Still, shall we all go into the back and get started?"

Mia tried not to smirk. She sensed there was something intense between these two, more than Sam was letting on, and she was determined to make it her mission to find out what. Sam had never been married, nor had he any children, always claiming to be too young to be tied down. He'd forever been a free spirit, wild and reckless, but something had changed and Mia was dying to get her hands on any juicy bits of gossip.

They entered Bell's office. There were two desks inside, both piled high with historical papers, strange artefacts and un-opened mail. Behind them lay a multitude of bolted steel shelves, each layered with objects which appeared to be tagged, ready to be catalogued. Mia's gaze swept the room. It was an Aladdin's cave, a treasure trove of rare antiques. Her nostrils flared at the smell of musty paper. This place was simply awe-inspiring. Her hand accidently brushed against a pair of reading glasses, and before she could stop them, they fell to the floor.

Bell and Sam both instinctively bent to pick them up—whack! Their heads banged together and Mia burst into a fit of giggles, unable to hide her amusement. Bell laughed as she rubbed her head whilst Sam turned bright red.

"Are you alright?" he asked, helping her to her feet, and it was then, right there, that Mia realised Sam was in love with Bell. She caught his eye and tipped him a wink, sure his neck had turned a darker shade of crimson.

"Don't fuss, I'll live," Bell insisted, clearly flustered. She placed the glasses on the end of her nose and headed for one of the desks scattered with layers of paperwork.

"So, shall we get started, have you brought the letter?"

Sam reached inside his coat pocket and drew out the yellowing paper.

Bell scowled. "Sam, you shouldn't be handling it without gloves. If this really is the real McCoy, it'll be worth a fortune and you can't afford it getting damaged."

Sam dropped his head, reminding Mia of a reprimanded schoolboy.

"Sorry, Bell, I didn't think."

Bell sighed. "Well, no harm done this time… Okay, leave it with me. I'll need a few hours, to run tests, etcetera. Shall we say we'll meet back here at five?"

"She's rather bossy," Mia later commented, once they'd left the auction house.

Sam shrugged. "Serves me right; I should have known better and protected the letter."

"But she was rather abrupt with you."

"No, not really. She's simply passionate about her job. She works hard to protect the past, restoring relics to their former glory, and I was completely thoughtless."

Mia was secretly impressed. Sam would never have defended a woman in this way before meeting Bell. She smiled to herself. Sam clearly had it bad.

To pass the next few hours, Sam took Mia out for the day. They headed off into the centre of London and visited Madame Tussauds and the London Dungeons. Mia loved being in the heart of the city and enjoyed the smells, sights and sounds of city life. The day simply flew by and all too soon they were heading back in the direction of the auction house.

"I've only just finished the tests," Bell stated, as they arrived. "I've managed to analyse the letter, find out whether it's a forgery or not." She carefully lifted the yellowing paper and smoothed it down with the flat side of her gloved hand.

Mia realised she was holding her breath.

"So, the burning question is…is it real?"

Bell's mouth turned down into a frown.

"No, I'm afraid not. It's a fake."

Mia glanced over at Sam, saw the look of bitter disappointment spread across his face.

"But how can you be so sure?" She was grasping at straws. "Perhaps you've made a mistake?"

"I only wish I had," said Bell, shaking her head. She pointed to the test results. "You see, firstly, it's the paper. I ran specific tests that showed it to be made from wood pulp and synthetic bleach. Neither of these were introduced to the manufacturing industry until the late eighteenth century. Secondly, the ink used has a fine resin, found in the recipes of a man called Stark. He was a chemist during the nineteenth century who dabbled with over two hundred different recipes. I'm afraid this is one of them.

Mia felt her shoulders sag. Her uncle would be crushed.

"Oh well, at least we know the truth and it was fun while it lasted." Mia put on her brightest smile. "To commiserate, I suggest we go out for dinner and have a few stiff drinks, try and drown our sorrows." She gave Bell a pleading look, hoping she'd agree to tag along.

"I can do better than that," she said. "Let's go to my place and I'll cook. I've got fillet steak and a couple of bottles of Prosecco in the fridge."

Mia was relieved to see Sam's eyes light up, "Really, are you sure? I mean, I wouldn't want to put you out."

"No, you're not putting me out, silly," Bell said, waving her hand dismissively. "And besides, Mia should meet my son."

"You have a son?" The words flew out of Mia's mouth before she could stop herself.

Bell smiled, her eyes shimmering with light.

"Yes, he's a real pain in the arse, knows everything of course, but I adore him." She grabbed her coat and a set of keys from off the top of a locker.

"Come on, let's go. You've both suffered a knock back, and steak fixes everything."

Within the hour, Mia found herself back on the tube with Sam and Bell, heading out of Central London. She was surprised, however, when they came out of the station, to find that Bell lived just a few stops from Sam. Within minutes, Bell was opening the front door to a rather swanky townhouse.

"Come in, and make yourselves at home," she insisted, taking their coats. "Please feel free to wander around. This place used to belong to my father. He was a lawyer, and left it to me when he died."

Mia's eyes widened at every step further into the house. This place was beautiful. The first reception room alone turned out to be bigger than Tegan's whole flat. It was bright and airy, with an ornate ceiling and a marble fireplace. In one corner sat a grand piano, and in the other a beige quilted chaise-longue. Mia, alone in this room, was simply in awe and pondered whether the luxurious chair might once have belonged to some rich Emperor. Her gaze was drawn to a gilded mirror that sat over the fireplace, then up to a pretty crystal chandelier. This house was simply a palace.

Bell strolled into the room, a tray of drinks in her hands.

"I know what you're thinking. It's all very decadent, but my father adored antiques and filled the house with things he loved.

"I think this place is amazing," Mia said, taking a glass of wine and thanking her hostess. Mia headed over to the expensive couch and sat down, albeit gingerly on its cream fabric upholstery, afraid she was going to stain it just by sitting there. Sam came in with a small tray of canopies and she was amused by the fact he'd already made himself at home.

"Mmm, grab yourself a couple of these, they're delicious,' he mumbled. Mia shook her head, and gently pushed the tray away. Out of the corner of her eye she saw Bell place the empty tray of drinks on a small table, before heading over to a cream chintz sofa. She plonked herself down—no heirs, no graces—then kicked off her shoes, rubbing the balls of her feet.

"Damned new heels near killed me today," she grumbled, but her eyes were bright, mischievous. Mia turned her head and grinned. She liked Bell. She didn't pretend to be someone she wasn't and Mia could see Sam was smitten.

Bell tucked her legs underneath her and then patted the seat, so Sam would come and sit beside her. He didn't hesitate, Bell's pleasurable expression lighting up her face. It was then that it hit Mia. These two people had clearly been seeing each other for quite some time.

"Is there anything I can do to help with dinner?" she asked, taking another sip of her Prosecco. Bell turned and shook her head.

"No, thanks, you just sit and enjoy your drink. Once Ethan gets here I can start preparing our evening meal."

Ethan? So that's his name… Mmm, sounds nice.

"So how old is your son?" Mia asked, intrigued.

He's nineteen and currently works across two sites. I wanted him to go to uni, but my work colleagues had other plans. He has a high IQ, you see; a member of MENSA. His knowledge of history is phenomenal and my boss, Professor Hickson, was willing to help him get the qualifications he needed by giving him an Open University placement."

"Wow. That's incredible," said Mia, feeling a little green with envy. "You must be so proud."

"Yes, I am," Bell admitted. "His father died when he was very young and so I took him to work with me far more than I should have. Thankfully, the auction house became a second home for Ethan, and my work colleagues, his friends."

"Then we have something in common," Mia stated, her voice a little flat. "We both lost our father at a young age."

Bell's smile slipped from her lips.

"Yes, I was so sorry to hear about your loss. I never met your dad, but it must have been a really tough time for you."

Mia felt tears sting her eyes.

"Yes, it was. He was a good man, the best." She glanced over at Sam and saw his pained expression.

"Anyway," she added, trying to salvage the moment, "where's Ethan now?"

"Why, I'm right here," and Mia jerked at the sound of a voice she didn't recognise.

"Ethan," Bell said, "I never heard you come in."

Mia felt her jaw drop. Bell's son was delectably *lush*. Her eyes devoured him from head to toe in an instant. He was at least six foot, blonde and with eyes that were the greenest she'd ever seen, like the ocean. Not to mention that smile—dazzling. Mia thought that if she tried to stand, she would simply keel over. She had never been affected by anyone like this before, and she didn't like it.

"So, you must be Mia?" he stated, making his way over. He was dressed casually: jeans, a grey hoodie and top-of-the-range trainers. Mia opened her mouth but nothing came out and so she closed it again. He took her hand in his. His grip was firm, a sign of sincerity.

"It's a pleasure," he said, and she swore she saw mischief dance inside his eyes.

I can assure you, the pleasure's all mine...

She found her voice. "It's nice to meet you, too," she croaked, pulling her hand away. She thought he was a little young to be so formal.

"We've just been hearing all about you," she explained, trying to distract herself from his gorgeous green eyes.

He chuckled before he replied.

"Then I insist on denying everything. Besides, my mother's renowned for stretching the truth –just a little."

Everyone laughed, the mood once again light. Bell came over and slipped her arm around her son's shoulders.

"Take no notice; he's always been modest."

"And you've always exaggerated."

"Nonsense," Bell insisted. "I'm sure any mother would be proud to call you her son."

Mia swore she saw Ethan blush.

"I think that's enough wine for you," he teased, taking the glass out of her hand. Bell pouted and pulled the wineglass back. "Hey, that's mine," she said, her brows furrowed. "If you want a drink, go and get your own."

"I will, but I'm just nipping upstairs to change."

He grinned at Sam and then turned his attention to Mia.

"Are you both staying for dinner?"

Mia nodded, took a large gulp of wine, unable to settle the butterflies fluttering about inside her tummy.

"In that case," said Ethan, heading for the stairs. "Just give me two ticks and I'll be right back."

Dinner turned out to be one of the nicest evenings Mia had enjoyed in a long time. Bell was an amazing cook and the meal of steak with mushroom puff tartlets was divine. She couldn't decide if it was the Madeira Bell had used in the sauce or the double cream that made her taste buds dance with ecstasy.

Ethan proved to be great company. He made Mia almost cry with laughter with his wit and wicked sense of humour. He told amusing stories of his youth and how he was rubbish at football after being born with two left feet. There was something about him that made her feel at ease and she felt a flicker of chemistry ignite between them.

He'd come down to dinner, dressed in a crisp white shirt, beige cargo pants and brown laced loafers, his blonde hair waxed into a modern style. He wore expensive aftershave and smelt so great she practically had to stop herself from pulling him close and nuzzling his neck. She shuddered inside, her reaction so unlike herself. She was a shy girl but there was something about him that drew the wild cat from its cave. How could he make her feel this way, make her senses burn with desire without even touching her?

"Would you care to help me with the washing up?" he said after they'd eaten.

"Excuse me?"

"The dishes: they need doing, and it's a great excuse for us to go and listen to some music?"

"Sure, that'd be great."

Mia excused herself from the table and followed Ethan into the kitchen. It was as she expected; elegant, stylish, chic.

Ethan headed over to an iPod, sitting between two loud speakers.

"What kind of music do you like?"

"Oh, anything. I don't mind; you choose." She liked the way his lip rose slightly at one side: a cheeky grin that was endearing.

He pressed a button and the room filled with Coldplay.

"Oh, I love this band," she announced, pleased with his choice. "My dad took me to see them play at the O2 arena just before he got sick."

"Oh, I'm sorry, I didn't mean to upset you."

"No, not at all, it was a great night, one I'll cherish forever."

He came and stood by her. Slowly, he reached out and gently took her hand.

"I know, it sucks, doesn't it: losing your dad."

Mia looked down, felt his fingers press against hers.

"Yes, it does."

He let go of her hand with a sigh. "Don't worry about the washing up, it was all a ploy to get away from the grownups. I have a confession: we own a dishwasher."

Mia grinned. That figured.

"Come on, we'll have to at least stack the dishes for our sins."

"Sure, I can help you do that."

Together, they cleared the plates, stacked the cutlery and did a general tidy up of the kitchen. All the time, they goofed around, laughing at one another's jokes as they listened to the music. Mia couldn't remember the last time she'd been so happy. Ethan was so easy to be around and although he appeared carefree, it seemed important to him that Mia enjoyed herself in his company. Then there was the way his eyes appeared to bore through hers, and that he made her weak at the knees with just a smile.

All too soon the evening came to an end and it was time to head on home. After grabbing their coats, Mia and Sam bid their hosts goodnight. Ethan and Bell saw their guests to the door, the night air sharp, the sky crystal clear. They each hugged one another one last time, then Mia and Sam waved goodbye from the street.

"Hey, Sam," Ethan shouted, miming throwing a ball, "catch this," and Sam, participating in the joke, ran backwards. He was tipsy from too much wine, though, and wasn't looking where he was going. As he leapt, pretending to catch the invisible ball, his ankle went over the kerb. He stumbled, lost his balance and Mia watched in horror as Sam fell into the busy main road. The sound of brakes filled the air, a loud screech, then a dull thud.

"Saaam!" Mia screamed. He lay in the middle of the road, blood and bone splattered everywhere. She stared in horror at his body, part of it crushed beneath the wheel of a lorry, as her mind strained to comprehend what had so quickly happened.

"Somebody…help him," she cried, desperate yet unable to move. Stunned, she watched the lorry driver clamber down from his cab and rush to her uncle's side.

"Oh, my God," he rasped, his face as white as a ghost's. "I think I've killed him."

"No," Mia cried, tasting bile in her throat, her stomach queasy with fear. She sucked air into her lungs then forced it out, overwhelmed by dread. She came to her senses and ran into the road, dropping to her uncle's side. "Someone…please…call an ambulance."

A voice, sharp, edgy, penetrated her mashed up thoughts.

"Mia, is he still breathing?"

She glanced up. It was Ethan, white faced, standing beside her. "I don't know," she said, "I can't tell. There's so much blood, and his head…"

Ethan bent to check, but Bell pushed him aside. "No, let me." She leaned over the still body, her fingers searching for a pulse.

"It's no good, I can't find one," and her hand moved from his wrist to his neck.

His upper body was unrecognizable, blood pouring from the back of his head, a crimson pool spreading along the tarmac.

Mia shivered uncontrollably as Bell crumbled before her eyes. Her head dropped forward and she shook, small whimpering sounds finally becoming gut-wrenching sobs. They pierced Mia's heart, and she turned and clung to Ethan. "No, no, no," she wailed, "please, tell me he's not dead."

He didn't answer, the silence stretching out between them, painful, like an open wound. She stared at the vacant look in his eyes, the kind Tegan's had possessed when she'd told her of their father's death. Mia's teeth now chattered, shock setting in. "No, Ethan, he can't be gone, there…there has to be some mistake—"

"I'm so sorry," Ethan's voice quivered, "I don't think he stood a chance."

The sound of a siren filled the night air, but its distant wail couldn't drown out her cry of anguish. Then lights flashed and doors slammed, and in what seemed like a haze of activity and hushed voices, the ambulance left, her uncle's body strapped to a stretcher, a white sheet draped over his face.

Mia felt numb, unaware of Bell talking with two police officers, Mia's mind now oblivious of it all. Deep inside her subconscious, white, sterile walls of a hospital exploded before her eyes. The memory of its clinical smell filled her nostrils, the odour so powerful she was almost physically sick. She remembered the doctors and nurses talking in whispered tones at her father's bedside, heard the beeps of his lifesaving monitors. An odd sensation now came over Mia. She found herself floating, her body light, arms grabbing at the air, fingers trying to reach a door, a way out…

"Mia?"

She was snapped out of her trance and stared into Bell's tearstained face.

"Are you alright?"

She didn't speak, couldn't. What was happening? Where was Sam?

Reality hit her like a punch in the face. She gave a heart wrenching wail, reliving Sam's moment of death. She couldn't breathe, her coat strangling her, and fought with its buttons to loosen the thick material from around her throat. Bell helped her, and Mia finally rubbed her neck, relieved. All she could think about was Sam. How could he leave her alone like this? She wasn't ready, the pain of losing her father still raw. She couldn't cope; she loved him, needed him. He was her friend. What would she do without him? It had all been so quick, like a switch. Click, and the bright light in her life had been snuffed out forever.

Ethan tried to comfort her but she fought against him, refusing to come to terms with her loss. She was deeply afraid, aware she couldn't face what came next, not again, not so soon. When he and Bell suggested they went back into the house, Mia realised she had no fight left in her, no energy at all, and so allowed them to take her back. When Ethan guided her inside, the police were already there, their faces grey, sombre.

Mia didn't want to go in, afraid of what they were about to say. Bell put her arm around her shoulders, pulling her close, but it only made her feel trapped. She tried to break away, but Bell's grip only tightened as she ushered Mia into the drawing room. She carefully placed her on the chintz sofa and Ethan came and sat beside her.

Although clearly upset, Bell eventually managed to explain to the police that Mia was Sam's next of kin. One of the officers cleared his throat, his voice low when he spoke, apologetic. Mia watched his lips move, heard him say, "I'm sorry. There was nothing anyone could do. Although your uncle died at the scene, please take some comfort in the thought that he wouldn't have felt much pain. He's been taken to the local hospital…" A strange buzzing noise filled her ears, her legs turned to jelly, and then everything went black.

Chapter 4

It had been three months since Sam had died. The funeral had been a blur, a painful memory and something Mia tried hard not to think about. Tegan had been a rock, an anchor in the storm, but her mother had been a perpetual thorn in her side.

At the funeral, Tegan tried to talk her into coming home, tempting her with her sisterly love. She'd refused, point blank. Her mother sobbed quietly at Sam's graveside, making all the right noises. As soon as she could, though, she'd helped herself to as many antiques and pieces of jewellery she could carry from his shop, then left for home.

It was nothing more than Mia expected.

Probate was surprisingly swift and Sam's property and worldly goods sold off to the highest bidder. In his will, the money was to be divided between his two nieces, his only living relatives. Mia was now a wealthy woman, but the money meant nothing to her. Consumed with grief, she could not look forward to the future.

Since Sam's death, Mia had become the welcomed guest of Bell and Ethan. At first she'd been grateful, but now they were a lifeline. Her mother had since tried to bully her into returning home. Mia understood it was the money from her benefactor that was the driving force behind her sudden bout of concern. However, her fear of Jacob Dallison meant she would not yield. She was terrified of him, and what he could do to her, yet she fretted over what the future would bring if she stayed in Islington. She didn't know another living soul apart from Ethan and Bell and the last thing she wanted to do was outstay her welcome. Yet what options did she have? Leave? No, she couldn't, not yet anyway.

She heard the front door open and Bell's voice ring out across the hallway.

"Mia, are you home?"

"Yes, I'm in here."

Bell entered the living room where Mia was sitting, reading a book.

"I've exciting news. I've got you a job."

"I'm sorry, you've what?"

Bell came and sat next to her.

"Listen, I hope you don't think I'm being pushy, but I spoke to Professor Hickson about having an assistant and he's agreed."

Mia sat up straight and put the book down.

"I still don't understand."

Bell let out a deep sigh and reached for Mia's hand, enfolding it within her own.

"What I'm trying to say is that if you like, you could come and work for me at the auction house?"

Mia felt a flutter in her stomach.

"That would be wonderful," she admitted, a smile sweeping across her face. "When can I start?"

I thought after the weekend, and….there's something else. I've found you a place of your own, if you want it. It's nothing much but the rent's cheap and it's close to work."

Mia felt her smile slide from her lips.

"Don't you want me here anymore?"

"No, don't be silly," Bell said, a little too quickly. "It's just I thought you would enjoy your own space. If you don't want to leave here, it's fine with me. I just thought…"

Mia let out a gasp. Inside, her gut twisted. Leave here? Why ever would she want to?

"No, it's great. You're right, I should stand on my own two feet."

Bell tightened her grip on her hand.

"Listen to me. It's not about standing on your own two feet, it's about moving forward with your life."

Mia felt a swell of tears but refused to let them fall. Instead, she put on her brightest smile. "So when do I get the chance to see this new place?"

Bell studied her face. "Tomorrow, but only if you're sure. I'll take you to the office first, show you the ropes and then we'll head over to the cottage."

"The cottage?"

"Yes, don't you remember? Sam left me Bluebell Cottage as a gift in his will. It's such a pretty place, but to be honest, I won't ever use it. Too many memories." A dark cloud appeared to shift behind her eyes. "Besides, I did think about selling it but it seemed wrong somehow. I've had it redecorated and your uncle's furniture, his photographs and everything he held dear are still inside. I thought that if you're seriously thinking of staying in London you should move in."

For a moment Mia didn't know what to say.

Her mind flew back to the day the lawyer had read out Sam's last will and testament. Her mother had been there, expecting a parting gift from her dearly beloved brother-in-law. It soon became apparent that he'd left her nothing except one line on a piece of paper that read: "Sandra, if you think I would leave you anything, you can go and kiss my arse!"

She chuckled, despite herself. Sam certainly had a sense of humour, even in death.

"Yes, I remember now. Didn't he call it his guilty pleasure?"

Bell nodded. "Yes, something like that. So why don't you pack a few clothes and essentials and stay the weekend in the cottage; see how you feel about the place?"

"Yes, I'd like that, it sounds a great idea."

"Good, then it's settled."

The next morning, true to her word, Bell took Mia to the auction house and gave her the grand tour. She explained that, along with making copious amounts of coffee, her job would be to catalogue the antiques that would eventually be sent to auction or to a private

43

collector. The building appeared much bigger than Mia first remembered. Bell showed her around the premises before getting down to the nitty gritty of how the business worked. Mia soon realised she had a lot to learn. After lunch, she found herself with Bell on a train heading for the village of Cockmoor, beside the Thames.

Bluebell cottage was just a few minutes' walk from the station and behind an old abbey.

"Wow! This place looks like something out of a Brontë novel," Mia proclaimed.

Bell laughed out loud.

"Yes, it does have that quality about it," she admitted, admiring the view.

"How did Sam find such a beautiful village so close to London?"

"Well, he always had a nose for a bargain, not to mention a knack for discovering hidden treasures in the most obscure places." Mia nodded, aware Bell's comment was true. Her uncle had a natural talent for finding diamonds in the rough.

Bell pointed to a pretty cottage set back on its own. She handed Mia a key. "Go on then, let yourself in."

Mia accepted the silver Yale key and headed up several quaint stone steps to its low garden gate, which she opened. Before her, a narrow path led to a light blue door. Even though winter was fast approaching, she could still see signs of honeysuckle and wild roses growing along the outer walls. She walked down the path, between rose trees growing on either side.

She opened the front door and felt a shiver of excitement. This place was to be her new home. A small vestibule led into a main living area. A wood burning stove sat in the grate of what was once an open fireplace. The room had little furniture: two leather armchairs, a drop-leaf table, a bookshelf filled with a multitude of DVD's and a few personal effects. The room smelt of fresh paint and turpentine.

She headed towards a room which turned out to be the kitchen. It was small, compact, pretty much like the rest of the cottage. Mia touched the granite worktops, noticed the blue and yellow tiles surrounded by light cream walls.

"Hmm, you've got good taste," she admitted when Bell joined her. Bell grinned. "I'm so pleased you think so. I really wanted you to like what I'd done."

"Yes, I do, it's lovely. The colours make the kitchen so bright and airy."

Something outside caught her eye. "Was that a black cat I just saw running along the garden fence?"

"Hmm, oh, yes, I forgot to mention, there's a stray that lives out back. Sam used to feed it, against my wishes I might add. It's very timid and won't come in the house but you might want to give it a saucer of milk once in a while."

Mia peered out of the window and craned her neck to see where it might have gone.

"Sure, I like animals and black cats are said to be lucky."

There was a knock at the door. "Who could that be, I wonder?" Mia said, pulling a frown. She hesitated before heading back to the front door and opening it to find Ethan standing there, two Waitrose carrier bags in his hands.

"I've brought supplies," he said with a grin. "Can I come in?"

"Yes, of course," she said, pleased to see him. She stepped aside to make way, and when he brushed passed, their chests connected. He stopped and gazed down at her and Mia felt a shiver of excitement rush down her spine.

"Right," Bell announced, "now you've got company, I'll be on my way. There's plenty of food in the freezer and I've noticed Ethan's brought fresh supplies so that should be enough to keep you going until Monday."

Mia turned to her, convinced her cheeks were burning.

"What, you're leaving?"

"Yes, there's a train in ten minutes and there's no need for me to stay. Besides, I have grocery shopping of my own to get before I can enjoy the rest of the weekend."

She switched on a lamp, flooding the room with orange light. "Let's get you settled in, see how you feel about staying here. If you like it, and you want to stay, we'll get a few direct debits set up for the electricity, gas, water, etcetera, so you'll be totally independent."

Mia nodded and watched Ethan take the shopping bags into the kitchen. She focused her mind on the fact that this was the first time they had ever really been left alone together.

"Hmm, if that's okay with you, then it's more than fine with me," she blurted, grateful for her help. Bell came over and gave her a hug, then shouted goodbye to her son.

"I'll see you Monday," she said to Mia, with a smile. "Oh, and make it nine o'clock sharp. I don't want you late on your first day." She kissed her goodbye and Mia snapped the Yale lock behind her.

Shoving her hands into her jeans pockets, she scurried through to the kitchen to find Ethan had already taken off his coat and had produced a bottle of wine. Mia opened a cupboard to find it filled with cereal bars, jars of coffee and a mountain of unopened biscuits. She opened another; bingo! Glassware. She grabbed two long stemmed wine glasses and checked for dust before offering them to her guest. He in turn opened a drawer and pulled out a corkscrew, the contents of the bottle soon filled both glasses.

"I'm guessing you're ready for this?"

Oh boy, if only you knew how much...

He offered her a glass, which she took, and he placed his own to his lips. "Mmm, tastes good, even if I do say so myself." Mia took a large gulp. She didn't care how it tasted, she just needed to calm her jangled nerves. What was he doing here, anyway? Why hadn't he left with Bell? Had they planned this encounter? She believed, deep

46

down, that Ethan felt the same way about her, but if that were true, why hadn't he said something sooner?

Unanswerable questions leapt around inside her head, like jumping beans.

She took another gulp of wine.

"So, I guess you've been here before?" she said, pointing to the corkscrew.

Ethan nodded.

"Yes, but only once," he admitted. "I visited a while back, earlier this summer. We went to the old abbey and then had a day down by the Thames."

"Did you stay here overnight?"

"Yes, in one of the guestrooms...Why?"

Mia shook her head.

"Huh, oh, just wondered. Does this place have three bedrooms?"

"Yes, haven't you seen them yet?

"No."

"Want to?"

"Excuse me?"

Ethan chuckled out loud. "Don't worry, you're safe with me."

Mia giggled, but inside she felt a stab of disappointment. She'd only ever had one boyfriend, one lover, not that he'd turned out to be much good in the bedroom department. She'd suffered nothing but sexual frustration ever since and was desperate to make up for lost time. Although she was hungry for sex, she wasn't easy. It had been over a year since the split and deep down she was an old fashioned girl. Ethan was clearly different—she'd read the signs—but didn't want to make the first move. Plus, if she'd got the signals all wrong, she couldn't live with the embarrassment.

"I thought I could stay over, you know, keep you company, but if you're not comfortable with that I can always take the last train home?"

"No, stay..."

The words were out of her mouth before she'd engaged her brain. Still, it's what she wanted, so why pretend? The thought of them being alone together all night made her shiver with delight. He smiled and placed his wine glass on the kitchen counter. The light from the window caught his gaze and his green eyes appeared to sparkle.

He was so good-looking, gorgeous even, that she almost had to pinch herself to make sure she wasn't dreaming. How she yearned to be held in his arms, to be kissed by those moist, sweet lips...

"Come on, I'll show you upstairs if you like?"

She hesitated for just a brief moment before placing her own glass on the draining board.

She had to be brave; she sensed this could well be a defining moment. He held out his hand and she grasped his fingers. A little nervous, she followed him up the stairs. The atmosphere felt charged and her stomach did somersaults, Mia mindful they were alone together at last.

A narrow landing led off to three rooms and a rather compact bathroom. Ethan pushed ajar the master bedroom door and Mia gasped with pleasant surprise. She'd expected a bachelor pad: black sheets and empty beer mugs littering the bedside tables. Instead, the double bed was covered with a beautiful red and gold bedspread. Crimson pillows lay at the foot of the bed, sparkling beads sewn onto their silky material. The sash windows were covered in delicate lace, manipulated to create swags and tails. In the corner, a white dressing table held an assortment of coloured perfume bottles. A silver mirror, brush and comb set sat idly by their side.

"Wow, this room's so pretty."

Ethan drew her inside and closed the door.

She spun around and stared at it. "Er, what...what do you think you're doing?"

He took a deep breath.

"Mia, would it come as a big surprise if I told you that I wanted to kiss you?"

Mia felt her jaw drop.

OMG! Did he really just say that?

She went weak at the knees, having waited so long for him to say something, to tell her he felt the same way. Now he'd come clean, she couldn't believe her ears. She didn't know what to say, how to react, just felt so stupid, standing here like a complete idiot.

"Er, really, you do?"

He chuckled, his dazzling smile then showing off a set of perfect white teeth. He was so handsome Mia thought she might have to pinch herself to awaken from this obvious daydream. His eyes, the greenest she'd ever seen, shone like glass as they gazed down at her.

He moved closer, and with an unexpected tenderness, lifted his hand towards her arm, his fingers stroking the back of it, his touch, so gentle, sending shivers down her spine. He touched her again, caressing her skin, and her senses became alive. Her heart skipped a beat when he entwined his fingers with hers and pulled her close.

Mia didn't resist when he reached up and stroked her long dark hair. His fingers slipped to her mouth and the ball of his thumb skimmed her bottom lip, provocatively. She shuddered, then closed her eyes, savouring the moment. When she re-opened them, his gaze was upon her face and she licked her lips in anticipation.

He bent his head and she leant forward, aware of his warm breath on her cheek, unable to deny he was making her hot and steamy. The chemistry between them was suddenly explosive and Mia struggled to hold back her desire. She wanted him so badly, her yearning so powerful that her body ached with sexual tension. His eyes grew wide with lust and she leaned in even closer. Gently, he held her chin before his lips crushed down on hers, his mouth warm and enticing.

The first kiss was deep, hard, needy. Mia gasped for breath when they finally pulled apart, her own lips swollen with passion. He smiled sexily, and she put her arms around his neck, her mouth nuzzling his throat. She caught a whiff of his cologne; God he smelt good.

With one arm wrapped around her waist, he tucked the other under her legs and lifted her off the floor, carrying her to the bed, where he laid her down. The muscles in her belly quivered. Alive with passion, she wanted him to possess her. The moment she'd dreamt of a thousand times was finally here and she desperately needed to be touched. He bent over and kissed each breast though her flimsy clothing. The pulse in her neck quickened. Stimulated, her lust ignited deep down in her belly and ran like a burning fire straight between her thighs.

His kisses became urgent, wanting more. Her fingers were quick to unbutton his shirt, to unfasten the belt on his trousers. They dropped to the ground and she stared at his black Calvin Kline boxers, tugging playfully at the elastic waistband until he slid them down and kicked them off. Mia's gaze devoured his manhood; she couldn't wait to feel him inside her.

Phwoah! Where have you been all my life?

She dragged her gaze up towards his upper torso. She could see he worked out: firm chest, arms that rippled with muscles. Not too much bulk—he was certainly no Arnold Schwarzenegger. Mia thought he looked like a Greek God and a moan of pleasure escaped her lips. She pulled him closer, and Ethan almost ripped off her skimpy top. Her jeans were next, then her bra and panties, all soon strewn across the floor.

They kissed, hungry for one another, but then Ethan pulled away, reached back for his jeans, scrambled for his wallet. He pulled out something small and silver and Mia helped him tear open the packet.

A wintry sun streamed through the window as they made love for the first time. It was an intense and passionate lovemaking, far more fulfilling than Mia could ever have imagined. She couldn't touch him, let alone kiss him, without her desire again igniting like a bonfire. Afterwards, when they lay in each other's arms, Mia came to the conclusion that being with Ethan was so much more than she could ever have dreamt of.

Chapter 5

All too soon the weekend was over and Ethan had to catch the early train home. Mia watched him leave, aware he needed to do more than just change his clothes. He had to come clean to Bell about their new relationship. She guessed his mother would not be surprised, after all, she'd already hinted that she'd sensed some chemistry between them. They'd both denied it of course, even laughed at her, but now they themselves had to admit their true feelings for each other. She still couldn't believe he'd stayed all weekend. He'd been unable to prise himself from her body and boy how she'd enjoyed every delicious moment they'd shared together. She understood that Ethan would head over to the Institute of Historical Research first thing, where he studied part-time. Mia was still in awe of him. He was so intelligent yet grounded, working at the auction house and travelling to the institute on a daily basis. Even though he was smart, he never made her feel stupid or inadequate. Instead, over the past two days they'd talked for hours, about family, their loss, history, music, who inspired them the most…the list had been endless, their bond quickly unbreakable.

She boarded the 8.15 train to London then caught the tube, which pretty much dropped her off at work. She headed on through the bustling streets, her thoughts filled with Ethan and when she'd get a chance to see him again. She admitted to herself she was obsessed with him, drugged by the novelty of endless hours of lovemaking. His kisses were intoxicating and she adored the smell and feel of his body.

She pushed open the doors to the Auction House and climbed the stairs. Just as she reached the top, her mobile went off.

"Hi, Tegan, bad timing. I'm just heading into the office. It's my first day."

"Mia, we need to talk."

"Oh, why, what's wrong?"

"It's Jacob, he's asking questions, throwing his weight around."

Mia felt her stomach do a somersault.

"What…what…do you mean?"

"He paid me a visit last night. Got a little heavy, but thankfully Jonas, one of the staff nurses from the ward, had popped round for coffee."

Mia tried not to panic, to stay in control.

"So what did he want…exactly?"

"He came here looking for you. God knows why, you haven't been here for months, but mum clearly doesn't talk to him. At first he pretended he'd called round to remind us the wedding's in two weeks and to ask what time we needed picking up in the car? When I explained you don't live here anymore, he got quite pissy. I tried to calm him but he said you'd agreed to go to the ceremony and that he'd be true to his word if you didn't turn up. Mia, has he threatened you? Is that the reason you ran away?"

Mia couldn't speak. She thought if she tried she might just vomit.

She sat down on the stairs, pushed her fingers through her long hair and tried to think clearly.

"You haven't told him where I live, have you?"

"No, I'm not that stupid, and mum doesn't know you've moved into the cottage, so don't fret about that. Mia, if he's threatened you, you need to go to the police."

"Oh, is that the time? I've got to go or I'll be late for work." She disconnected the call, switched off the mobile and stuffed it into her jacket pocket.

Her nerves were shaken. What should she do? She couldn't go back for the wedding, but then, perhaps it would be better if she did. Tegan wouldn't like it but they'd have both made a point, tried to make a stand at least. Clearly their protest had fallen on deaf ears. Her mother was still marrying Jack Dallison even if it did mean losing both her daughters. Mia knew when she was beaten. If she went to the ceremony, she'd meet Jacob's demands and he'd then leave her alone, so she could forget that godforsaken town forever and never return. She warmed to the idea, saw logic in her decision. Yes, she'd ring Tegan tonight, explain the situation and talk her into going with her. It wouldn't be easy, not without revealing Jacob's sinister hold over her. She shivered; she'd have to make it convincing. If Tegan saw through her plan, it would be a complete disaster

With her mind made up, Mia headed into the office. Bell was on hand, ready to show her what to do, as promised. She guided Mia, helped her find her way around, for which Mia was grateful. She was surprised to find she wasn't the only assistant in the auction house. She was introduced to Angel, Felicity and an undergraduate student called Jonathan. They were all pretty similar in age and she soon found out that Felicity and Jonathan were an item. Whenever possible, they disappeared for a spot of canoodling, much to Bell's frustration. Angel, on the other hand, was single. She dressed like a goth and wore thick black eyeliner and half a dozen studs in her ears. Her smile, though, was stunning and she made Mia very welcome. Mia warmed to her immediately.

"Don't worry, we're all crazy in here so I'm sure you'll fit right in," she assured Mia with a grin. She had short purple hair and a ring through her nose. Mia admired her. She had style and wasn't afraid of showing off her personality, unlike herself.

The morning rolled along swiftly, and much to her delight, Ethan popped in to say "Hi" at lunchtime.

Mia caught Bell giving her son a knowing smile.

"Oh, so the wanderer finally returns," she said, pulling on her coat. "Mia said she was taken with the cottage. I wonder if you had anything to do with that?"

Ethan gave her a lazy smile.

"Well, I showed her around, made her see what she'd been missing staying at yours."

Bell chuckled heartily. "Oh, I see, so my place sucks?"

"No, not at all," Mia quickly butted in, but Bell laughed.

"I'm just happy you've decided to stay. As far as I'm concerned, the cottage should have been left to you but, well, there you go. Anyhow, it's lunchtime and I'm hungry so I'm off to Subway to grab myself something to eat. Can I get you two anything?"

Ethan grinned broadly.

"That would be great; I'm famished. No disrespect to Mia, but I burned off too many calories over the weekend. It must have been mowing the lawn and being the general handyman that did it." Ethan's gaze rested on Mia and she felt her cheeks burn. She wanted to berate him, knowing full well that Bell was aware she didn't own a mower, but she had to admit, he was certainly handy. She smiled despite herself, knowing he was teasing her but deep down liking it.

Bell smiled and grabbed her bag. "Okay, don't tell me, the usual for Ethan, but what about you, Mia?

"Oh… I'll have a spicy Italian six-inch sub, only easy on the mayo, please."

Bell chuckled again. "So you both like the same sub; why am I not surprised."

Mia lifted an eyebrow.

Bell left with a wave of her hand and Ethan came straight over and pulled Mia close.

"I'm glad she's gone. I've been dying to do this all morning." He bent his head and kissed her hungrily on the lips. "Hmmm, you still taste real good," he murmured, huskily.

Mia's body melted. She felt so alive in his arms, her whole being on fire.

"Let's make babies?" he whispered softly in her ear.

"Seriously, are you insane?" She giggled, aware he was simply trying to get into her knickers. Not that she would mind, but this was certainly not the time or place.

He nuzzled her neck and chuckled. "Why not? I've always wanted a boy, a cute little mini-me."

Before she could reply, she heard the door open and jumped back in surprise to see an elderly gentleman standing in the doorway: white hair, watery blue eyes and skin the colour of pale mustard.

"Oh, hello, Professor Hickson," Ethan said, awkwardly. He wiped his lips with the back of his hand and looked a little guilty. "We were just…"

"Yes, I can see what you were doing. I'm not blind."

The professor entered the office, his face devoid of humour. He let out a heavy sigh and cast Mia what she thought was a look of distaste. "Listen, what you do in your own free time is no concern of mine. Tell your mother I have this mountain of paperwork I wish her to attend to. I'm heading over to my office, so she can find me there when she's ready."

"Yes, sir, I'll tell her."

The professor handed him a huge bundle of correspondence.

"Good. Make sure she gets these and I'll see you back at the Institute tomorrow morning."

Without a backward glance, he left.

"Huh, well, nice to meet you too."

Ethan dropped the pile of paperwork onto Bell's desk.

"Oh, don't mind him, he's old school. Thinks everyone's here just to work."

"So, aren't they?"

Ethan smirked, "We all need a little fun, after all, all work and no play…"

He grabbed her gently, his fingers sliding down her cheek.

Bang! The door flew open and Bell barged in.

"So that's two spicy Italian subs, easy on the mayo as requested."

Ethan rolled his eyes and let Mia go, causing her to suffer a fit of the giggles.

Bell stared back at them, bewildered.

"What?"

Ethan grabbed the sandwich bags out of her hand and passed one to Mia.

"Nothing. Forget it. Everything's fine." He tugged at Mia's sleeve and they headed towards two computer chairs. Ethan unwrapped his sandwich and took a huge bite.

"You're eating as though you haven't eaten for weeks," Mia said under her breath.

Ethan grinned, a slice of lettuce sticking out of the side of his mouth.

"Don't worry, I'm only starved of one thing." He tipped her a wink and Mia thought her heart would burst with happiness.

*

Later, that evening, Bell helped Mia move the rest of her belongings into the cottage. It didn't take long; she didn't have much in the way of possessions but already the place felt like home. Once she was alone, Mia rang Tegan. She'd had it all planned out in her head, what she would say, but when she was actually on the 'phone, it didn't come out quite the way she'd hoped.

"What? Are you out of your tiny frigging mind?" Tegan fired back. "Tell me, honestly, have you been taking drugs?"

Mia squirmed in her armchair. Tegan knew her better than anyone and there was no way she could pull the wool over her eyes.

"Yes, I know what I said, but I've been thinking. If we don't go, it'll only cause more bad feeling, create a huge rift."

"Since when did that matter? And besides, she's not exactly mother-of-the-year so who cares?"

"I hear what you're saying, but dad would be so disappointed in us. He raised us better than this. He would want us to support her regardless of whether we agree or not."

There was a long pause…

"I don't understand what's got into you. The last time we met you couldn't bear being in the same room as her and now you're acting as though you want to be best buddies? I may be a lot of things, Mia, but I'm not stupid. What's really going on here?"

"Nothing, I just think we should try and keep the peace."

"By which you mean keep Jacob sweet?"

God-damn-it, why did she always have to hit the nail right on the proverbial head.

"No, of course not. It's mum I'm thinking about."

"Sure you are. Now I know you're lying."

"Look, just do this one thing for me and I promise I'll never ask another favour of you again. Regardless of how we feel, we should be there."

Another long pause…

"Okay, I'll go, but only because you asked me. As far as I'm concerned, you're going because you're scared of Jacob Dallison, and if I find out my hunch is right, I'll cut his balls off and use them as earrings."

Mia swallowed. Considering her sister was a nurse, caring for the sick and infirm, she did appear a little sadistic at times. "Look, let me ring mum and tell her the good news. I'm sure deep down she'll be pleased, no matter how frosty the reception might be to begin with."

"You always were a soft touch."

If only you knew the truth, Mia thought with a shudder.

Much to her surprise, Sandra was simply delighted when Mia called and told her the good news. She gushed down the 'phone when Mia explained that both her daughters were willing to attend the wedding after all.

"Darling, I knew you'd come to your senses. I was only saying to Jack last night that the day simply wouldn't be the same without my girls."

Mia knew she was bullshitting. She couldn't have cared less whether either of her daughters attended the ceremony, but Mia didn't bite. Instead, she made all the right noises, made her mother believe she was happy for her to marry Jack.

"Yes, well, it's your decision at the end of the day, and who are we to hold you back. Tegan wants you to be happy just as much as I do." The lie caught in her throat. Her mother was totally oblivious.

"That's just wonderful; you've made my day. Now, although I'm not having bridesmaids, I have ordered you both outfits that I want you to wear."

"Er, what outfits? You didn't say anything about any outfits before."

"Oh, it was all Jacob's idea. He said you would change your mind about coming and he was right. Of course, I've always wanted you to be a part of my special day, so please don't start pouting and upset me now. The dresses are on order and we're running out of time. I understand it's short notice but could you make it up from London at the weekend, just so we can have a fitting? It won't take long and we can go out for dinner; just the four of us."

"The four of us?"

Yes, silly. You, me, Tegan and Jack."

Mia relaxed and tried to hide the suspicion in her voice. Her fear of Jacob was making her paranoid. She really didn't want to leave the safety of the cottage or cancel her date with Ethan, which she'd only just arranged. However, if she wanted to keep the peace, there was nothing she could do. If she said "No", it would only cause a fight.

"Yes, okay, I'll be there, but I'm leaving early Sunday morning."

"That's fine, dear. I have golf first thing and wouldn't want to be late for the Country Club."

Mia sighed. Some things never changed.

The rest of the week flew by. She didn't see as much of Ethan as she would have liked due to his commitments and studies. At work, she found that Angel was a fun person to be around and that Felicity and Jonathan were thinking of moving in together. Before she knew it, Saturday morning raised its cloudy head and Mia was back on the train, heading north.

To her delight, Tegan was there to meet her off the train.

As soon as Mia opened the passenger door and stepped onto the platform, she heard her familiar voice calling out her name. She glanced up to see her sister wave, a huge bright smile spread across her face. Mia grinned. She'd missed Tegan so much and it was lovely to see her again.

She dashed through the throng of passengers, pushing past those who were happy to dawdle. "Mia, you're here. And on time." Tegan hugged her tightly and Mia had to laugh.

"Steady on, you're throttling me."

Tegan finally let go and held her at arm's length. "You look much better than the last time I saw you."

"Well, that's hardly surprising considering the circumstances at the time."

Tegan linked arms, then pulled her towards the exit. "Is everything settled now, I mean with the let of the cottage and everything?"

"Yes, I've moved in and I adore the location. It's close enough to the city that I don't feel out on a limb, and it's just a couple of tube stops from work."

"Ah, work. Such a dirty word. How's that going, and more importantly, how's that gorgeous man of yours? I was so pleased to hear you two had hitched up together. I remember him from the funeral, and even then I could see he only had eyes for you."

Mia blushed and raised an eyebrow.

"He's fine, mighty fine if you want to know the truth." They both burst into fits of giggles as Tegan manoeuvred Mia over to where her car was parked.

"Tell me all about him. I'm dying to know everything, but first we need to meet mum at the dressmakers. She's booked us in for the 3.00 pm slot so we may as well just drive straight there."

Mia nodded, dropped her overnight bag onto the back seat and then got in on the passenger side. Tegan was soon at the helm, heading them into the centre of town. The roads were busy, a typical Saturday afternoon, and Tegan drove like she did everything in life, with fire in her belly.

"Hey, stay in your own lane, moron," she cried when a red Chrysler cut across the car in front. It then swerved back, causing her to brake—hard. "Stupid prick!" she yelled, brows furrowed. She thrust her middle finger towards the windscreen then beeped her horn.

Mia rolled her eyes.

"Calm down or you'll be the one to cause an accident. You're driving like a loon. Haven't you heard of road rage?"

Tegan chuckled and put her foot on the accelerator. "Road rage? Seriously?" she scoffed. "Don't be silly, I'm a good driver; the best."

With a flick of the indictor, she swerved off the main road and down a cobbled street. She practically did a handbrake turn to get the car parked right outside the shop.

"Here we are," she said, grabbing her purse. "All safe and sound and in one piece."

Only just, thought Mia as she stepped out of the car and onto the pavement.

The shop was situated along the High Street, its windows filled with elegant gowns and beautiful wedding dresses.

Mia whistled through her teeth.

"Those look a bit pricey," she commented, aware most were designer labels.

Tegan held the door open for her. "Are you really surprised? Only the best will do for our dear mother."

They were soon ushered upstairs by a rather glamorous shop assistant, where a glass of wine was thrust into their hands.

"Darlings, you've arrived on time." Sandra rushed over and gave them both a peck on the cheek. She was dressed elegantly, as ever: pearls around her throat, her skirt cut just above the knee, showing off her long slender legs. There was no denying she was quite a catch for her age.

She pointed a manicured finger towards the changing rooms. "Your outfits are hanging up in there, so off you go and try them on."

"Still a bossy cow, I see," Tegan muttered under her breath. Mia caught her eye and they both grinned at one another.

"What was that, dear?" Sandra asked with a frown. "Are you trying to be difficult already?"

Tegan didn't reply. Instead, she shrugged her shoulders and made her way into the large cubicle. Mia swiftly followed, drawing the curtain over so they couldn't be seen.

"Just ignore her, and don't bite; you know what she's like."

"Yeah, only too well. She's a pampered bitch and it makes me sick."

Mia sighed. "Let's just get through today. We're almost at the last hurdle."

Tegan didn't reply, too busy unzipping the bag which contained her dress. The material was silky, the colour of champagne. Her face lit up with pure delight.

"Hmm, this shade's gorgeous," she said, admiring the material.

Mia couldn't agree more. The dress was simply beautiful. It had a princess scoop neck, the bodice covered in beaded sequins and decorated with pretty Tulle lace. It fell just below the knee with a swirl of netting underneath. Her gaze caught sight of matching heels.

Mia couldn't wait to try them all on. Within seconds, both sisters were dressed and twirling around the dressing room, smiling and admiring themselves in the mirror.

"You both sound pleased," Sandra called out. "Come on, let's see if they fit."

Mia threw back the curtain, her warm smile radiating happiness. "It's beautiful and fits like a glove," she confessed, smoothing the material with her hands. She had seen how the colour complimented her big brown eyes, made her dark hair look striking against her pale skin.

Sandra clapped her hands with glee and the shop assistant cooed encouragingly by her side. Sandra fussed over the girls, eager to ensure their dresses fitted perfectly. "I think Tegan's needs a slight nip in the waist," she declared, gathering the silky cloth to prove a point. The shop assistant grabbed her pins and began to tuck, fold and manipulate the material.

"Remember I need to breath," Tegan protested, and in the distance the shop bell tinkled.

A few moments later, a gruff male voice caught their attention.

Mia turned, expecting to see a stranger, but to her horror saw Jacob standing there, gloating.

Mia gasped, her hand flying to her throat.

"Long time no see, babe." He gave her a wolfish grin. "I have to say you look very tasty in that dress." His eyes devoured her in an instant. Mia backed away, afraid of him even with other people in the room. He was dangerous and she knew it. Her heart skipped a beat when the memory of his rough hands touching her skin came to the forefront of her mind. She closed her eyes, but all she could recall was being thrust against a wall, his fingers pressed into her thigh. She opened her eyes to see him licking his lips; the gesture made her stomach turn.

Tegan came to her rescue.

"What are you doing here? I don't remember sending out any invitations."

His eyes shifted, whilst his mouth turned down into a hard line.

"What's it to you? Still on your high horse? Think you're a cut above me, princess?"

His laugh was brittle, mocking.

"That's enough, you two," Sandra interrupted. "Where's your father? He said he'd meet me here?"

Jacob shoved his hands into his jeans pockets and turned to face her.

"Don't panic. He's on his way. He asked me to let you know that he's running a little late and will meet you at the restaurant."

"Oh, I see. In that case, there's no need for you to hang around, I'll see you next Saturday, at the wedding."

Jacob gave a nod and took a step back. "Okay, next week it is, then. I'll pick you up at twelve o'clock, Cinderella?" He winked at Mia and gave her a predatory smile. Mia shivered. Did that idiot really expect her to agree to get into a car with him, alone?

"Mia won't be travelling anywhere by herself," Tegan interjected. "We'll arrive at the wedding together, so you can pick us both up at twelve." Before he could reply, she grabbed Mia's hand and dragged her into the dressing room and out of sight.

*

On Sunday morning, Mia caught the first train back to London. The weekend hadn't been unpleasant, but seeing Jacob had brought her loathing of him back to the surface.

It was early evening by the time she approached her home. She'd left the station and climbed the hill to see the pale glow of a lamp in the downstairs window. She smiled to herself; Ethan was waiting for her, just as she'd hoped. Her step quickened, relieved at the thought that she wouldn't be alone tonight. She lifted the latch to the small wooden gate and went up the path to Bluebell cottage. Opening the front door, she allowed the tension in her shoulders to melt away. She was safe now. No more Jacob for a few days at least.

She kicked her overnight case into a corner and closed the door behind her.

"Hey, how did it go?" Ethan met her with a long kiss and a beer. She put her arms around his neck and drew him close. Stuff the beer, she thought, she needed to touch him, to hold him close.

He pulled away, his eyes searching hers.

"Was it really that bad?" She didn't reply, but grabbed the beer and dropped into an armchair, throwing back her head and closing her eyes.

She felt Ethan sit beside her and she held out her hand.

His fingers entwined with hers and she let out a sigh.

"No, it wasn't so bad, but I'm glad it's the wedding this weekend and it'll all soon be over."

"You going back Friday, after work?"

"Yep, for my sins."

She lifted her head and gazed into his eyes. He gave her a sexy smile.

"So we'd better make the most of the time we have together."

Mia grinned.

"Honestly, is that all you ever think about?"

He laughed and took a swig of his beer.

"What else, and how can you expect me to think otherwise when you're so beautiful?"

Mia felt a warm glow inside.

"Mum said I can bring a friend, you know, to the wedding."

Ethan sighed. "I'd love to go with you, but I have a twenty-thousand-word assignment I need to finish by Monday. Normally it wouldn't be a problem but with me being here so often..." He lunged forward and kissed her mouth. "Well, I have been just a teeny weeny bit distracted of late."

He turned, placed her beer bottle onto the table and dropped to his knees, kneeling between her thighs.

"What are you doing?" Mia asked, but she could see a twinkle in his eye.

He pulled her gently off the chair. She giggled as she slid on top of him, straddling him. His arms wrapped around her waist, his hands stroking her back, her own hands feeling the muscles beneath his shirt.

He laid her down on the floor and pressed himself against her. She could feel he was already hard.

"What, here on the carpet?" she said, aroused.

He leaned closer and nuzzled her neck.

"Yes, baby, right here, right now."

"Hurry," she whispered, kissing his mouth and quivering inside. "I've missed you more than you could ever know."

Chapter 6

For the record, and despite herself, Mia thought her mother looked beautiful on her wedding day. The venue, a swanky local hotel, was simply perfect. The ceremony had gone without a hitch and Sandra Stevens was now Mrs Jack Dallison.

Tegan and Mia sat in a large ballroom that had been transformed with exquisite taste into Sandra's dream wedding reception. Each of the tables oozed with style. A large glass vase placed at the centre, held a handful of pebble sized crystals, showcasing at least a half dozen stems of crisp white lilies. The flowers were magnificent, boasting large trumpet heads and orangey yellow centres. Everything about the wedding shouted elegance, and of the bride and groom having copious amounts of money. The sashes on the chairs were the same colour as Mia's dress and the tables were laid with polished silver cutlery and cut glass crystal.

There were at least two hundred guests mingling around, most of whom Mia had never met. It was obvious they were Jack's side of the family; Mia's own having pretty much all died off over the last few years.

She moved over to the bar to get herself a drink. She'd already had a few flutes of champagne and wanted something a little more fun. She ordered Malibu.

Turning, she caught sight of Tegan dancing with her new boyfriend, Jonas. He was deliciously tall, dark and rather handsome. She smiled, watching their relationship blossom, glad to see her sister so happy. She liked Jonas, sensed they were a good match.

"Can I buy you a drink?"

She turned sharply but relaxed a little when she realised it was Daniel, Jacob's younger brother.

"No, thanks, I've already got one." She shook her glass, the ice tinkling as though to prove the point.

He nodded, then caught the bartender's eye. "Another one for young missy here, and I'll have a Whisky, on the rocks." Before she could refuse, he held up his hand. "It's just a peace offering. I understand Jacob's been a little rough on you lately."

Mia took a large gulp of her drink.

"Rough? That's pretty much an understatement."

"I don't always agree with his tactics, but we were both getting a little desperate. You know how it is; you start to get cabin fever when there's no escape."

Mia simply stared at him, the alcohol in her system making her mouth a little loose.

"Look, Danny, don't try and justify Jacob's actions. What your brother did to me was despicable. You don't use sexual harassment to get your own way."

He took a sip of his Whisky.

"Unfortunately, that's the way he works. Plus, he always wants what he can't have."

"What! Are you saying you condone what he did?"

"Hell, he got you here, didn't he?"

Anger flooded her face and she felt her cheeks burn.

"Why, you creep."

She couldn't stop herself. His smug face grinned down at her, his words rattling inside her head: *Hell, he got you here, didn't he?* Without thinking, she flung the last of her drink in his face, hearing a gasp from those standing close by as they realised what she'd done.

Danny's face filled with fury.

"Why, you pathetic bitch. You've just made a big mistake."

He pulled a fresh handkerchief from one of his pockets and wiped himself down, then flung it towards her before storming off.

"What the hell did you just do that for?"

She turned. Tegan stood behind her, eyes wide with concern.

"They were both in on it."

"In on what?"

Mia bit her lip.

"Nothing. Just leave it."

Tegan reached out and grabbed her arm. Her fingers dug into Mia's flesh.

"No, I won't. What the fuck is going on?"

Out of the corner of her eye Mia could see Jack and Sandra heading straight towards them.

"I told you: nothing ... Just drop it." She snatched her arm away and dashed out of the ballroom and headed straight for the main foyer.

"Where are you going in such a rush?"

She spun around to see Jacob standing there, a girl on each arm. He was dressed impeccably in a blue suit, white shirt and classy tie.

"I'm getting some air," she blurted. "There's too many Dallisons around here taking up my breathing space." He chortled and gave her that same wolfish grin she'd seen at the dressmakers. She fled, feeling his eyes bore through the back of her skull.

In the hotel grounds, she stared up at the night sky. Cool air embraced her bare shoulders and she could smell an oaky scent in the air. At last, she breathed in deeply, and when she exhaled, she felt refreshed, no longer stifled by overbearing guests.

In the distance she could make out a lake, surrounded by a dark circlet of trees. The way the moon shone down onto the water made it look so mysterious she found herself drawn towards it. It was far too late for there to be any signs of wildlife, which was more the pity. She adored wild creatures, the great outdoors, and so, as she walked across the lawn, she enjoyed the calming influence of being that bit closer to nature.

Although the incident with Danny had been unpleasant, at least after tonight it would all be behind her. She could then move on with her life, forget about all these idiotic Dallisons.

An owl hooted softly in the trees and Mia glanced up to see its golden eyes gaze down at her. She gasped in delight when it took flight, astounded by the sheer length of its wingspan. She smiled lazily as it flew off towards the moon.

She made her way nearer the lake, enjoying, as she drew closer, the silvery ripples that swept across its surface in the wake of a solitary fish. She felt her earlier tension ebb away as she took advantage of this stolen moment.

But then she heard something...a noise. Was someone moving about in the bushes? She glanced over her shoulder and peered into the darkness... Nothing. She hesitated, a chill sliding down her spine. Someone was definitely out here and she became on edge. Perhaps she shouldn't have come here alone after all; better to play safe and head back to the hotel.

Somewhere in the darkness a twig snapped. Frightened, she spun on her heels, hurried away from the lake.

"Hello, is anybody out there?"

No reply.

Don't panic. It's probably just an animal. Don't let your imagination run away with you. She rushed back towards the hotel, her heart pounding, then she tripped. Her stomach knotted with fear when she felt a hand grab her ankle, dragging her to the ground. She screamed, unable to shake it off, the sound of heavy breathing in the darkness sent a wave of sheer terror to course through her entire body.

She scrambled in the dirt, her fingernails tearing at the soil, but it was to no avail. The strong grip at her ankle left her helpless. Another scream welled within her when she felt the weight of a man's body creep on top of hers, pinning her down. Before her mouth could open, though, she felt a crack to the back of her head, then remembered nothing more.

When Mia opened her eyes, she saw a multitude of stars. She winced, a splitting pain raging across the back of her skull. She felt nauseous, dizzy, confusion flooding her mind like the saline taste of seawater.

It was still dark, the moon now hidden behind thickening cloud, and she shivered in the freezing cold.

Glancing around, she wondered why she was lying on the ground. Had she fallen asleep? She gently rubbed the back of her head until the pain eased a little, then sat up on her elbows, trying to remember, to get her bearings. But then a pain between her legs made her sit bolt upright, seeing in horror that her dress was hitched over her belly, her underwear around her ankles.

She let out a gasp of repulsion as panic engulfed her.

No, this can't have happened... But why couldn't she remember? She scrambled backwards in the dirt until she hit something and cried out, the memory of the weight of that man's body flashing back to her mind. She was terrified to face it, to comprehend what it all meant. Was he still here? Hiding in the darkness, ready to finish off what he'd started? Whimpering, she brought her hands to her mouth as she turned only to find she had come up against a tree. The floodgates opened and finally she cried, believing Jacob had done this to her. She may not have remembered the attack, but she could still feel it.

Shaking, she got to her feet, pulled up her underwear and covered her naked body with what was left of her tattered dress. Her head still hurt, her mind in complete turmoil, as she tried to decide what to do next. Should she call the police? Oh, no, the humiliation, the shame. She couldn't bear the thought, only wanted to crawl into a hole, lay down and die. How could she possibly live a normal life now? Fearful he might come back and violate her all over again.

Ethan jumped into her thoughts and she cried even harder. If he ever found out about this, she could lose him forever, or worse, witness repulsion in his eyes every time he touched her body. What was she going to do?

Shivering, her teeth chattering, she stared at the entrance to the hotel. She could hear loud music, lingering trails of laughter, yet she couldn't go back inside, couldn't face everyone or risk the chance of coming into contact with that monster once again. But then, wasn't this all her own fault? Hadn't she been mean to him and his brother, left him the only one form of retaliation and revenge he could understand? Yes, she had brought this on herself, for why else would he have wanted to ruin her? This would be her secret now, her own shame. She couldn't tell anyone, not even Ethan or Tegan.

When the cold became unbearable, she made her way back inside. She waited until no one was about and went straight to her room, locking the door behind her before she ran to the shower. Still sobbing, she tore the dress from her body and flung her undergarments straight into the bin. When she stepped over the edge of the bath and into the shower, the water was scalding, but she didn't care. She needed to rid herself of the smell, erase the thoughts that someone had violated her flesh, her secret place. She scrubbed at her skin until it almost bled, and then scrubbed even harder. Not satisfied, she ran a bath to make sure there was nothing left of him inside her. As she lay in a mountain of bubbles, she cried until she could cry no more.

How could she have been so stupid? Why had she gone down to the lake alone? It hadn't mattered that it was a beautiful evening and the stars were out in their hundreds. She had put herself at risk, gone where Jacob had been able to hurt to her.

There was a knock on the door and she jumped, terrified.

"Mia, are you in there?"

It was Tegan. Mia held her breath, a lump rising in her throat. She couldn't talk to her sister, not in this state.

Another knock, louder this time.

"Listen, if you're in there, just tell me everything's okay."

Mia felt fresh tears pour down her face. She would never be okay again, never be the same person she had once been. She heard her sister's footsteps move away. Left alone, she slipped under the water and blanked out the world for as long as she could hold her breath.

The next morning at breakfast, Mia struggled to eat. "What happened to you?" Tegan asked, nudging her arm. Mia recoiled, not wishing to be touched, not by her sister, not by anyone.

"I tripped and fell last night," she lied.

"It must have been all the champagne," Jacob said, walking into the breakfast room, all casual smiles. "That's what you get when you can't hold your drink."

The sight of him, displaying no remorse, made her feel physically sick. She wanted to hit him, to scream at him "Why did you do this to me?" At the same time, she was afraid of him, afraid of the power he now held over her and the fact he could come and hurt her again whenever he wished.

She found she was shaking so she left the table and backed away, trying not to run.

"Hey, steady on."

She gasped, spun around and saw Daniel holding onto her with one hand, a glass of fresh orange juice in the other.

"You nearly fell on top of me. I guess you've still got plenty of alcohol in your system from last night, huh?"

"No, I didn't drink that much," she blurted, pushing his hand away, but then she stumbled and he lifted an eyebrow.

"Hmm, so I see."

Tegan rushed over, grabbed her hand and pulled her to one side. "What's wrong with you this morning? You seem unsettled, jumpy."

Mia shrugged. "I've told you: nothing. Can't you just leave me alone. It's been a long weekend. Mum and Jack will be heading off on their honeymoon soon and then I'm on the first train home."

Tegan's grip tightened. "I know you, and I know when something's wrong. Where did you go last night?"

"When?"

"After you had that spat with Danny? I tried to find you, but you'd disappeared."

Mia was beginning to feel numb all over. Too many questions and too many answers to keep secret. She shook her head, trying to stall and think of a good excuse. "I was upset over Danny being a dick so I went for a walk in the grounds and then to bed."

"That's it? You just left the party without even saying 'Goodnight'?"

"Yep, that's about it. And besides, you had Jonas to keep you company."

"Oh, I see, you got jealous because I had a date and Ethan was too busy to escort you?"

Mia's jaw dropped.

"No…I didn't mean… it's… Look, let's forget it, okay?"

"Fine," Tegan said, throwing her hands in the air. "I can't take much more of this cloak and dagger stuff, anyway."

She hurried back to Jonas who was sitting with a few other guests at the breakfast table.

"Family tiff, eh?" She recognised Jack's voice, that of her mother's new husband.

"Morning; sleep well?" she asked, trying to think of something polite to say.

His eyes appeared to twinkle. "Is that something you normally ask a man after his wedding night?" He winked and Mia blushed.

"Huh? Oh, sorry… I didn't mean…"

He gave out a loud chuckle. "At least when you're our age you don't have to worry about contraception."

Mia felt the blood drain from her face. Birth control... she wasn't using any. Last night hit her like a brick in the face. On top of everything, she could also be pregnant. No, she mustn't let that happen. She needed to find a chemist, and fast. She could ask neither Tegan nor her mother to take her, either would immediately be suspicious. She'd have to grab a taxi, then get back as quickly as possible.

She raced upstairs, grabbed her purse and rang down to reception to arrange a cab. Within minutes she was heading into town, her mind racing along with the traffic. Was this horror what other women went through in similar circumstances? Not only had she been violated but it was down to her to ensure there would be no repercussions.

She soon dived out of the taxi and into the nearest pharmacy. Inside, her stomach was a fistful of knots. She had to try and put on a brave face, get through this ordeal as best she could, then put it all behind her. If she let the trauma of last night consume her, it would ruin her life. No, she needed to stay strong, blank it all out if necessary, then find that hidden strength she believed she possessed.

At the counter, the elderly woman in glasses who served her reminded her of Cruella De Vil.

"Good morning, dear; can I help you?"

Mia found she couldn't look her in the eye.

"Could I have the morning after pill, please."

The woman's voice now appeared clipped.

"Can I ask whether you've had unprotected sex in the last five days?"

Mia hung her head.

"Yes, last night," she confessed, still unable to make eye contact. She believed that if she did, the woman might sense what she'd been through and she didn't want her pity. The assistant moved to a shelf at the back of the counter and pulled out a small blue and white packet.

"Here, take this as soon as you can." She pushed the box closer.

Mia glanced down at it. *Just take the tablet, then all will be over.* She pushed a nagging doubt to the back of her mind, added a bottle of water to the bill and paid for it all. She opened the packet there and then and swallowed the tablet in one quick gulp.

"It's done," she breathed, letting out a sigh of relieve and handing the empty packet to Cruella.

She left the shop seconds later, only to find the taxi hadn't waited. "God damn it," she cursed under her breath, "that's all I need," then turned tail and headed for the taxi rank.

Footsteps approached from behind and frightened, she spun around, her heart in her mouth, and saw Daniel.

"What are you doing in town, I thought you were still at the hotel?"

His eyes widened in surprise and it was clear he'd got over last night's clash.

"We've hit a last minute hitch. I need string to tie some old tin cans behind the car when the honeymooners leave. I thought Jacob had it all in hand, but obviously not."

"Oh, there's a card shop on the High Street which sells that kind of stuff."

"Great; I'm on it. Look…about last night."

Mia shook her head, eyeing him coolly.

"Forget it, Danny, our tiff is the least of my problems."

"You sure?"

"Yes, all I want is for you and your brother to leave me alone."

He shifted his weight from foot to foot and glanced down at the floor before saying: "I doubt we can do that. You know, with us practically being neighbours and all."

Mia felt the cold hand of dread grip her heart.

"What do you mean? What are you saying?"

"Why, didn't your mum tell you? Jack's bought us a flat in London, not too far from a place called Cockmoor, to be precise."

Chapter 7

It had been a while since Mia had taken a good look in the mirror. Since her ordeal, she couldn't bear to do so, hated seeing her own reflection. She never used to mind. She had been quite proud of her clear chocolaty eyes, rimmed with thick black lashes, and her rosebud mouth which hid small, straight teeth. Even her hair was often admired, thick, dark and luxurious.

After what she'd suffered, she avoided mirrors of any kind. Glass fronted shops were the worst, always trying to get her to take a peek. She would throw her head back, look away and often cross the street.

Today was different.

In a few minutes time, Ethan would be here, and if she didn't do something soon, she would lose him forever. She'd been up since the crack of dawn, and within that time had showered and put on her sexiest underwear. With care, she'd blow-dried her hair, then brushed it until it shone. She'd applied enough makeup to look smoking hot and then dug out the tightest pair of jeans she owned. She couldn't lose him, not even if she now saw herself as damaged goods.

Once she finished, she moved over to the window and glanced down at a photograph sitting on the windowsill. She picked it up and smiled. It was of her and Sam when she was just a babe in arms. Sam's expression screamed 'It's a baby, it might break', his eyes showing how petrified he was of dropping her.

"You were always such a scaredy-cat," she mused out loud, "but I wish you'd had children of your own." She espied Ethan coming up the hill and so replaced the picture, the moment already forgotten.

She let him in and could tell he was surprised by her sexy appearance. Since she'd returned from the wedding, she'd barely let Ethan come near her. She'd become frigid and her actions had made him confused. He'd become angry, and in the end he'd left after they'd had a blazing row. He was hurt, believing she didn't want him anymore. That simply wasn't true. She loved him with all her heart, needed him, but after Jacob… It was hard to explain, even to herself. She wanted to be touched by her lover so badly, but felt dirty, used. She realised she was letting Jacob ruin her life and she couldn't let him do that, he'd done enough damage already.

She offered Ethan a chair and he sat down, his expression grim, guarded.

"What is it? Your text message said you needed to see me face-to-face."

"Yes, I do… It's…" Mia wasn't sure where to begin. She still couldn't tell him what had happened to her by the lake, but she needed to make amends, to show him she still cared for him, before it was too late.

"Can I get you a beer?"

He nodded and so she made her way into the kitchen, where she opened the fridge and grabbed a Carlsberg. She closed the door… "Ethan? What are you doing?"

Before she could say another word, he reached out and pulled her close. His lips searched for hers, and in return her mouth welcomed him. His arms embraced her and she wrapped her own around his neck, wishing only for them to become one. Heat and hunger flooded her veins, fire exploding inside the pit of her stomach. Before she realised what she was doing, her fingers tore at his shirt, trying to get to his flesh. Within seconds they were both naked and Ethan took her, right there, on the kitchen worktop. She didn't care, she loved him, wanted him more than she ever thought possible. When he entered her, she thought she would explode with sheer ecstasy. As one, they came together and their passion consumed them both. Only once they were spent did Mia grab his shirt and put it on. He still wore his trousers and lifted them to his waist, buttoning them up.

"Babe, I've missed you," he whispered in her ear and she shivered with delight. "Listen, I know it's bad timing, especially after such great sex, but I can't stay."

Mia didn't like the sound of this and pouted. Ethan pulled her close. "It's not like that. It's just I promised Bell I'd go to a party tonight, meet some of her old buddies. It's the same old faces, but I think Angel might be there. Do you want to come with me?"

She grinned and kissed his mouth. "Only if you make love to me again before we go." He took a deep breath and held her close.

"I don't think that's going to be a problem," he replied, his hand slipping down into the front of her shirt...

By early evening, they'd headed into London, and by the time they reached the address, the party was in full swing. For Mia this was the first time she'd been invited to meet any of Bell's close friends. Whist she had been a guest at their home, she'd been invited to a few social events, mostly dinner in a restaurant with a client or an opening at an art gallery. This night would be different, the first time she'd see Bell let her hair down.

As they passed a few young people gathered outside on the steps and entered the property, loud music boomed out from two gigantic speakers.

"Wow! How many have been invited?" Mia asked, in awe.

"Too many by the looks of things," Ethan said with a smirk. "However, that's typical of Walter. Always inviting the groupies."

Mia tried not to laugh. "Walter? That's so old fashioned. Is he an old man?"

"Nope, but his mother was a big fan of Disney."

"You can't be serious?"

Ethan grinned and gave a chuckle. "No, I'm just messing with you."

"Well then," she said in a quiet voice, "who is he?"

"Come on in and I'll show you." He guided her up a flight of steps and they entered an elegant hallway. To one side was a grand marble staircase.

"Just look at the size of this place," she said, in awe.

Ethan laughed, tightening his grip on her hand. They pushed their way through a throng of revellers, some writhing and dancing to the music, others drinking and laughing, making new friends. Mia's eyes rounded. The walls were decorated with gold music discs, platinum records and pictures of world famous bands.

Mia felt a flutter of excitement. She pulled Ethan close, so she could shout in his ear "Is Walt a rock star?" He shook his head and pointed to a portrait of a man hanging over a gigantic fireplace. "No, he's a music producer, the best in the business."

She stared, opened mouthed, at the painting. The subject had slick dark hair and what she guessed were designer shades. He wore tight leather trousers and held a blue electric guitar in his hand. His shirt sleeves were rolled up to the elbow, showing off some pretty impressive ink. The backdrop was a music studio. He was imposing, standing there, a king amongst peasants, and Mia was a little overwhelmed, not wishing to meet such a daunting individual.

Ethan dragged her over to the bar, where a handsome guy, who looked to have walked out of a modelling agency, gave them drinks. Mia stared at the crowd, scanning the many faces, searching for any sign of Bell. Yes, there she was, tucked away in a corner. Mia tugged at Ethan's arm, pointing in Bell's direction. He nodded, and they made their way through the sea of dancers. She caught sight of someone who she thought looked familiar. Hang on… Wasn't that…Kate Moss?

She arrived at Bell's side, and the moment she recognised Mia, Bell flung her arms around her and kissed her cheek. "Hey, so glad you could make it. You look stunning." She dropped her arms, turning her attention towards Ethan. "Walt's been asking for you."

Ethan grinned, flashed that smile Mia loved so much.

"Where is he? In his studio?"

Bell nodded and took a sip of her drink.

Ethan glanced down at Mia. "Would you like to meet him?" Mia shook her head. No, she certainly would not. She felt out of place here as it was, and knew she would only stand there, tongue tied.

"He won't bite, I promise," but Mia wouldn't be swayed. She was happy in Bell's company, hidden out of sight. He bent over and kissed her lips. "Okay, I won't be long; I'll just say 'Hello' and have a quick catch up. Mum'll keep an eye on you until I get back."

"Sure. Tell him I said 'Hi'." She gave him a reassuring nudge and he headed off in the direction of the stairs. Within minutes, Mia had finished her drink. She tapped Bell on the shoulder, gesturing that she was off to get a re-fill. Bell pointed to her own empty glass. "Vodka and Coke," she shouted over the din and Mia headed straight to the bar.

Sweaty bodies bumped into her as she made her way across the dance floor. The heat was stifling and Mia was glad when she reached the counter. If she were honest, she wasn't much of a party animal. Tegan had always been the one who liked to party until dawn. She was more of a stay in and enjoy her sexy boyfriend's body kinda girl. She was impressed with Bell's connections, but all she wanted at this moment was to be in her PJ's, eating a tub of Ben & Jerry's.

"Well, look what the cat's dragged in."

Mia felt dread sweep across her soul. It was so powerful she gasped out loud.

She turned, her eyes wide with despair. "You!"

Jacob lifted his hands. "Yes, at least I was the last time I looked."

"What are you doing here?" Her eyes darted past him, searching for Ethan.

"I was invited of course. Dad still has some pretty cool connections."

"Your dad?"

"Yes, he used to be in the business. How do you think he made his fortune?"

Mia couldn't have cared less. She couldn't breathe, needed to get away from him, and fast.

She bolted, but his hand shot out and grabbed her arm.

"Hey, stay, have a drink with your...*brother.*"

"Let go of me." She glared at him, her hands pushing against his chest. She was scared, shaking. He pouted like a spoilt child but his eyes were hard and mean.

"Now, now, let's not make a scene. I'm only trying to be friendly."

"Then do as I say and let go of me," but his grip only tightened.

"This is no way to treat me," he warned, "especially when we're so close." He licked his lips whilst his eyes slowly devoured her body.

Mia felt the blood drain from her face. She was trapped, here, with this vile predator.

"Hey, Mia, I didn't know you were going to be here tonight; how lovely."

Mia swung around, her eyes connecting with Angel's. She felt Jacob ease his grip, drop his hand, turn his attention towards the bartender.

Angel pushed closer, her heavily made up lids narrowing. "Mia, are you okay? Only you don't look so good."

Mia tried to smile but couldn't quite lift the corners of her mouth.

"Yes, I'm fine. Er, actually you could be right. I don't feel at all well, probably too much alcohol. I'll just nip outside and get some air."

"Would you like me to come with you?"

"No, thanks, I'll be okay." Somehow she managed to lift those corners. "Honest."

She dashed for the door, bumping into a group of young men who cursed her as she flew past. She didn't hear their taunts, all that mattered was getting away from that monster. Flashbacks of that fateful night now plagued her until tears threatened to fall. Jacob had ruined her life, and no matter how much she tried to forget, he would always be around to remind her. The only thing she had been grateful for was her period.

She'd just reached the front door when strong arms gripped her around her waist, and she gave out a great sigh of relief, assuming Ethan was back.

Spinning around, a smile already on her lips, she found to her horror it wasn't Ethan but Jacob. Before she could react, his lips forced themselves upon her. She squirmed as his embrace tightened and she tried to push him away but he was far too strong. Her back hit a wall and his hand cupped her breast.

"Mia, what—?"

She gasped out loud and Jacob let go. She turned her head to find Ethan standing there, opened mouthed, his face pale, anger in his glare. "How could you?" he rasped.

"No, it's not what you think," but Jacob was laughing, mocking her. "Yeah, mate, she's a right vixen. Made a beeline for me the second you were out of sight."

She saw Ethan clench his fists, take a step forward.

"Hey, she came onto me," Jacob insisted, lifting his hands in self-defence.

Ethan lunged, his fist connecting with Jacob's mouth.

"Liar!" he roared, his voice filled with fury, but Jacob scoffed. "Nice right hook, I'll give you that." He wiped away a trickle of blood with the sleeve of his jacket. "But be warned... I won't let you do that again." Ethan went to take another swipe, but two men, bystanders, grabbed his arms and pulled him back.

"That's enough, mate," one of them shouted. "We don't want any trouble."

Ethan shrugged them off, then straightened his shirt.

"He's not worth it," Mia said, trying to defuse the situation. She could see he was shaking with rage and needed to calm down. Jacob, though, winked, lifting his hand to his ear. "Call me," he mouthed, "you have my number." Before she could deny it, he headed back towards the bar.

Ethan now glared down at her, clearly still furious.

"You know the guy?"

"Yes...but..."

His mouth twisted with distaste and he turned away and dashed out of the building. She quickly chased after him, but got caught up in a throng of revellers. Her heels clattered on the pavement outside, but it was no use; he was getting away.

"Ethan, wait!" she pleaded, but he chose to ignore her, whistling down a taxi into which he soon climbed. Her shoulders sagged as he was driven away, no longer able to hold onto her emotions. How could he believe she would ever betray him? Or even think for one second that she would go off with someone else the moment his back was turned? She loved him with everything she possessed, believed in him, in their relationship. She was convinced he'd blame her for what happened here in Walt's house, that he would never forgive her. This was not her doing, but why was Jacob so determined to ruin her life?

All the way home, she tortured and blamed herself. Cleary, everything must be her fault? If only she hadn't gone to that stupid party. At least, if she'd stayed with Angel, everything would have turned out alright.

On the tube, her mobile rang at least half a dozen times, but none was from Ethan: three missed calls from Bell, two from Angel with a text message asking if everything was alright. There was also a withheld number. *Probably bloody PPI*, she thought, miserably.

On arriving at the cottage, she flung her 'phone onto the kitchen table and headed for the fridge. She pulled out the bottle of wine she'd never had time to drink when Ethan had been over earlier. She poured herself a large glass and took herself off to bed. Her mind was consumed with having lost him. What was she going to do? She couldn't tell him about Jacob and what he'd done to her. He would despise her all the more, even hate her, and the thought made her cry. Would Jacob torment her for the rest of her life? It was looking more likely, and now, because of him, she'd lost the one person she loved most in the world. How would she ever live without him?

In her bedroom, she reached for her iPod and hit random. Coldplay began to sing *Paradise* and her lower lip trembled. It was official, her life was a complete and utter disaster. She went to close the bedroom curtains and glanced down at the windowsill. She frowned: the picture of Sam wasn't there. Through teary eyes, she scanned the room, knowing she had glanced at it just before Ethan had arrived. She finally saw it on the dressing table. Funny, she couldn't recall having put it there. She shrugged and went to pick it up, but the moment she touched its carved wood frame a cold shiver shot up her arm, as though she'd put her hand inside a freezer. For a moment her tears were forgotten as she stared at the photograph, Sam still smiling nervously up at her. A familiar odour then seemed to surround her. Could that be…Aramis aftershave? The hairs on the back of her neck stood on end. She took a deep breath, but just as quickly, the aroma disappeared, her hand feeling warm again.

Mia put the photograph in its rightful place and the odd sensation she'd just suffered out of her mind. After all, it had been a very stressful day. She undressed, wiped the makeup from her swollen eyes and got into bed, from where she stared down at her 'phone. Part of her wished it would ring, the other, frightened Ethan would call and tell her it was all over. What could she say, though? Playing the scene with Jacob over and over in her head, she had to admit it had looked as though she'd willingly kissed him. Explaining would mean telling Ethan everything. She sipped her wine but it tasted like vinegar, and so she put the glass down on the bedside table, switched off the light and snuggled under the duvet. When she closed her eyes, she could see Ethan's face filled with sadness and regret. She cried herself to sleep, but dreamt of being safe, wrapped in her lover's arms. No one else could make her feel like he did, only his lips, his kisses would ever do for her.

Chapter 8

Monday morning came around far too quickly. Mia caught the tube and braced herself for the moment she would see Ethan again. He'd refused to answer any of her calls and she'd cried over his messages, telling her to leave him alone.

She'd texted back, pleading for him to let her explain, to make it up to him, but she hadn't got through to him. She'd lost his trust and didn't know how she was supposed to win it back.

Bell was in the office when she arrived. For some strange reason she thought the place smelt of lavender and chilli. Someone had clearly been staying here over the weekend and had tried to mask the evidence.

"Mia, can—"

"Please. Don't." She raised her hand and gave her a look she hoped told Bell not to try and lecture her. Unfortunately, Bell was stubborn.

"All I wanted to say was…let him cool down and he'll come round."

Mia shook her head.

"I don't think he'll ever forgive me."

Bell gave a deep sigh, picked up a pair of glasses and stuck them on the end of her nose.

"He will, you'll see. Okay, enough said; let's get to work. We've got a heavy schedule this week. At least a dozen manuscripts came in over the weekend and I have several miniatures that need restoration. I'm going to be out of the office quite a lot, too. Professor Hickson has a project he's been working on that he now feels needs my full attention. There's plenty for you to do, though, so I'm leaving you in Angel's capable hands.

Mia lifted an eyebrow. "So where's Felicity?"

Bell came over, tugged at her hands, made her look at her.

"Jonathan's dumped her."

"Really? There must be something in the water."

Bell again sighed. "Seems that way, but whatever happened at the party is between you and Ethan. He's staying at the Institute this morning but said he'd drop by later this afternoon. Why don't you take the opportunity to talk to him, get your side of the story across?"

"I've tried but he won't listen. I can't imagine what you must think of me, but I swear I didn't cheat on him. I would *never* do that."

Bell dropped her hands, a slight smile skimming her lips. "I believe you; it isn't in your nature. Now, do as I say and speak to Ethan this afternoon, clear the air." She grabbed her handbag, lifted a mountain of paperwork into her arms and headed out of the office.

"Life's too short," she shouted from down the hall. "So fix it before you both live to regret it."

At lunchtime, Mia grabbed a sandwich and a diet Coke from the vending machine and headed out towards the back of the auction house. Although the front of the building was on a busy main road, to the rear sat a quaint little terrace. It wasn't very grand, actually quite small, but it was rather pretty. A few shrubs were dotted about in tubs, a wooden picnic bench at its centre. Wall art covered the brickwork in an attempt to give the place an Italian feel, and along the fence wandered a couple of grapevines. Although the fruit had long since decayed, the leaves had yet to wither and die. Winter was indeed upon them, but the terrace was protected by the surrounding buildings, granting no biting wind to chase them indoors, just a wintry sun to help keep the chill at bay.

"So what are you going to do?" Angel asked, joining her for lunch. She opened a plastic bowl filled with green salad and drowned it in dressing.

Mia eyed her from her side of the bench.

"About what?"

Angel narrowed her eyes and gave a little huff. "You know full well. Ethan of course."

Mia stared at her new friend. She'd changed her hair colour to a fluorescent orange with black tips. Her lipstick, a dramatic Goth black, made her teeth appear whiter than white and the kohl around her eyes resembled a sleek cat's. Mia didn't like her hair, thought it made her look like a feather duster, but her face was beautiful, even with the weird makeup. Mia decided there was something most alluring about her personality. She had a way of calming people, not to mention she'd tried to protect her, changing the subject whenever Ethan came up in conversation.

A few of her colleagues were also on the terrace, some enjoying a smoke, others busy on their mobile 'phones. After a while, Mia and Angel were left alone to eat their lunch in peace.

Angel reached inside her jacket pocket and pulled out a can of Irn Bru.

"So, you still haven't answered my question?"

"What can I say? I can't explain to him what happened when he won't answer my calls?"

"Give him time. He's stubborn, like Bell, but he'll come round, you'll see."

Mia wanted to change the subject. Just talking about Ethan brought back the misery of Saturday night.

"Have you worked here long?"

"Hmm, not really, just a couple of years. My mum went to school with Bell's husband. They both went to the same university, promised they'd look out for one another, you know how it is: I'll scratch your back if you scratch mine."

"But your mum didn't need any help?"

"Hell no. She's a real ballbreaker. It was me, I needed the support. I fell in with the wrong crowd, started taking drugs and acting all crazy. My mum couldn't control me—"

"But what about your dad?"

"He left when I was little. Went out for a loaf of bread and never came back."

"Oh, I'm sorry, I didn't know."

"It's fine, all water under the bridge. I've been clean for three years now and Shane—that's Ethan's father—well, he near on saved my life."

Mia didn't know what to say. She hadn't expected such a revelation from Angel. She was a tough girl, Mia only had to look at her to see that, but there was also an air of vulnerability about her too.

A dozen sparrows flew down from the sky. Within seconds they were foraging for food. Mia ate the last of her sandwich, brushed the crumbs from her fingertips and onto the ground.

"I was sorry to hear about Felicity and Jonathan. They seemed good together."

"Huh?" then Angel nodded. "Yeah, me too."

"It just goes to show you can't judge what's inside someone's head," Mia said, feeling glum.

Angel shrugged. "I have to admit I was surprised when I heard he'd dumped her. He appeared keen, always the one to make sure she was happy."

"I guess some people pretend to love someone when really they're just waiting for the right excuse to get out."

Angel raised a quizzical eyebrow. "Is that what you think happened with Ethan?"

"Maybe. After all, what kind of guy doesn't let you explain? Unless, of course, he *wanted* an excuse, a way out, only he didn't have the balls to tell me."

"Or maybe you're completely wrong and he just needs time to cool off?" Angel concluded. "By the way, I think you've got company." Mia heard approaching footsteps, and out of the corner of her eye, spotted Ethan making his way over.

Her heart missed a beat. What was *he* doing here so soon? She pretended she hadn't seen him, which was really quite difficult considering he was only a few feet away. He came and stood beside her and she heard him clear his throat.

"Hi, Mia, Angel."

Angel gave him a sideways glance. "I was told, 'two's company and three's a crowd,' so that's my cue to leave." She grabbed what was left of her salad and picked up her drinks can.

"No, wait, stay," Mia pleaded, but Angel's expression told her otherwise.

"I've some tests I need to run in the lab. I'll meet you back there when you're done."

She winked at Ethan. "Do me a favour, kiss and make up. I can't stand seeing her moping around any longer." She made her way back inside and Ethan came and sat down.

"Mia, we need to talk."

She glanced at her hands.

"So, go ahead... I'm all ears."

She played with a piece of black cotton on her sleeve, anything to distract herself from catching his gaze. Finally, she found the courage to lift her head, to peer into his face, shocked by his appearance. He'd dark circles under his eyes and that smile, the one she loved so much...gone.

He let out a deep sigh. "How about tonight? I can come over after work."

She tried to smile, to look enthusiastic.

"Great. I'll cook." Mia fought back her tears. She wanted to be with him so badly, to hold him close, but she couldn't, not until he knew the truth. The lies, the deceit, were eating away at her like a festering wound, the guilt simply intolerable.

He stood up quickly and she blinked, sensing he was feeling awkward.

"Shall we say seven?"

"Sure, or you can come earlier if you like?"

He didn't reply. Instead, he headed off back inside.

The afternoon seemed to drag, but as soon as she got home it was all hands on deck.

At seven o'clock the doorbell chimed.

Right on time, Mia mused, feeling rather nervous.

She let him in, took his coat.

"I've brought dessert," he said, with an awkward smile.

"Thanks, but you didn't have to. I have everything we need." She stepped back, allowing him to pass.

"Shall I take it through?" She ducked past him, straight into the kitchen, balling her hands into fists to stop them from shaking. As she started getting their dinner's ingredients out of the fridge, Ethan dropped a carrier bag onto the worktop.

"I'll leave it here," he said with a sheepish grin, "unless you want me to put it away?"

"No, its fine; I'll do it in a minute." She pushed her hair behind her ears, a gesture she often did when nervous, then placed fresh vegetables onto the worktop; fennel, onions, garlic, red and yellow peppers.

"So what are we having?" he asked, leaning against the doorframe.

She didn't reply at first, too on edge… too scared to speak.

"I'm… I'm making Chinese."

"Anything I can do?" His voice sounded different, gentler, not so hurt.

"Chop onions?"

"Sure, I can do that." He went over to a drawer, helped himself to a knife and grabbed the chopping board.

"Mia, I—"

"Dinner won't be long. Would you like a drop of wine with your meal?" He nodded, so she reached for a bottle and thrust it into his hand—anything to stall him, to keep him from asking questions.

She heated a little oil in a wok and threw in some raw chicken. It all sizzled noisily and then she added the vegetables. Eventually, she took the food off the hob and splashed a few dashes of Soy Sauce into the mix.

"Sit yourself down and I'll bring the food over." The table was already set for two. Nothing fancy, no candlelight or pretty flowers in a vase. Mia didn't want this evening to be seen as romantic. She had to reveal a terrible secret, tell him the truth about what had happened, then trust him enough that he wouldn't run away. Her mind was in turmoil as she set the plates down onto the table. How could she eat at a time like this? The last thing she wanted was food.

Ethan poured the wine and eyed her warily.

"Are you alright?"

She forced a smile. "Yes, of course, don't worry about me. Long day. Tuck in. Don't let your meal get cold." She lifted the first mouthful to her lips, trying to entice him, then took a bite and chewed slowly, the chicken tasted like ash in her mouth. She reached out and took a large gulp of wine to wash it all away.

"Mmm, this isn't bad at all," Ethan said, with a slight smirk.

She waited until he'd eaten, until they were both on their third glass of wine, before she allowed their idle chitchat to steer towards Saturday night. She needed as much Dutch courage as possible.

"So why did you do it? Kiss him, I mean?" There, he'd said it, the burning question which would lead to so much more... She licked her lips nervously. This was never going to be easy. "There's a lot I need to tell you and I want you to hear me out before you make any hasty decisions."

Ethan eyed her coolly, sipped a mouthful of wine.

"Okay, I'm listening."

Mia took a steadying breath.

"The man you saw on Saturday night wasn't a stranger to me."

She saw the muscles in his jaw tense, watched the light in his eyes diminish.

"So, he's an old boyfriend?"

"No, he's nothing of the sort. Do you remember when I told you my mother was getting married and that the man she was marrying had two sons?"

"You mean those two idiots you told me about?"

Mia nodded. "Yes, those two." She took a large gulp of wine. "Jacob's the eldest. He's the man you saw kiss me."

Ethan looked appalled.

"I'm sorry, I'm just not grasping any of this?"

She pushed her fingers through her long dark hair.

"Jacob and his brother were desperate for the wedding to go ahead. Jack, his father, had agreed to buy them a place of their own, once he got hitched. When I said I wasn't going to the wedding, he was worried my mother might call the whole thing off. Of course, he doesn't know her, because she'd rather sell her soul to the devil than give up a rich meal ticket. So, one night, not long after their announcement, he waited for me after I'd closed the bookstore. He told me in no uncertain terms that if I didn't attend the wedding there'd be consequences."

"You mean, he threatened you?"

Mia nodded. "Yes, he warned me off. Said that if I didn't attend the ceremony, he'd do unspeakable things to me, and I believed him. That night I packed by bags and came to stay with Sam."

She could see fury in his expression, saw tension build in his body, but she continued: "In the end, I thought it would be better if I just kept the peace and agreed to go. I talked Tegan into attending too, and I thought that would be the end of it."

"But it wasn't?"

"No, not by any stretch of the imagination."

He reached out and cupped her hand in his, and she felt tears sting her eyes.

"The night of the wedding, I needed some air. I'd seen Jacob in the foyer and he watched me go into the hotel gardens, alone. It was so hot inside that all I wanted to do was get away from the crowd for a while."

She now did begin to cry, tears soon sliding down her face.

"It was a beautiful evening. The stars twinkled and the air was cool on my skin. I walked down towards the lake but then heard something, someone… I called out, but no one answered and I felt a moment of vulnerability, sensed someone standing there, in the darkness."

Ethan's grip tightened around her fingers.

"He attacked you?" A muscle twitched above one of his eyes. There was no going back, not now. This was the moment she had been dreading for weeks: the confession she had never wanted to reveal.

A painful sob broke from her throat.

"I… I…woke up on the ground, half naked, my clothes ripped. I couldn't understand what had happened at first. I must have been hit over the head and was feeling woozy, sick inside. But then I felt pain between my legs and reality hit me… It was Jacob; he'd followed me down to the lake; a coward and a vile monster who used his brute strength to get what he wanted."

It was all too much. Reliving that moment was as painful as having a knife thrust into her gullet. She felt unclean all over again and had to close her eyes, her body becoming wracked by her sobbing. She heard a chair scrape back, then felt strong arms enfold her.

"Oh, my God, Mia, why didn't you tell me this sooner?"

She cried like a baby, her face pressed against his chest. He guided her into the living room and they sat on the floor together, holding each other tight.

"Baby, you need to go to the police."

"No," and she pulled away, "you mustn't tell anyone."

"But he can't get away with this."

She began to cry harder.

"It's not about him. It's about me. If everyone finds out, my life won't be the same again. Those closest to me will pity me, and I couldn't bear it. Up until now I've managed to block it all out, learned to live with it. I don't want to remember; I just want to forget."

"But to keep all this pain and torment from me… Why?"

"I was afraid I'd lose you, that you wouldn't want me anymore."

Ethan held her at arm's length.

"Listen, sweetheart, you're never going to lose me. But this animal must pay for what he's done."

"No! You don't understand, he's dangerous, we've got to stay away from him."

"But I can't stand by and let him get away Scott free. What kind of a man would I be to allow him to do that?"

Mia looked into his eyes, saw his pain and squeezed his hand tight.

"You must…if you care for me. He's a monster and doesn't have any moral code. If you go to the police now, it's his word against mine. I should have reported him straight away, but I didn't. His dad's stinking rich so he'll have the best lawyer. They'll simply wipe the floor with me."

Ethan's expression turned morose.

"I feel as though I've let you down somehow."

"Don't be silly, far from it," Mia chided gently. "You're standing by me, and that's all that matters."

He shrugged.

"This isn't making me feel any better." He paused, his face blank in thought. "Was that perverted prick at the party because of his father's connections?"

Mia nodded. "Yes, apparently Jack earned his money in the music business. He's a friend of Walt's and that's why Jacob was invited. He must have seen me on my own and made his move when I went to the bar. I tried to get away, but he followed me out. Of course, the rest is history."

Ethan paled. "How can you ever forgive me? I'm truly sorry for ever doubting you. I'm such an idiot. I realise now he was playing me for a fool. I was hurt and my pride took a blow, and then I didn't believe you but him instead. Oh, my Mia, the truth is: I have deep feelings for you and… And I was a little scared."

Mia felt her heart soar.

"Do you still care for me now, after hearing all the sordid details?"

He pulled her close, his nose nuzzling her hair.

"Oh, Mia, what I'm trying to say is 'I love you'."

Through all her pain and suffering came a moment of pure joy.

"You do?" she whispered in his ear.

"Forever," he whispered back.

Crash! A picture came off the wall, flew across the room and landed by the fireplace, shards of broken glass now lying on the hearth.

"What the f—" Ethan said.

"Oh, bugger, I really liked that picture."

"Did you see that? It didn't just fall."

"I think you're right; I think Sam just threw it. I'm guessing he's a tad upset because you just declared your undying love for me."

Ethan froze to the spot.

"You're kidding me, right?" he barely breathed.

"Nope. Strange things started happening the night we had our first fight. I came home and found the picture on the windowsill had been moved. At first I thought I'd just forgotten doing it, then worried Jacob had somehow found a way in. I reckoned I was becoming paranoid, but then other stuff started happening."

"What other stuff?"

"Spooky goings on. You know? Like a radio coming on all by itself, playing songs that Sam loved. Then there's the aromas that remind me of specific times we shared together: the whiff of popcorn from when he'd take me to the cinema, the smell of his aftershave."

Ethan got to his feet. "Are you sure you're not reading too much into all this?"

"Not at all. Although, like you, I was sceptical at first. I thought it was all just coincidence, but then I unplugged the radio and removed its batteries, even left it in the garden. It had no power, but the same songs just kept on playing over and over."

"Weren't you a little freaked out? I mean, the thought of a ghost trying to connect with you?"

"No, Sam would never hurt me, and if he's here, there's got to be a reason. I just haven't figured it out yet, but I will."

"And you're not afraid?"

"Don't be silly; this is my home. Besides, I like having Sam around, he keeps me company."

Ethan scratched his forehead.

"Let me get this straight. You're telling me that this house is haunted by your dead uncle?"

"Yes, but he's a friendly ghost. Although he does drives me crazy when he messes with my clothes. He mixes them up in my drawers, so I'm forever late for work. He does the same in the kitchen. I found my teabags stuffed in a box of Weetabix yesterday."

Ethan's eyes had grown wide in disbelief.

"Do you think he's here for good?"

Mia shrugged. "How the hell should I know? I'm not a bloody psychic."

Chapter 9

That night Ethan stayed with her and they made sweet, passionate love. At first, she sensed he was afraid to touch her, not wanting to force himself upon her. She was grateful for that, for being so kind and gentle... so considerate.

Together in bed, Mia guided his large hands over her naked body. His thumbs stroked her nipples, pleasure ricocheting in all the right places.

"I love your touch," she said, huskily, "almost as much as I love you." His lips found hers and his tongue explored her mouth. Shivers of desire exploded from every orifice, her nerve endings alive, on fire. He stroked her abdomen, down between her thighs and she shook with sexual desire.

"I need you," she coaxed, drawing him closer. "Show me how much you want me."

He didn't hold back, and she rode the wave of passion that threatened to consume her until they both climaxed together. The explosion between them was so intense, so intoxicating, she was convinced she would never experience anything as earth shattering with anyone else but him. Wrapped in each other's arms they slept, and for the first time in weeks, Mia was content. No more nightmares, no more worrying that she was about to lose the man she loved.

The next morning, she refused to get out of bed when the alarm clock blasted music in her ear. She hit "Snooze" and slept for ten more minutes, awaking to find Ethan in the shower, calling out her name.

"Mia, give it back," he shouted, "you're going to make me late for work." Mia rubbed the sleep from her eyes and got out of bed, her bare feet silent on the carpet. She padded over to the bathroom.

"Who're you talking to?" she yawned.

"You. Come on, it's too early to be playing games. Hand it over."

"Hand what over?"

"The towel, of course."

Mia glanced around, not a towel to be seen. "Which one did you use?"

Ethan turned towards her, a smile tugging at the corners of his mouth.

"You know full well. I always use the stripy one."

"Hmm, you mean Sam's old towel?"

His smile vanished. "Oh, don't start that mumbo jumbo stuff again," he said. "I barely slept a wink."

Mia laughed out loud. "You're such a liar; you slept like a baby. You were snoring in my ear most of the night."

He chuckled and gave her that sexy smile.

"Wanna join me?"

She shook her head. "Much as I'd love to, I've a train to catch."

"Spoilsport." He turned off the shower, pulled the curtain back and climbed out over the edge of the bath. "It's freezing in here, everything's shrivelled up with the cold."

Mia rolled her eyes and checked behind the door for the missing towel—nothing.

She went out and past one of the spare bedrooms, a quick look inside revealing nothing but a cute teddy bear sitting on top of a pillow.

Humph. No sign of it in here.

She popped her nose into the small box room. *No, nothing in there except a mountain of dust.* Then she stared at the linen basket at the top of the stairs. *I wonder…*

Jackpot! There, beneath the lid, was the towel, all neatly folded.

"For heaven's sake, not in with the dirty laundry."

She snapped the lid closed. "Really, Sam, for a ghost you're pretty transparent."

She threw the towel at Ethan, found a clean one for herself and dived into the shower.

Minutes later, Ethan shouted, "I've made breakfast," so she quickly finished off and clambered out.

"Do you have any plans for this evening?" Ethan asked, biting into a slice of toast.

Mia smirked and stirred her coffee. "Well, I thought, after work, I'd go and see my doctor. I think, now we're officially *together*, I should get myself some birth control."

Ethan's smile warmed her heart. "You're thinking about making me permanent?"

"Maybe, and if I do, we need to be sensible."

He came over and wrapped his arms around her waist. "Hmm, that sounds like a great idea, and then I won't need to wear my socks in bed."

She gave a comical splutter then said, "Socks? What on earth are you talking about?"

It was his turn to be amused. "That's what I call condoms. You see, you never really get a true sensation when you wear them."

She pulled him closer. "Don't worry, lover boy, you won't have to wear them for much longer." His kiss was long and passionate until the clock on the wall started vibrating, violently.

"Jeez, what the hell's going on?" Ethan cried, alarmed.

Mia laughed and grabbed a slice of toast. "It's nothing to worry about, it's just Sam reminding us we're going to be late for work."

That night, Mia stopped off at her local GP's, having been lucky enough to have been given a cancelled appointment. Considering she'd never met her doctor before, having only registered a few weeks previously, he surprised her with a welcoming and warm smile.

"What can I do for you?" he asked, offering her a seat.

Mia felt a little shy. Although he knew about these things, talking about her sex life was rather embarrassing.

"Well, I have a serious boyfriend and I wish to be in control of my own contraception."

The doctor gave her an approving nod.

"That's the safest thing to do," he acknowledged and grabbed a small plastic pot. "First things first, could I ask you to take a routine pregnancy test, then we can discuss what kind of birth control is right for you."

He offered her the pot.

"The bathroom's just behind you."

Mia accepted the white tub and trotted off to the toilet. She'd never done a pregnancy test before and found it all quite fascinating.

Within minutes she was back with the doctor and he was dipping a floppy stick into her urine. He glanced up, got another stick from out of a pot and tried again.

"Is something wrong?" Mia asked. For some strange reason her mouth had gone dry.

The doctor sighed and pushed his glasses further up his nose.

"I take it you aren't trying for a family at the moment?"

Mia frowned; her stomach was beginning to feel a little queasy.

"No, why?"

"I'm afraid the test's positive."

Mia's brows furrowed more with confusion.

"Positive for what?"

"You're pregnant. You're going to have a baby."

Mia sat back in her chair. Did he just say she was *pregnant*?

"That's impossible, we've been so careful," she spluttered, refusing to believe him.

The doctor shook his head. "I take it from your reaction that you've been using some form of contraception?"

She nodded. *Why did his voice seem so far away?*

"Can I assume you used condoms?"

Again she nodded.

The doctor let out a sigh and folded his arms.

"I'm afraid it's quite common for them to split or tear."

Mia could feel the blood drain from her face. Why was he telling her this now? Wasn't it a bit like closing the stable door after the horse had bolted? The doctor picked up the 'phone and pressed a button. "Can you ask the nurse to come in, please."

The next half hour was a complete blur. She was taken to another room where the nurse offered her advice. "I can see it's all been a bit of a shock," Mia heard her say, "but it's early days yet so you still have a couple of options."

Numb, she left the surgery clutching a few pamphlets and an appointment to see the midwife. She was *pregnant*; what the hell was she going to do? The thought of a termination repulsed her. The nurse said it was something to think about but she'd ruled it out straightaway. She understood that for some, other girls in the same situation, it might be the right thing to do, but Mia couldn't go through with something like that. She wasn't mentally strong enough, she couldn't deal with the emotion, the guilt afterwards. The nurse had said she was just a couple of weeks pregnant and that the baby was due early September. It seemed a lifetime away, and yet, the baby would be here before she knew it.

The problem she now faced would be telling Ethan. What would he say? Would he be happy? Sad? She felt a stab of apprehension. Would he still want her? Although only the day before, he'd said he'd love her forever.

She got off the train and headed for the cottage, thankful for the first time ever that Ethan wasn't staying over. She needed to think, to clear her head, come to terms with such devastating news. The truth was she wasn't ready to be a mother, to have a child, but something inside told her she couldn't face a termination. She was trapped, confused, terrified. What should she do next? Surely this was all a bad dream and at any moment she would wake up and everything would be okay.

To calm herself, she made a hot chocolate and hunted out her iPad. She googled 'Four weeks pregnant – what to expect' and found a picture of a blob of something she wasn't sure was even human. It said underneath: 'Your growing baby's not much bigger than a poppy seed'.

She felt the first tremor of doubt deep inside. Was she doing the right thing by keeping this baby? Was she both mentally and physically mature enough to bring up a child? Perhaps, but she would need Ethan by her side.

She grabbed her mobile. The urge to talk to someone, to share her secret, overpowered her.

She rang Tegan.

"You busy?"

"Hell yes; I work for the NHS so all I do is work and sleep. Besides, I have a sister who hardly ever 'phones me, so what else should I do with my time?" Her voice was filled with the usual sarcasm.

"Hey, yes, sorry. You know how it is, work, life...stuff."

"By 'Stuff' I take it you mean Ethan? How is that gorgeous man of yours?"

Mia smiled then curled herself into an armchair.

"He's good. Stayed over last night, but he's got one of his famous assignments to finish so he's with Bell tonight."

Tegan tutted. "Shame, so no cuddles for you then."

Mia took a deep breath.

"I'm pregnant."

"Sorry, bad line. For a moment there I thought you said you were pregnant."

"Yes, that's what I said."

"Ha-ha. Stop messing about; be serious."

"I am, and it's no joke."

"WHAT. YOU'RE PREGNANT!"

Hey, don't shout. I know it's a bit of a shock. Think about me, I only found out just over an hour ago."

"Honey, I'm sorry, but *you're pregnant*. That's really hard to digest. Does Ethan even know?"

"No, you're the first person I've told."

"So what are you going to do about it?"

"I'm not sure, maybe keep it. I haven't made my mind up yet as I haven't had a lot of time to think."

"Are you sure you want to do that?"

"Not really, but I'm not having a termination. I'd rather put the baby up for adoption than do that."

"Well, don't you think you should discuss these options with Ethan first?"

"Why, he's not having the baby?"

"No, but he's still the father. Anyway, you shouldn't be making any decisions without him."

Mia chewed the inside of her mouth. Tegan was right. This was his baby too and she shouldn't exclude him.

"Okay, I guess you're right."

"So when will you tell him?"

"When I feel the moment's right. We've only just got over one bad experience; I really don't fancy another just yet."

"So you don't think he's going to take it too well?"

"Honestly? I don't know. However, I'm sure we'll get through this; I just need to choose my moment carefully."

"I don't like the thought of you going through all this on your own. Look, if you need me, just give me a call. I'm due some annual leave so I can come up pretty much anytime."

Mia smiled into the 'phone.

"I'm okay, so don't worry; I've just got a lot on my mind, that's all. I'll keep you updated on my progress and I've got my first appointment with the midwife soon, so I'll know more then."

Down the line, Tegan let out a heavy sigh.

"Just promise me you won't do anything rash. You have a few weeks to think things through before you have to make your final decision, after all, a baby's a huge responsibility."

And on that note, Mia ended the call.

She went upstairs, ran herself a bath and had a good soak. Her hand drifted to her belly. She couldn't quite believe there was the start of a new life growing inside.

She experienced equal quantities of pleasure and blind panic. Part of her was afraid, yet another was excited. This was Ethan's child. She felt a glow warm her. He would stand by her, she was sure of it.

Once she'd finished in the bath she put on her PJ's and headed for her bedroom.

The cute teddy bear she'd seen in the spare room earlier that morning was now lying on her pillow. She walked over, picked it up and gave it a hug. It smelt of Aramis cologne.

She smiled and placed the bear back onto the bed. "Thank you, Sam," she whispered, "that's just the sign I needed."

Six weeks passed and Mia still hadn't told Ethan she was pregnant. It wasn't as though she hadn't tried, it was just that the golden opportunity, the one she'd been waiting for, hadn't materialised. This very day was Mia's twentieth birthday. For a special treat, Ethan had suggested they make a day of it, go shopping in the city, eat a lavish lunch and then go to the theatre.

Mia decided: "Today is the day".

They met on Oxford Street. It was a cold February morning, a wintery sun barely able to break through the thickening cloud.

He grasped her hand inside his and kissed her cheek.

"Happy birthday, sweetheart." He gave her a small black box tied with white ribbon.

"Is this for me?" she asked, thrilled.

Ethan glanced around. "Is there someone else celebrating a birthday today?"

She giggled. "No, I guess not. Shall I open it now?"

"Well, that's generally the idea with presents."

She let go of his hand and opened the box, peered inside. She gasped with delight. "You've bought me a Pandora bracelet. Oh, Ethan, you shouldn't have." She reached up on her tip toes and kissed him hard on the lips. "Thank you; I love it."

"Shall I help you put it on?"

"Please."

She admired her gift, noticed a love heart charm in the centre with the words "I love you" engraved on it. She thought her heart would burst with joy. "It's simply beautiful," she declared, stroking the silver with her fingertips.

They made their way down the busy East End of London main street. The pavement was crammed with busy shoppers, a stream of red double-decker buses rolling on by. Taxis carried tourists to and from landmarks or headed to fancy bars and restaurants. Mia soaked up the atmosphere, enjoyed every minute, especially the big department stores. Soon her arms were laden with fancy bags of every description, and by early afternoon, so were Ethan's.

"Haven't you had enough," he moaned, eventually. "Only, my feet are killing me."

Mia smiled and pulled him close. "Okay, let's have a mini break," and she dived into a Café Nero. As soon as they entered, she realised she'd made a big mistake. The overpowering aroma of coffee beans made her stomach queasy and she instantly felt nauseous.

"Perhaps we could go somewhere else," she pleaded, but it was too late. Ethan had already put down the bags and was heading over to the shop counter. Mia tried not to breathe through her nose and gave a weak smile. "Hot chocolate?" he mimed when he caught her eye, but Mia shook her head. Water would suffice. She sat at the table nearest the door. For the first time in her life she was grateful for the cold blast of air that swept over her each time a customer opened it.

Ethan soon came back with a tray filled with goodies: a large cappuccino, two pieces of carrot cake and a bottle of water. The strong smell of the coffee literally turned her stomach. She jumped up, already retching, and cupped her hand over her mouth.

"Mia, what's wrong with you?"

She couldn't reply. Instead, she ran to the lavatory, her mouth filled with bile. She made it inside a toilet cubicle, coughing and spluttering as she vomited. She'd been suffering from morning sickness for a couple of weeks, but this was the worst she'd been. She gave herself a few minutes, rinsed her mouth out with cold water from the tap and then stared at herself in the mirror. She looked awful. Her skin was deathly pale and she had dark circles under her eyes. She scoffed at her reflection as she washed her hands. So much for pregnancy making her bloom.

She came out of the toilets to see Ethan waiting patiently, his face tight with concern.

"I hope you're not coming down with a stomach bug?" he said, offering her the water.

Mia sat down and unscrewed the top off the bottle, guzzling the cool liquid whilst she decided what to do next. Now was the perfect time to come clean about the baby. It was a public place, so if he didn't take the news too well, he wouldn't overreact. She patted her mouth dry with a cheap serviette. This wasn't the way she'd planned it but she couldn't chicken out now. He sensed something was wrong and she couldn't prolong the agony.

She took a deep breath.

"The thing is…" Now she realised she didn't quite know where to begin. After all, how does one tell someone they are going to be a father when it's not expected? She'd played the scene over and over in her head a thousand times, but now this life changing moment had arrived, she felt her courage slip away.

Ethan shuffled his chair a little closer and grabbed her hand. "Is everything okay? I mean, you're not sick are you? You know you can tell me anything… Right?" Anxiety shone in his eyes and a shiver of guilt ran down her spine. This was the defining moment. She couldn't keep this secret to herself any longer.

She licked her lips and glanced around to make sure no one else was listening.

"Do you remember when I went to see the doctor a couple of months ago?"

Ethan nodded and lifted a brow, as much as to say… *What does that have to do with anything?*

"Well, when you first go to discuss contraception, the doctor makes you take a pregnancy test." She could see he was taking in every word but that the penny hadn't yet dropped.

"Yes, I remember, and you said you'd decided to go on the pill."

Hmm, and that hadn't gone to plan, she thought in despair. She faltered, afraid of what came next. "The thing is, Ethan, there's no way to break it to you gently."

She saw him pale, felt his hand tighten around her fingers.

"Go on; what is it?"

She bit her lower lip, then forced the words out. "I'm pregnant."

"You're what?" He flung himself away from her as though hit by a bolt of lightning. His mouth gawped with disbelief.

"How? When?"

She ignored his first question. "I think it was the day you came around to the house after our first tiff. The doctor told me that condoms are known to split, so I'm guessing that's when it occurred."

She caught his stare, as though he were seeing a two headed monster.

He rubbed his hand over his jaw. "Are you positive?"

She nodded, breaking eye contact, and stared down at the table, feeling ashamed, as though she were to blame. "I'm so sorry," she whispered. She was trying not to cry, to hold it together. She'd convinced herself he would be thrilled, dreamt of him hugging her and being excited about the imminent birth. He'd even joked one time that he'd wanted a mini-me. But his expression said something completely different. He was angry, confused, but most of all, she could see he was devastated.

107

His skin had turned a deathly pale and the light in his eyes had disappeared.

He pulled his chair closer.

"So, what are you going to do?"

Her mouth went dry and a shiver of fear rippled down her back.

"What do you mean?" and her fingers gripped the bottle of water so tightly it spilt all over the table.

She watched him lick his lips, contemplating his reply. Slowly, he lowered his head, his voice a mere whisper.

"I mean, you're not planning on keeping it are you?"

"Yes, I thought…"

"Christ, tell me you're not serious." He threw his hands up, other customers stopping what they were doing to stare.

Mia felt a lump grow in her throat. This was definitely not going as well as she'd hoped.

"Ethan, please."

He shook his head. "No, this can't be happening. We've only been seeing each other a few months. There's no way we're ready for such a huge commitment."

Mia could feel her resolve slipping, felt the tears start to flow.

"I know this is a huge shock, but what else can I do? I'm not prepared to go through with an abortion. I… I thought you'd understand."

At that moment, he reminded her of a man on the run. He looked…hunted.

He got to his feet and grabbed the few carrier bags that were his.

"I've got to go. I need to think…to get my head around everything you've just told me."

He moved to the door, pulled it open, but then turned and stared at her one last time. "This is not how it should have been," he said, and then he was gone and she was left all alone.

Chapter 10

Misery comes in many forms and for Mia it came with the feeling of abandonment. Since the scene at the café, she hadn't received a single word from Ethan. She'd left a stream of messages and several voicemails, but no matter how much she begged, he never returned any of her calls. Mia was in utter turmoil. She had never expected him to react so badly. Yes, sure, he would be shocked, even suffer misgivings, at first…but then he'd come around, or at least that was what she'd expected.

On Monday morning she felt so ill she rang in sick. It wasn't just that at ten weeks pregnant her body was adjusting; it was also because she now realised Ethan had deserted her in her hour of need and she couldn't face rejection.

By Tuesday, she found eating dry toast was enough to keep the morning sickness at bay and so reluctantly forced herself to return to the Auction House.

Her nerves were as tight as piano strings when she entered the office. To her horror, she found Bell sitting at her desk, in floods of tears. Mia had never seen her in such a state, not since Sam's tragic death. She shuddered, remembering that fateful day with hallucinatory clarity, then dashed over to Bell, her heart almost breaking at seeing her so distressed.

"What's wrong? Has something happened to Ethan?" Fear exploded inside her mind. Of course, that was it, why else wouldn't he have been in touch?

Bell shook her head and wiped her eyes with a sodden tissue.

"No, it's nothing like that," she rasped, "it's just…he's gone."

Mia felt the blood drain from her face.

"Gone? Gone where?"

"To Leeds with Professor Hickson. He only told me yesterday morning and I just can't get my head around it. Said he'd agreed to be the professor's assistant whilst he's on secondment at the Henry Morgan's Institute."

"But for how long?" Mia heard desperation in her voice. Was this his way of punishing her for telling him about the baby?

Bell stared vacantly up at her, her eyes still shining with tears.

"He said he'd be away for at least six months, possibly longer."

Six months... Mia felt her heart break. How could he do such a cruel thing, leave without saying goodbye? Why would he do that? But deep inside, she already knew the answer. It was obvious he didn't want the baby and this was his one chance to escape.

"Did he tell you I'm pregnant?"

Bell stopped crying and looked dazed.

"You're having a baby?"

"Yes, I'm afraid so."

"And he knows?"

"What do you think?"

Bell got up from her chair, her expression guarded.

"So, do you think that's the reason why he left?"

Mia shrugged.

"I don't know for sure, but I'm guessing it's the most likely answer. I broke the news to him on my birthday, but...er...he didn't take it too well." Bell came over and brushed a lose curl away from Mia's cheek. "Did you tell him you're planning on keeping the child?" Mia nodded and Bell reached out and gently touched her face.

"It's such a big commitment and he's not ready. He's far too young and immature to be a father, plus he has a glittering career ahead of him."

"There was always room for his career," Mia said. "I would never have stopped him doing what he loved. All I needed...all I hoped for was for him to be by my side. I haven't given up on him yet. It's still early days so he may change his mind. I just need to give him time." Her voice trailed away. She had to stay strong and believe her own words.

"And if he doesn't come around?"

"He will; he has to."

Bell dropped her hand, shook her head, then made her way back to her desk.

"I'm not so sure. For him to just up sticks and go...to leave you...me...this." She flung her arms into the air. "Look around you, Mia; this is Ethan's home, his life. The fact he's walked away from everything speaks volumes. I wouldn't be surprised if he contacts me to say he's never coming back."

"No. Don't say that," Mia cried, and tears bubbled to the surface. "I know you think I've chased your boy away, but it takes two to make a baby and I'm the one left holding it."

Bell's expression softened and then she let out a deep sigh.

"I'm sorry; you're right. I blamed you and I had no right. Everything is such a mess and I don't know what to do to fix it."

"It's not your mess to fix," Mia sniffed, "and if anyone can sort my life out, it's got to be me."

Bell let out another sigh, grabbed a few files off her desk and headed towards the door just as it flew open and Angel stormed in. "Bell, Felicity say's the publisher's on the 'phone and he's in a right mood." Her cat-like gaze flicked from one to the other. "Shall I ask him to call back?"

Bell threw the files back onto her desk. "No, I'll get it. He'll only keep on ringing until I agree to the new layout for this month's magazine." Without a backward glance, she headed down the Hall.

"What's got into her?" Angel asked, closing the door, her large eyes wide with curiosity.

Mia felt herself crumble.

"Ethan's left because I'm pregnant."

Angel whistled through her teeth. "No wonder Bell's pissed. You know that as far as she's concerned the sun shines out of his arse."

Mia nodded. "That's pretty much the half of it, but he is the only family she has."

Angel plonked her backside on Bell's desk, pushing the paperwork to one side.

"That's not strictly true. What about the baby you're carrying? That's her granddaughter or grandson in there."

Mia sniffed again; she hadn't really given it much thought.

"I guess you're right. It's just I've been so wrapped up with Ethan that the rest of the family have taken a back seat."

"Then it's time you put everything into perspective. Bell should be grateful you've stuck around and she's going to get to see the baby."

Mia was grateful for Angel trying to make her feel better.

"Do you fancy coming over to the cottage for dinner? You could stay the night if you like?"

Angel smiled, her jet black lips stretching into a grin.

"Have you got any beer?"

"Yes, plenty."

"Then it's an offer I can't refuse."

That night they travelled on the tube together. Angel had dyed her hair jet black. "I like your hair that colour," Mia remarked as they made their way towards the train station.

Angel grinned. "I can get a similar shade for yours if you like?"

Mia chuckled and headed for the platform. "Thanks for the offer, but no thanks. I'll stick to chestnut."

"You're boring," Angel scoffed, opening a carriage door and letting Mia go first. Mia laughed for the first time that day. "Let's just say I'm a little more conservative than you are."

"It's good to let yourself go once in a while," Angel insisted, grabbing two empty seats. "After all, you only live once."

They chatted all the way home and it wasn't long before they arrived at the cottage. Mia dived straight into the kitchen and rustled up one of her famous stir-fry's with some left over chicken. They sat down and ate together, Angel with a bottle of beer and Mia with a glass of milk. Angel was good company and they appeared to have a lot in common. Both loved to read, watch chick flicks and were huge fans of The Vampire Diaries.

"So who's your favourite vampire?" Mia asked with a smirk.

"I'm into Klaus," Angel confessed. "I've always been a sucker for the bad boys."

Mia grinned. She wasn't surprised. "My guilty pleasure's Damon," she admitted. "It's those big, beautiful green eyes."

Angel tugged playfully at her sleeve. "Why, because they remind you of Ethan's?"

It was true, they were very similar in shape and colour. Mia's good mood vanished.

"Oh, don't be so glum," Angel chided. She got up from the table, headed over to the fridge and helped herself to another beer. "I'm sure it'll all work out in the end."

Mia wasn't convinced. She got up from her chair and headed into the lounge. Angel followed.

"Do you know what I'd do?"

"No, what's that?"

"I'd write him a letter."

"Are you serious, and does anyone even use the mail these days?"

"Sure they do, and at least it'd give you the chance to write everything down, get it off your chest."

"Then why shouldn't I just text or email?"

"Because it's not personal, it's not the same as a letter. As far as I'm concerned, what he did to you sucks...big time, but if you want him back, get writing."

113

"And what would I say…exactly?"

"I dunno. Tell him how you feel, that you miss him and you're prepared to wait until he gets back."

"And what if I don't want him back?"

"Oh, don't be such a martyr, that simply isn't true."

Mia slouched forward as she pondered over Angel's idea. Would it really work? She guessed there was only one way to find out. She went over to a small cupboard and dug out some writing paper and a pen.

"I'll blame you if this makes matters worse," she announced, and she sat down in an armchair, her feet tucked under her legs. She bit her lip as she thought about what she would say. What could she say to make him come home?

Dear Ethan,

I'm writing this letter because I don't know what else to do. Your mum told me today that you've left to go to Leeds with Professor Hickson and that she doesn't know when you'll return. I can't believe you're gone. Already there's an open chasm in my heart that's so deep I don't know how to fix it. The news of you leaving was like a physical blow. An invisible injury that will never heal.

There's other stuff too. Already I yearn for the fleeting touch of your hand, your kisses on my lips. I'm heartbroken; the pain of losing you so powerful that my mind thinks part of me is missing. They say that when you love someone they become a part of you. Well, I want that part back so badly I could scream.

I miss watching you sleep, the warmth of your body next to mine, All that I loved about you has gone, yet I refuse to believe you've abandoned me, our baby. It hurts. It hurts so much to think that you could ever leave me like this. I believed you when you said you'd love me forever, and because love is such a powerful emotion, I cannot accept you'll not come back to me.

I understand how the news about the baby was not what you expected and that it will forever change our lives. But, Ethan, this is our child, our flesh and blood. Please don't give up on us. All I'm asking is for you to give us a chance, to try and make things work.

I love you, always and forever,

Mia

Once she'd finished she handed the letter to Angel.

"What do you think? Is it too mushy?"

Her companion shook her head. "He's an idiot if he doesn't realise how much he means to you. Personally, I think he's a lucky man to have someone love him the way you do."

Mia let out a deep sigh as she folded the paper in two. She hoped it would make him realise that she wasn't trying to trap him.

"Would you like another beer?"

Angel nodded. "Sure, but I'll get it." She went back into the kitchen whilst Mia searched for an envelope.

"I like your fridge magnets," Angel called out. "Who bought you the alphabet letters?"

"I think they were Sam's, my uncle," she explained, unable to find any envelopes.

Angel arrived back with two beers. "Just one won't hurt," she said, shaking the bottles gently.

Mia hesitated. She really shouldn't, but what the hell. She went into the kitchen to leave the letter on the table, to remind her to buy a packet of envelopes and some stamps. Out of the corner of her eye she caught sight of the fridge magnets. The letters had been rearranged to spell "Angel is cool," which made her smile. There was nothing like being a little in love with one's self.

She made her way back into the sitting room and switched on a small radio.

"So what's your next step?" Angel asked, taking a swig of beer. Mia sighed and sat down next to her friend.

"I'm going to have to tell my mum about the baby."

"What, you haven't told her yet?" Angel's eyes grew wide. "Why?"

"Well, firstly, I wanted to wait until I was three months pregnant. I didn't want to tell her and go through all the shit that will come with it only then to lose the baby by some force of nature."

Angel nodded. "I see your point. So you don't think she's going to be happy about the forthcoming event?"

Mia lifted an eyebrow. "Would your mum?"

Angel laughed out loud. "I need a man first, but Jeez, she'd probably kill me."

"Then you get the bigger picture."

"Sure, but I've noticed you don't talk about your mum much. Don't you get on?"

Mia took a mouthful of beer. "Huh. This tastes disgusting."

Angel chuckled. "I guess your taste buds no longer enjoy the finer things in life."

Mia wiped her mouth, ignoring Angel's comment. "My mum and I have never seen eye to eye. I was always a daddy's girl."

"And your dad died, right?"

"Yes, after a battle with Leukaemia. He tried everything to stay with us, two bouts of chemo plus clinic trials in a prestigious hospital, up in Manchester. He turned out to be just another lab rat."

"I'm so sorry," Angel whispered. "I didn't mean to pry."

"No, it's fine, honest. It's just my mother hardly went to see him. It was me and Tegan, my sister, who made the effort, whenever we could. It was mostly weekends, mind, and my mum was always otherwise engaged. I know it hurt him, but he tried not to show it."

"What a bitch."

"Oh yeah, and now she's married to this guy who's loaded. He's nice enough but has two sons who are nothing but trouble."

"And you don't see much of them?"

"Not if I can help it. The only problem is that those two morons have moved down to London."

"London's a big place," Angel insisted.

"Maybe, but I've already found out it's not big enough."

"You've seen them?"

"Only Jacob, the eldest, and that didn't turn out so well."

"What do you mean?" It was at that moment that Mia felt she needed to unburden herself. Something inside told her Angel could be trusted. As they sat talking together, she confessed to what had happened at Walt's party. Angel turned out to be a great listener, but Mia found she couldn't tell her about what he'd done to her at her mother's wedding.

Angel huffed when Mia had finished. "No wonder you want them to stay the hell away. What an arsehole, and I certainly wouldn't want him related to me either."

Without warning the room went as cold as ice, as though someone had opened the front door and let the night air in.

"It's freezing in here," Angel declared, jumping up and rubbing her arms. "Has a window blown open upstairs or something?" Mia stared at her friend, knowing all too well it was Sam making his presence known. Just as quickly, the temperature in the room went back to normal.

"That was weird. I just suffered the most peculiar sensation," Angel gasped, confusion written all over her face. "It was as though someone walked right through me."

Mia thought it best not to tell her about her uncle. The last thing she wanted was to scare her away. She didn't have any other friends her age and so Angel was now extremely precious.

"Don't worry. The heating often plays up," Mia said, unable to look her in the eye.

Angel cleared her throat and glanced up, Mia catching her expression of scepticism. "Really, are you sure? Because that's not all that happened."

"What are you talking about?"

Angel licked her lips, and Mia noticed how her skin had turned pale.

"Please don't freak out, but I just heard a man's voice whisper in my ear 'Help me, keep her safe'."

"That's impossible," Mia murmured, her mind racing ahead. Why would Sam speak to Angel?

Angel reached over and grabbed Mia's hand. "I sense there's a ghost in this house," she declared. "Do you know who it is?"

Mia stared at her new best friend. "It's Sam," she quietly confessed.

Angel squeezed her fingers. "Your uncle? I thought as much."

"You're not scared?"

"No, of course not. Did I forget to mention I'm a medium? I have psychic powers, the ability to connect with the dead, and the reason why I'm known as Angel."

Chapter 11

After Angel's revelation, the two of them became virtually inseparable, pretty much stuck together, as though glued. Mia figured that for the first time in her life she'd found herself a true friend. She guessed the relationship worked both ways. Angel was a loner, and having such a rare gift, which meant she could reach out to dead people, didn't appear to make her very popular with the living.

At least three times a week they got together. They mostly stayed at Angel's flat because it was closer to work and also because, since the incident with Sam, she wasn't all that keen to return to the cottage.

This night, however, was the night Mia was going to stay home and tell Sandra about the baby. She'd been putting if off and putting it off, and now Tegan was getting on her case.

When she arrived home from work, the first thing she did was check her mail. It had been two weeks since she'd sent Ethan the letter, begging him to return.

With a sigh, she threw the junk mail onto the table and went and made herself a hot drink. There was still no word from him. She'd heard on the grapevine that he'd settled down in Leeds and that the Professor was very pleased with how quickly he'd established himself. The news did nothing to make her feel better. Instead, she felt him slipping away.

She went upstairs and lay on the bed, grabbing her mobile phone. After a deep breath she rang her mother. It seemed ages before she answered.

"Hello, this is the Dallison residence."

"Hi, Mum, it's me."

"Oh, darling, how lovely to hear from you, it's been ages."

"Huh, sorry... Yes, I've been busy, you know, work and everything."

"Yes, I understand, but I do wish you'd call a little more often. Sometimes I feel as if you don't care about me."

Mia rolled her eyes. Here we go, she thought.

"I know, but the 'phone does work both ways."

There was a brief pause. When her mother spoke, her voice carried an edge.

"So, what have I done to deserve the pleasure?"

Mia squirmed on her bed and thought she may as well get straight to the point.

"I've some news," she blurted, noticing her voice had gone up an octave.

Her mother now sounded pleased. "Oh, really? Have you been promoted? Or have you found yourself another boyfriend? I did like the sound of the last one but...well, you let him get away."

Mia felt anger build up inside. Would her mother always blame her for everything that went wrong in her life?

"Well, seeing as you've brought Ethan into the conversation, I think I'd better tell you."

"Oh, you're back together again; I knew it."

Mia gritted her teeth. Just for once, would her mother shut up and let her finish?

"No, not exactly, but it does concern him."

Her mother fell silent and Mia felt her resolve slip away.

"Er, the thing is, Mum...I'm pregnant."

"You're what?"

"I'm pregnant...with Ethan's child."

Her mother gave a huge gasp.

"No, I... I...can't believe it. You've always been such a good girl."

Mia sighed. "Good girls get caught out too."

"Does he even know?"

"Yes."

"And what's he going to do about it?"

"He's gone to live in Leeds."

Another gasp.

"You mean he's left you?"

Mia felt tears slide down her cheeks, her resolve finally broken.

"He packed his stuff the minute he found out." She began to weep, unable to bear the pain of losing him any longer. She'd been so brave, believing he would see sense and return, but telling her mother made it all so real, so final.

"What a bastard!" Sandra's fury exploded like a rocket launcher. "So he thinks he can have his wicked way with you and then leave you in the lurch? Why, I have a good mind to tell Jacob and Daniel and get them to pay him a visit."

Her threat abruptly stopped Mia's tears.

"No, don't you dare. This is between me and Ethan, and the last thing I want is him being beaten up."

"He deserves it after what he's done to you."

"No, Mum, please, I'm begging you, don't get them involved."

Clearly, the tone of her voice had calmed Sandra down a little.

"Oh, very well, but only because you're so insistent. I can't believe it, not of him. Still, he's not the first man to run away from responsibility. Are you keeping the baby, and if you are, will you be coming home to have the child here?"

Mia had already thought about that.

"Yes, I'm having the baby, and no, I'm staying here. This is my home now and I'm booked in with a regular midwife. Besides, my friends and job are here."

Sandra gave a deep sigh.

"As you wish. So when's the baby due?"

"Early September."

"So soon?"

"I guess."

"Well, if you need anything, you know where I am."

Mia smiled into the 'phone. "Thanks, Mum."

She ended the call and threw her mobile onto the duvet. *Thank God that's over...*

A heavy sigh escaped her lips. She was relieved that her mother had taken the news better than she'd expected. Grateful, the tension in her shoulders started to ebb away. Was she really worried about what her mother thought about her? No, it was more her reaction, and the fact she'd come close to getting Jacob and Daniel involved. She prayed silently that Sandra would keep her word. It was raining outside, yet another wet weekend. She snuggled down, pulled the pillow close and allowed the rhythmic patter of rain to lull her into a deep sleep.

Mia never heard a word from Ethan, but as the weeks rolled on, she still refused to give up hope that he would change his mind once the baby was born. She took Angel with her when she had her first scan at twelve weeks. It should have been a joyous occasion but instead it fell flat. All the excitement of the pregnancy had simply evaporated along with Ethan. It was Angel who stood by her, held her hand and became a shoulder to cry on.

Mia watched the baby on the TV monitor move inside her. It was sucking its thumb and she cried with relief when she was told the child seemed healthy. Measurements were taken, and when she had a further scan at twenty weeks, the midwife asked if she wanted to know the sex. She'd refused. It didn't matter one way or the other, it was Ethan's child and she would love it unconditionally. She left the local hospital holding five scan photos: one for herself and the others for each of her close female friends or relatives. It made her sad to think she had no men in her life; no brother, father or boyfriend. Things really were bleak.

Although she was unhappy, the next few months passed quickly. To keep her mind occupied, she concentrated on getting the nursery ready. Money wasn't an issue; she had her monthly salary and Sam had made ample previsions for her in his will.

Angel helped her transform the back bedroom into a nursery. They painted the walls pale lemon and hung up matching curtains. Once the paint pots were put away, they enjoyed a day in the city, buying furniture in one of the big department stores. In contrast, the cot, baby unit and wardrobe arrived all in white. Mia was impressed to learn Angel was quite the artist and watched in fascination as she stencilled images of Peter Rabbit, Jemima Puddle-duck and Mrs Tiggy-Winkle on the walls. Mia, who was by now eight months pregnant, was delighted with the end result.

Her bump, as she liked to call it, had grown considerably over the past few months and she was due to start maternity leave the following week. She now found the journey to work tiresome. Her ankles were beginning to swell, especially when she was on her feet too long, and by mid-morning she was always dog tired. She was looking forward to having nine months off work, although the thought of raising a child alone still scared her to death.

She was sitting at her desk one lunch time, glancing through a glossy magazine, when she heard someone running down the corridor. The door burst open and Angel flew in.

"Thank God you're sitting down because you're not gonna believe who I've just seen."

She dashed over, her large eyes wild. Mia rose to her feet in alarm. "What the hell... Are you okay?" Her friend didn't reply but Mia could see she was trembling.

"Angel, talk to me... You... You...look as though you've seen a ghost."

Angel bit her lip and glanced over at the door.

"I may as well have, and there's no easy way of breaking the news to you... He's back."

"Who?" but even before Angel could speak, a feeling of utter dread washed over Mia. "Ethan?" She found she couldn't breathe, had to grip the chair to stop herself from falling.

Angel nodded, "Yes, I've just seen him drop off some files in the Professor's office."

It felt as though a dagger twisted in her heart, and she fell back into the chair. He was back. He'd finally come home. For a moment she was elated, yet frightened at the same time. Had he returned to be with her, or perhaps even with the baby? She tried not to build her hopes up, feeling the baby kick as her pulse quickened.

"Your daddy's home," she whispered softly, stroking her stomach with affection. She couldn't believe it. Not a word and then he was here, *puff*, as if by magic.

"What should I do?" she asked Angel. "Should I go to him?"

"I'm not sure," Angel admitted, biting her nails. "I still can't get my head around him showing up unannounced."

"No, me neither, but I can't just ignore the fact he's here in the same building."

"I know, but I don't think you should go running to him, either. He's the one who left you up the duff remember."

Mia lowered her gaze. Those words had stung like a horsefly. She didn't want to be reminded that he'd left her to cope alone. God knows what she would have done without Angel these past few months. She'd been a rock, always ready to listen, and whenever Mia had hit an all-time low, it had been her who had picked up the pieces.

"Perhaps I should wait, see if he comes looking for me."

"I think that's a good idea, after all, he's the one who should do all the chasing."

Mia felt a moment of panic. "But what if he doesn't want me anymore? What am I going to do then?"

"Don't think like that," Angel chided, "just take one step at a time. However, he's going to have to face the music at some point."

"Yes, but when? Look at the state of me." She rose to her feet, her stomach large and swollen, and rubbed out an ache in the small of her back. "He's not going to want me like this." For the first time, Mia saw doubt cloud Angel's eyes. "You won't always be pregnant, and besides, it's *his* child."

There was a cough, someone cleared their throat and Mia lifted her head to see Ethan standing in the doorway. He looked so well, his face slightly tanned, his clothes immaculate as always. Angel jumped, clearly taken by surprise. She squeezed Mia's hand before leaving the room without uttering another word.

Mia didn't know whether to laugh or cry.

"It's so good to see you," she blurted, feeling awkward. "Northern air must really agree with you."

She noticed he tried to smile, but his attempt failed miserably.

"Hello, Mia. Long-time no see."

He stepped into the room, closing the door behind him.

Mia rushed forward, wishing only to make him welcome, but he held up the palm of his hand and she stopped dead in her tracks.

"There's something I need to get off my chest. You know…clear the air."

It was Mia's turn to attempt a smile. She felt cumbersome, and if she were honest, a little wary. She wasn't too sure how this would end, yet she couldn't let go of that spark of hope. Perhaps he'd made plans for them to be together, maybe move to Leeds? Didn't he realise she would follow him to the ends of the earth?

"Hmm, that sounds ominous," she muttered and sat back in her chair, pointing to Bell's empty one. "Please."

Ethan went and sat down, then pointed to her stomach.

"My, but that's big," he announced without a trace of tact.

Mia grinned, taking no offence as she stroked her belly lovingly.

"Do you wanna feel?" She reached out to grab his fingers, but Ethan pushed his chair back and looked horrified.

"Er, no, thanks, that would be…weird." He ran his fingers through his hair. "Mia, we need to talk."

"Okay, so talk. I've been waiting over six months to hear what you have to say."

Ethan glanced away then; she had clearly hit a nerve.

Mia tried not to hold her breath, aware he hadn't tried to kiss her or hold her in his arms. The man in front of her had become a stranger, not the Ethan she remembered. A distance had come between them, she could sense it.

"The thing is, I've had time to think about things these last few months."

Mia eyed him critically. "You mean the baby?"

He nodded and then jumped to his feet.

"Christ, Mia, I don't even know how we landed in this mess. I mean, I know *how*… It's just… I'm not ready to be a father. I haven't graduated from my uni' course yet and there are so many things I want to do before I settle down and have kids."

Thwack! Like a butcher wielding a meat clever, he'd severed her heart in two. The bottom simply fell out of her world, yet it seemed impossible that one man could wield so much power over her. If Mia had been less crushed, she might have lost her temper.

She rose to her feet, her legs shaking, and went to stand beside him. "I need you," she whispered, trying to take his hand, "we both do. You said you loved me, that you'd love me forever; didn't you mean it?"

She watched him grapple with his emotions and saw despair resting deep within his eyes.

He snatched his hand away.

"I do… I did, but not with a child in tow. It was your decision to keep it. I just can't do this. Call me a coward, what you will, but I don't want to feel—"

"Trapped?"

His shoulders sagged.

"Is that what you think I've done to you?"

He nodded, then threw himself back into his chair.

"I'm sorry, Mia, but yes, I do." At his words, Mia felt her own despair ambush her. It was so powerful she couldn't stop tears bursting from her like a river bursting its banks.

"But I love you," she cried, those tears now streaming down her face. "Doesn't that count for anything?"

It was clear Ethan couldn't cope with her being upset. Once again he jumped to his feet, but then pushed her gently aside and ran for the door before he turned and sighed. "It's over between us," he rasped. "Just move on, Mia, forget about me and get on with your life."

"No-o-o-o, wait..." and she rushed after him, but he simply slammed the door in her face. She stood motionless, shocked at what he'd done, before sliding to the floor. She broke into uncontrollable sobbing, unable to hold onto her emotions a second longer. It was over; it was official; he no longer wanted her. She lay on the floor, curled into a ball, and wrapped her arms around her unborn child. Part of her wanted to die, to make the pain in her heart go away. *He doesn't love me anymore...*

His love had given her strength, the courage to carry on. But how could she ever recover from the knowledge that their relationship was truly over?

Now wracked with sorrow, her cries drifted along the hallway like a lost soul. She didn't hear the footsteps that rushed along that corridor, nor see the door fly open, only felt the strong arms that enfolded her. Through bleary eyes she saw Angel trying to help her to her feet, but all Mia could do was drop her head to her chest and let out a stifled scream.

That night, she hadn't wanted to stay at Angel's. Although her friend had pleaded, she explained she simply needed to be alone. With a heavy heart she made her way home. Her eyes were swollen, red rimmed, her hair dishevelled and messy. When she entered the cottage, she was both physically and mentally exhausted.

At three am she awoke, sharp pains cutting across her abdomen. At first she thought they were Braxton Hicks, something the midwife had described as false labour. She couldn't quite put her finger on it, but something just didn't seem right. She threw back the duvet and headed for the bathroom. The pain was so sharp, excruciating, that it felt like a knife slicing through her stomach. Doubled over, she turned on the light, then heard water hit the floor.

Shit, my waters just broke. What the hell do I do now? She'd planned to stay at Angel's for the last week of her pregnancy, but that was four weeks away yet. She opened a cupboard door, grabbed a hand towel and shoved it between her legs. Flustered and a little scared, she at least had the sense to ring the number she'd been given by the midwife. Another contraction wracked her body as a nurse answered.

Mia managed to explain that she was having contractions every five minutes, that her waters had broken and that she lived alone.

"Call an ambulance immediately," the nurse advised. "Get here as soon as you can." Mia did as she was told and rang '999', threw on some sweats and grabbed her already prepared bag of baby things and spare clothes. She rang Angel, who'd agreed to be her birthing partner, feeling the first tremor of fear when she got her voicemail. Mia cursed under her breath; Angel was also renowned for forgetting to charge her mobile.

She started to shake, afraid of what was yet to come, but tried not to cry. She wouldn't be the first woman to have a baby alone. Secretly, though, the thought terrified her and for a moment she contemplated ringing Ethan. The pain had already become unbearable but at the last minute she changed her mind, afraid of being rejected yet again. The contractions were now more frequent, and this only added to her anxiety, not knowing if this was still the first stage of labour.

A blue light flashed outside her window and she hobbled down the stairs to greet the ambulance crew. Just before she opened the door, she felt an odd sensation, as though a cold draught had brushed across the nape of her neck. She shivered as the light above her head dimmed and a DVD dropped from a small wooden bookcase and landed at her feet. Her hand cupped her stomach as she struggled to bend down to retrieve it. She flicked it over and grinned despite a sharp tightening across her abdomen. She stared down at the picture of Danny Devito and Arnold Schwarzenegger before letting out a loud titter. "Seriously Sam... *Twins*. Are you kidding me?" She clicked the tip of her tongue inside the roof of her mouth to hide her amusement. "Very funny, but let's make this clear; one child's more than enough for me so don't go giving me double trouble." She pushed the DVD back into its rightful place, welcoming the unexpected distraction. She knew it was Sam's way of helping her through her uncertainty. It had worked too because her fear of the unknown had disappeared for the time being.

Mia opened the front door and headed towards the paramedics. The two men gave her warm smiles of reassurance and soon had her strapped onto a stretcher. The contractions were coming thick and fast by the time they arrived at the hospital, where the crew wheeled her straight into a birthing suite.

Chapter 12

Present Day...

Mia stared out of the window and watched a thin spiral of smoke leave a nearby chimney. It swirled in black coils toward the heavens and she wished, at this very moment, that she too could disperse into the atmosphere and never be seen again. It wasn't even remotely possible, already another day, the early morning sun having risen, a golden ball against a backdrop of light blue. Mia turned away from the window and stared at the sleeping babe lying in the hospital cot. This very day she would have no choice but to leave this sanctuary and go home, without the man she loved beside her.

The guilt of how she reacted during and after the birth still haunted her every waking moment. She had been furious, hurt and deeply upset with Ethan, but that was no reason to take it out on the child. She was ashamed of her outburst, but there was no going back now. What was done, was done. The words could never be unsaid, and the pain and sorrow of Ethan's betrayal would stay deep within her heart forever.

A knock at the door shook away her dark mood and one of the staff nurses came scurrying in.

"All the paperwork for your discharge is complete," she said, "so you can go home as soon as you're ready."

Mia tried to look enthusiastic. Inside she was frightened, afraid of going home alone. She put on a bright smile, prayed it would be enough to fool the world.

"Great," she said. "I'm just waiting on my friend to pick me up. You see, I don't drive and she's bringing the baby's car seat."

"That's just as well, really, as you're not allowed to drive so soon after the birth." The nurse popped the discharge papers onto the bed, then paused at the cot and patted the baby gently. She'd clearly had an afterthought, though, for she stopped and said, "Your baby's thriving, and it's good to see you've finally bonded, but if you've any concerns or need advice, just ring the number on the bottom of the sheet and one of the midwives will help all they can." She glanced down at the fob watch pinned to her chest, let out a deep sigh and then hurried away.

Mia sat on the bed and her depression quickly returned. Inside, she felt hollow, dead. How had she come to this crossroads in her life? She'd had such a great future ahead of her: a job she enjoyed, a wonderful home and a gorgeous boyfriend to call her own. Now she had a baby, a child to raise alone. Her eyes filled with tears and she allowed them to fall. Although she felt love for the child, she worried she had made a huge mistake. Perhaps Ethan was right and she shouldn't have kept the baby. Her life would now follow a different path, all because she'd thought she knew best.

Another knock on the door forced her to pull herself together.

Angel popped her head in, but her initial broad grin slipped from her lips as she rushed to Mia's side. "Hey, chick, whatever's the matter?"

Mia turned her face away, refusing to make eye contact. "I don't think I can do this," she blubbered, dabbing her eyes with a paper tissue. "I know I'm being pathetic but I can't look after a baby, not on my own."

Angel sat down on the bed, put her arm around her friend and gave her a quick hug.

"Of course you can, but no one ever said it was going to be easy, especially with your baby being premature."

Mia sniffed loudly. "I'm such a fool, I thought it would be a walk in the park. I'm already exhausted and I haven't had a wink of sleep in days."

"It will get easier, I promise. They always say the first few weeks are the hardest for all new mums. Anyway, look on the bright side, at least your baby's out of the incubator and already fit enough to go home." Her voice adapted a curious tone.

"Oh, I meant to ask… have you chosen a name yet?"

For the first time, Mia's lips curved into a smile. "Yes, I've decided on Alex."

Angel nodded her approval. "Good choice, I like it. It's kinda short but sweet."

Mia glanced over to where her child still slept. A wave of guilt surged inside her mind, crashing into her thoughts, causing her to take a deep breath. What gave her the right to blame an innocent child for the wrong choices she'd made? After all, it wasn't the baby's fault how everything had turned out. She tried to block out any feelings of remorse, but it was no good, Alex had already stolen her heart.

Her gaze flicked back towards Angel who was busy fiddling with something inside her jacket pocket. To her surprise, she produced an iPhone.

"This is for you," she said. "It's my old mobile, although I don't want you losing your temper again and smashing it up—like you did your last one." Angel hugged her again before she could reply. "I've sent a text to my entire contact list to let them know I have a new number. I've also wiped the 'phone, but have kept a few contacts I knew we shared." Her face turned serious. "I haven't told anyone this is your new number. I thought you could do that…when you're ready."

"Thanks, I appreciate your thoughtfulness," Mia said, genuinely touched by her act of kindness. She was still angry with herself for having destroyed her mobile but had been too upset to control her despair. Her grief had been all-consuming, and the fact that Ethan had only been interested in the baby when he thought he had a son had only made her fury rise. Why was it that most men wanted boys anyway? Was it a macho thing? She wasn't sure, although she'd once heard her mother say it took a man to make a girl. Either way, during labour, her emotions had taken over her senses. She'd made her mind up, Ethan wasn't going to see the baby. He couldn't just decide to be interested when he realised the sex of the child. No, he couldn't do that, not after everything he'd put her through.

Neither Ethan nor Bell had visited the hospital to see the baby. She hadn't expected Ethan, but Bell... Well, that had stung.

Angel soon gathered Mia's belongings, went down to the car and then came back up with the car seat.

"Are you ready?" she asked, scooping up the baby's sleeping form into her arms.

Mia nodded and grabbed the last of her things. "Mm, I guess. I mean it's not as though I have a choice, do I?"

"No, that's true; you don't. Let's face it. Alex is here to stay so why not make the best of a bad situation."

Mia knew when she was beaten. Angel wasn't the type of girl to let anyone shirk their responsibilities, no matter how bad the circumstances.

"Okay, you're right, let's get out of here and take this little mite home."

Angel's face appeared to relax, just a little, before she moved towards the door.

The three of them made their way downstairs, heading outside the maternity unit to where the car was parked. The baby and its passengers were soon strapped inside, although the drive home was slow. Angel drove as though she were carrying something so fragile it might break at the slightest bump, so by the time they hit the village of Cockmoor Alex was screaming for a feed.

Mia let herself in the front door whilst Angel hurried behind with the baby.

To her surprise, the living room was filled with several helium balloons and the kitchen table held a stack of cards and presents.

Mia grinned then chuckled. "Who arranged all these?" she asked. "I know I've had a baby but I wasn't expecting such a wonderful homecoming."

Angel placed the car seat on the floor. "Who do you think?" she huffed and headed off to get the rest of Mia's things from the boot.

After the ordeal of giving birth, Mia admitted to herself that it was good to be home. There was a Moses basket sitting on a stand in the corner, brightly coloured baby toys draped around the hood; a small card attached told her it was a gift from her dear sister.

Mia bent down and unclipped the baby from its restraints.

"Okay, we've got this covered," she said, carefully taking off the baby's hat and coat. She rummaged inside a changing bag and pulled out a fresh bottle.

"There you go," she said, popping the teat into its mouth, "it's clearly feeding time at the zoo." She watched the baby guzzle down the milk.

Angel came back and dumped the last of her belongings onto the floor. "That's all of it," she exclaimed. "Time to put the kettle on."

She dashed into the kitchen whilst Mia settled in the armchair. Within minutes, Angel was back with two hot, steaming mugs of tea.

She plonked them down onto the table.

"So, how's little Alex doing?" she asked.

Mia relaxed as her friend cooed over the baby. "Fine; although hungry as ever."

Angel came and sat beside her, then gave a deep sigh.

"Good, cos I've something to tell you."

Mia stared at her serious expression, and felt a stab of apprehension. "Oh, what is it?"

"I've had a text from Ethan."

Mia gasped out loud unable to control her reaction. "When?"

"Just now."

"What did it say?"

"He asked if he could come over."

Mia unconsciously pulled the bottle from Alex's lips and the baby started to cry.

"No, he can't… I don't want to see him."

Angel's eyebrows furrowed.

"Don't be silly, this is what you've wanted all along."

Mia jumped to her feet, practically throwing the baby into Angel's arms.

"No, I've made up my mind: he can't come over. He said he didn't want us, so why the change of heart? No, it's just idle curiosity. I bet he'll come and see the baby once and then he'll never visit again."

"I don't think that's true," Angel argued, quickly shoving the bottle back into the baby's mouth. "I know he's been a shit, but perhaps now the baby's here he's trying to make amends. It's probably only just hit him that he actually has a child of his own."

"NO!" Mia almost spat out the word. "He mustn't come here. He isn't welcome. Plus, he made his choice, so now he can stick to it."

She watched confusion sweep across Angel's face.

"I don't know what's got into you. Just days ago you would have done anything to get him back."

"Yeah, well, things change, people change, and if he's so fickle, I don't want him in my life."

But Angel was like a dog with a bone. "I don't care what you say, something isn't right. You still love him; I can see it in your eyes."

"That's enough, just let the matter drop," but her words were like oil to a flame.

"No, I won't. I know you; this isn't you talking. Has something happened? Something you're not telling me?"

Mia bit her lip, feeling she was being backed into a corner.

"Why does there have to be something the matter? Can't you see I'm simply ready to move on with my life? There's no point getting my hopes up just for him to dash them all over again."

Without uttering a word, Angel got to her feet and took the now sleeping child over to the Moses basket. With care, she placed Alex inside. She then came and stood beside her friend, but to Mia's surprise, her voice was hard, unrelenting.

"You're lying to me and I want to know why."

Mia took a deep breath. "I think it's time you left."

Angel's eyes widened but her anger refused to diminish.

"What? You think you can cut off anyone who ever challenges you?"

"I said get out."

Angel's eyes became slits.

"You're serious aren't you?"

Mia didn't reply, instead she bolted towards the door and flung it wide.

"Thanks for everything, but I need you to leave."

Angel hesitated before snatching up her coat from the chair. She raced towards Mia, but then stopped abruptly. "I will get to the bottom of this," she said, and before Mia could reply, stormed off down the garden path and into her car.

As soon as Angel drove away, Mia burst into tears. She wrung her hands, her emotions all over the place. How on earth had she managed to have a row with her best friend? The one person who had looked after her like a sister all these months? She became wracked with guilt. She should have come clean, been honest. She couldn't think about that now, though; she couldn't even admit it to herself.

Torn and alone, she felt the need to talk to someone… anyone, and picked up Angel's gift. She flicked through the numbers, found no one she wanted to confide in. She needed to talk to Tegan but couldn't remember her number off the top of her head. Her sister was now in a serious relationship with Jonas. Over the last few months her calls had become less frequent; love did that to people.

Mia decided to ring her mother. She'd spoken to her from the nurse's station, the day after she'd given birth. Her mother had sounded pleased but didn't gush over the safe arrival of her first grandchild. She simply wasn't that maternal.

Having keyed in her mother's landline, Mia saved it and then waited to be connected.

"Hello, this is the Dallison residence."

"Hi, Mum, it's me. I've just got home."

"Hello, dear, this isn't your usual number."

"No, I told you, I accidently broke my 'phone."

"Oh, yes, so you did. Are you back at the cottage?"

"Yes, we arrived about an hour ago."

"All settled in?"

"A little. It's early days…you know… I need to get into some kind of a routine."

Her mother hesitated. "This may be a bit out of the blue but… are you up for a visit?"

Mia's voice was guarded when she replied, "Like, who?"

"Me and Jack of course. He's got a business trip arranged in the city that he needs to attend, and I thought I could come along, perhaps stay with you for a couple of nights?"

Mia tried to hide the surprise in her voice. "Sure, that would be really nice… When?"

"Jack's first meeting's tomorrow evening at the Hilton. I know it's short notice but it's just a thought. I can arrive by mid-afternoon, although if you haven't the room we can always stay at the hotel."

Mia was actually pleased. She needed her mother and this was the perfect opportunity.

"Why, I'd love you to come and stay."

"You would?" She could hear the pleasure in her mother's voice.

"Yes, it would be great to see you and I can introduce you to the new arrival."

Sandra chuckled down the line, "I've got you a present; it's a baby carrier."

"Aww, that's lovely, thanks."

"Well, Tegan told me you already had a pram, so I was stuck what else to get you."

"Mum, its fine, I'm really grateful."

"Is everything alright, dear?"

"Yes, why? Shouldn't it be?"

"Oh, I don't know… You just don't sound yourself."

"Don't worry, I'm fine; a little tired perhaps but that's only to be expected."

"Okay, darling, if you're sure. I'll see you tomorrow."

By the time the conversation had ended, Mia felt much better. Her mother would finally be there when she needed her the most. A little happier, she unpacked the rest of her things and tidied the house while the little one slept. It wasn't long before the baby needed feeding again, and before she knew it, it was early evening. By ten o'clock she was shattered and dying for her bed. When she was finally able to dive under the duvet and close her eyes, all the guilt of what she'd done slithered snake-like into her mind. It flicked its forked tongue at her conscience, keeping her awake. She flipped her pillow and stared at the ceiling.

Why had she been so hard on Angel, her one ally? She turned on her side and punched her pillow into some kind of shape, then chewed over the fat as she tried to sleep. Ethan wanted to see their baby but now it was for all the wrong reasons. If only he'd wanted them both from the very beginning, she wouldn't be in such a dilemma.

She eventually fell into a fitful sleep but the baby was unsettled and awoke every two hours. By the time she'd fed, changed and settled Alex, it was almost time to start all over again. The night was a long one, and by six o'clock the next morning, the sound of a screaming baby woke her from yet another short-lived forty winks. Through bleary eyes, she went down to the kitchen and filled several bottles with cooled, boiled water before storing them in the fridge. She noticed the alphabet letters had been rearranged on the door. Now they said "Tell the truth and shame the devil". She slammed the door shut and jumbled up the letters. "Shut up, Sam," she grunted, annoyed. "You're really not helping matters at all."

She gave Alex a bath before the next feed but still the baby cried. No matter what she did, Alex wouldn't settle. It appeared that the more formula the baby had, the more Alex cried, and by the time Jack and Sandra arrived that afternoon, Mia was beside herself and in a state of sheer exhaustion.

Her mother stormed the building and soon took charge, Jack ambling in behind her.

"Have you seen yourself? You look as though you've been dragged through a hedge backwards."

"Hello, Mother, it's nice to see you, too."

There was no denying, both Mia and the cottage were in complete disarray. The cards and presents were still on the kitchen table, all unopened, and dirty baby clothes were strewn across the kitchen worktop. Empty bottles were sitting on the draining board, still waiting to be washed and put into the steriliser. It was also evident that Mia hadn't even had time to take a shower.

Sandra hung up her coat and got down to business. "Why is this baby continually crying?" she demanded.

Mia shrugged and tried not to weep. She was dog tired, having hardly slept and still in her pyjamas. "I don't know?" she whimpered. "I've tried everything, but nothing seems to work."

Sandra picked up the crying infant. "Colic," she announced. "There's nothing worse. Have you been trying to get the wind up halfway through feeds?"

Mia nodded weakly, feeling like a reprimanded schoolgirl. She had never realised looking after a baby could be so hard, so exhausting.

"Yes, every time, but hardly anything comes out."

Her mother gave her a knowing look. "Poor little mite will have terrible stomach-ache." She turned to her husband. "Jack, would you be so kind as to nip to the nearest chemist and see what you can buy over the counter." Jack didn't appear too happy but grabbed his car keys nonetheless and headed back to the car.

"Thanks, Jack," Mia called after him. He waved but didn't turn around as he closed the door behind him.

"It's a good job I arrived when I did," Sandra said, "otherwise you'd be suffering another sleepless night."

Mia tried to smile but was too tired to lift the corners of her mouth. She watched her mother gently rock the baby, noticing how her features had softened.

Her mother caught her eye.

"Darling, why don't you go and grab a couple of hours sleep? I can look after Alex and then you'll be able to cope through the night much better."

Mia didn't need asking twice, so dragged herself up the stairs and threw her tired form onto the bed. She didn't even have the energy to get under the duvet.

She awoke a few hours later to find a blanket had been draped over her shoulders. She sighed, grateful to her mum for having come up to check on her. She yawned and stretched her tired limbs, her ears listening out for the baby. Alex appeared to be asleep, but she could hear raised voices and so jumped out of bed and crept to the top of the stairs. She could hear both Jack and her mother arguing.

"I don't care if she's an unmarried mother, this isn't the flaming sixties."

"It doesn't look good, my step-daughter having an illegitimate child. I have a reputation to uphold and people will think she's an easy lay."

Sandra's voice turned into a low hiss. "That's rich coming from you. How dare you judge my daughter for having a child out of wedlock. Perhaps you should look a little closer to your own doorstep, especially after what your sons have been accused of."

She heard Jack take an indignant gasp. "I've already told you: they were both innocent," he roared.

"Bullshit. They're about as innocent as Jack the bloody Ripper."

Mia had heard enough, and more importantly, if they carried on arguing, they'd have woken the baby.

"Hey, what's going on down there?" She rushed down the stairs and barged into the kitchen.

Sandra stared guiltily at her, her eyes still full of fury. Unexpectedly, she dashed over to the other side of the room and switched the kettle on.

"Anyone for tea?" she asked, her voice too bright.

Mia sensed the smile she wore was for her benefit only. Jack appeared agitated and refused to look Mia in the eye.

"Sorry," he mumbled. "I didn't mean to… well… hurt your feelings."

"It's okay, you haven't. I understand we all have our own principles, but you need to realise this is the twenty first century and there are a lot of women out there who are single parents."

His cheeks turned beetroot. "I think I should stay at the hotel tonight. Give you ladies time to talk about baby stuff and whatnot."

He glanced at Sandra, her face as hard as steel.

"Yes, I think that would be for the best," she replied curtly. "You can pick me up tomorrow night after your business meeting."

Jack nodded and headed into the living room, where he picked up a small overnight case. He grabbed his jacket and car keys and, without saying goodbye, left.

"What was all that about?" Mia asked, glancing out of the window to make sure he'd gone. "I never realised he felt that way about unmarried mothers and I certainly didn't realise he was so judgemental."

"There are a lot of things you don't know about him," Sandra said, grabbing two cups. She opened one of the cupboard doors. "Darling, tell me you don't use red label teabags."

"What did you mean, just then… about not knowing Jack?"

Sandra continued her hunt for tea bags. "Ha, here we are, an unopened box of Yorkshire tea hidden at the back. I bet they belonged to Sam."

"Mum, answer me."

"Right, let's have a well-deserved cuppa, before that gorgeous grandchild of mine wakes up. It appears the Colic drops are working. Jack said the chemist assistant was very helpful. She explained that you just put a few drops into the bottle before the feed, and hey presto, out pops all the wind."

"I'm so grateful," Mia confessed, Jack instantly forgotten. "You know, before today, I'd never even heard of Colic."

Sandra gave her hand a tight squeeze. "That's what mums are for," she said.

Mia furrowed her brows.

"Mum, are you alright? I mean, I'm grateful and everything, but this just isn't like you. I don't wish to sound rude, but you've never liked kids… much."

Sandra smoothed her skirt and took a sip of tea. "Well, in that case, I guess being a grandmother agrees with me." She spotted the pile of dirty laundry sitting on the kitchen worktops. "Enjoy your cuppa," she said, scooping up a load of clothes and heading over to the washing machine. "It won't take me two ticks to get this place shipshape."

That evening, once Alex had gone to bed, Mia had a shower and then brought out a bottle of red wine. She decided Sandra seemed different somehow but couldn't really put her finger on why. Her mother appeared more relaxed than she'd been in years, sitting there in the living room, listening to the DJ talk on the radio about the weather and the usual congested state of the roads.

Sandra's eyes were half closed when Mia handed her an empty wine glass.

"I like this place," her mother muttered, softly. "It has a good feel about it, as though it's friendly." Mia poured the wine, then placed the bottle on the table.

"Hmm, I know what you mean. The first time Bell brought me here, I just knew I'd be happy here."

"And are you?"

Mia pulled a slight frown, then went and sat next to her.

"Well, things haven't exactly gone to plan, but yes, I'm happy enough."

Sandra swilled the wine glass beneath her nose and took a deep breath. "Ah, Chateau Du Cedre, my favourite." Mia grinned; she'd been saving the bottle for a special occasion, secretly thinking she'd have shared it with Ethan, but that would no longer be the case. The truth was, her mother would probably appreciate it far more, anyway.

"Did Angel bring you and Alex home?"

Mia nodded, then looked guiltily into her glass.

Sandra raised a perfect eyebrow.

"Something happened?"

"We had a fight."

"Over what?"

"Ethan."

"Why?"

Mia threw herself back into the armchair. Her frustration bubbled to the surface.

"Because, after everything he's put me through, he wants to see the baby."

"But I don't understand, isn't that what you wanted?"

Mia again lowered her gaze and stared into her wine glass.

"Yes, no, oh, I don't know. I guess."

Sandra shook her head. "Darling, you're not making any sense, and what does it all have to do with Angel?"

Mia lifted her lashes and stared intently at her mother.

"She went against my wishes. Said I should let him see Alex."

"And so you should. He is the father, after all."

"But it isn't that simple anymore."

"Life never is, dear." A shadow, something dark, flickered behind her mother's eyes. She cleared her throat. "Mia, there's something I've been meaning to tell you." Mia caught her mother's pained expression. It was as

143

though she was fighting some hidden demon, and the mellow mood they had just shared, disappeared.

"What is it? Is it Jack?"

Sandra tried to salvage the moment but failed miserably. "No, darling, not this time, but there's something I need to tell you, something I fear you're not going to take too well."

Mia hadn't the foggiest idea what she was on about. "Mum, you're talking in riddles and you're not making any sense. What exactly are you trying to say?"

Sandra took a deep breath and bent her head a little closer.

"Mia, as you know, your dad was ill for a very long time. Much longer than either you or Tegan were aware. Long before he was diagnosed, your dad appeared to lose interest in life, in me..." She took a large gulp of her drink. "I was still young, and Tegan had just started school. I was lonely, your dad always at work, closing the next big deal. Your Uncle Sam came to stay while he was having the shop refurbished. He was so much fun to be around, he really was a breath of fresh air."

Mia didn't like where this conversation seemed to be leading. "I'm sure it's all water under the bridge," she said, grabbing the bottle from off the table and refilling both their glasses. "As the saying goes: 'What happens in Vegas stays in Vegas'."

She watched Sandra struggle with her emotions, aware her face appeared pinched, strained.

Her mother took a large slug of wine.

"One night we went to see a movie. Your uncle always did love the silver screen and I jumped at the chance of a night out. We went for a drink afterwards, to a wine bar I knew which played the most amazing Jazz. It was a fantastic night, and we danced until dawn and then went home. Tegan was staying over at a friend's house and your dad was away on yet another business trip, and..."

She emptied the final dregs of the bottle into her glass. "It just happened, Mia. It was only the once but there were such consequences."

Mia suddenly felt sick. Unable to erase the vivid images of Sam and her mum from her mind. Sam and her mum together? She closed her eyes, fought back the tears. No, it wasn't possible, surely not. She thought of how much Sam had hated her mother, but all along it had been a ruse, a way to hide his true feelings?

"I don't understand," she whispered. "Why would he be so cruel to you when you once had a fling with each other?"

A single tear rolled down her mother's cheek.

"He never forgave me for what I did."

"What do you mean? Because you were the one who finished it?"

Mia realised her mother was trembling.

"I did something far worse, something terrible. I... I... passed off his only child as another man's."

Confusion exploded inside Mia's brain. What on earth was her mother talking about? What man? What child? Her mother's tears were falling harder now, Sandra almost crumpling into a complete wreck before Mia's eyes.

"What I'm trying to tell you is that you're Sam's child, and I allowed his brother to raise you as his own."

Mia felt her world fall apart in an instant.

"No, that's simply not true!" she cried, aghast. "It can't be. You're lying. Sam isn't my real dad."

"Why would I lie?" Sandra insisted. "What would I gain?" She tried to reach out and touch her hand but Mia snatched it away.

"No, I refuse to believe you; this is all just a bad dream and I'm going to wake up any minute now." She jumped from her chair, her own tears running down her cheeks.

She turned towards her mother.

"How could you do such a thing to Sam, and to my father?"

"I'm so sorry," Sandra said. "I should have left your dad then, I know that now."

"Left him?" Mia's despair exploded like an atom bomb. "Why, you're nothing more than a cheap slut. My own mother is a whore, for God's sake."

"That's enough!" Sandra cried, her voice shrill. "How dare you of all people judge me. I may not have been the perfect wife but I've always been a good mother to you."

"Seriously, do you really believe that? Is that why you were so quick to marry Jack and choose his sons over your own flesh and blood?"

Sandra finally crumpled before her eyes.

"I was scared of being left on my own. I didn't know what else to do. Jack wanted to move in and he promised me the boys would be good."

Mia's anger flared, like a candle in the wind, her voice gaining an edge. "Oh, well, if Jack says they're going to behave then that makes everyone happy—right?"

Sandra placed her empty wine glass on the table. "On that note, I'm going to bed before we both say something we'll regret, before everything turns ugly." She headed towards the kitchen but just as she reached the doorway, Mia threw her glass, just missing her mother's head. It smashed against the wall beside her and Sandra stared down at the broken shards, her eyes wide with disbelief.

"That's for dad," Mia yelled and promptly folded her arms and turned her back on her.

Chapter 13

The next morning, in that hazy state between sleep and wakefulness, Mia remembered all that had been said by her mother the night before. Her confession flooded Mia's mind like the tide. The previous night she'd come to bed and sobbed for the fathers she'd loved and lost. Her whole being suffered inner turmoil. So many emotions consumed her, threatening to drown her in despair. The betrayal of her mother was the worst thing she'd ever had to deal with. Then there was Sam—the knowledge she was actually his daughter, a daughter whose life he could never be a part of. Her head was messed up and her heart broken, her beloved dad now no longer her father.

She threw back the duvet and got out of bed. Her bare feet padded silently over to the window and she drew back the curtains. She picked the picture up off the windowsill, the one of her and Sam. It no longer cried out to her 'It's a baby, it might break'. Now it told a whole different story. She saw misery in his eyes, read a different message, one that said 'This is my daughter, and I want her in my life'. She bit back the tears. All she appeared to do these days was cry, but who could blame her? Her life was a mess, a complete lie, and so many people had been hurt in the process.

Alex stirred in the Moses basket, then started to moan. She heard her mother in the bathroom and so replaced the picture, feeling guilty at having the image of Sam in her bedroom. She went over to the basket and picked up the baby, aware Alex would need changing and a bottle. She made her way into the nursery, placed Alex on the baby unit and grabbed a nappy and some wipes. The bathroom door opened and she felt herself tense.

"Good morning, sweetheart, did you have a better night?" At that moment, Mia wanted to swing around and hit her mother in the face with something hard. She wasn't normally an aggressive person but now she wanted to hurt her, to give her as much pain as Mia was suffering inside. With some reluctance, she held onto her anger and kept a lid on her despair. Sandra came and stood beside her, bent and cooed over the baby. She appeared so calm, so composed, but there were new marks of strain around her mouth and eyes, perhaps even a sign of vulnerability which was hardly surprising after last night's revelation.

"I see you were only up twice in the night," she commented, letting Alex grab her little finger.

Mia bit back the scream that bubbled in her throat. She wanted to say so much, to punish her for all the upset she'd caused, but what would be the point? What was done, was done. There was no going back—no reconciliation, no happy ending. Her father was dead, Sam too. Opening old wounds and refusing to let them heal would, she knew, only tear her apart.

She reached out and grabbed her mother's arm.

"You mustn't tell anyone else what you told me last night," she warned. "Not Tegan, not Jack, not anyone."

Sandra appeared shocked at the venom in her voice. "Alright, dear, if that's what you want."

"It is. If you tell, you will split this family forever. I don't want Tegan to think I'm only her half-sister. It would crush us both."

"She wouldn't do that to you," Sandra insisted, but Mia's fingers dug into her flesh.

"Promise me," she hissed, "that this will always be our secret."

"If that's what you want… I promise."

Mia finally let go.

"Good, now you can pack your bags and leave. I don't want you here a second longer."

"But Mia, I—"

"Please, just give me time. You've blown my world apart and I need to deal with this catastrophe in my own way."

Her mother's shoulders drooped. "Very well, I'll get my things together and ring for a taxi."

"There's a number in the kitchen. It's on the wall by the cooker."

Sandra leant forward and kissed the baby on the forehead.

"You should be proud you have such a beautiful child," she whispered, but Mia didn't reply. She was trying not to lose it. Her mother walked back to her bedroom to get her things, leaving Mia wanting her out of the house not a moment too soon.

Mia headed downstairs, made up a fresh bottle and dropped a few colic drops into the formula. After what seemed like forever, she heard the beep of a horn and saw her mother standing at the front door, a small suitcase in her hand.

"Can you ever find it in your heart to forgive me?" she asked.

"I don't know; there's such a lot to forgive."

"I understand it will take time, but I'll be here when you're ready. I sense him, you know, Sam. I feel him here, with you. It's all he ever wanted... to be with his daughter."

"Then why?"

The taxi beeped again. "Oh, that's my cue to leave, but remember, if you change your mind, just give me a ring and I'll come and stay."

"Thanks," said Mia, and she meant it.

Not long after her mother had left, the health visitor paid a visit. She examined the baby, appeared pleased with the results and then asked a few basic questions.

Mia had a few of her own.

"When can I go out?"

"Oh, not yet, dear," the woman said, shaking her head. "Your baby was premature, and although over five pounds you should really stay in until full-term."

"But that's three weeks away."

"Indeed, but your baby is still a little delicate yet. Thriving well, but needs a few more ounces of fat on those tiny bones before it braves that big old world out there."

Mia heard her 'phone vibrate and glanced down to see a missed call from Ethan. Her stomach did a somersault. *How the hell did he get her number? Only one other person knew it: Angel...* Regardless, there was no way she was going to call him back. Mia thought she was about to go mad. She needed to make it up with Angel first, to explain what she'd said to Ethan.

Once the health visitor had left, Mia toyed with the idea of ringing Angel and explaining. She went over in her mind what she would say but each imagined conversation quickly snowballed into a disaster. Overcome with frustration she chickened out and decided to text instead.

Mia...

Hi, I'm so sorry about the other day. I need to explain, to tell you the truth. The thing is...I'd come and see you but can't go out of the house for three weeks due to Alex being prem. I know I'm asking a lot but would you come over and see me? Please...xx

Angel...

You have a nerve, especially after practically throwing me out of your house.

Mia...

I know. I'm so sorry. Please forgive me, I need my friend xx

Angel...

Okay, I guess, but it won't be until this evening. I'm on a date!!!!!

Mia...

No way... You never said?

Angel…

You never asked, you were too busy…chucking me out into the street.

Mia…

I'm such a rubbish friend, I don't deserve you xx

Angel…

For once I have to agree with you. See you tonight around eight.

Mia sighed with relief as she placed her mobile onto the table. So Angel was on a date; how wonderful. Her friend deserved so much and she missed her like crazy. The last few days had been brutal, not just the birth of Alex but the whole thing with Ethan and her mum's confession. She sat in the armchair as her baby slept in the Moses basket by her side. With care, she gently bent over and stroked the child's face. Her baby was so beautiful, so perfect in every way.

She thought about her father, then about Sam. She understood now why she had always been his favourite, why he'd been so keen when she'd asked if she could come and stay. It must have been terribly hard to watch another man bring up his child, even if it was his brother. Did her father even know? She thought probably not. Her mother would have cuckolded him, afraid of losing her status and the lifestyle she'd become accustomed to. Not that Sam didn't have money. It was clear after he died that there had been plenty. So what was the reason? Had it just been a fling? Sam was notorious for having one night stands. Perhaps her mother had been nothing more than a conquest? No, she didn't believe that for one second. He may have been a womaniser but even Sam wouldn't have stooped so low. So why hadn't they got together? Was it because of the affect it would have had on Tegan, or even herself? So many questions swirled about in her head, questions that would have to be left unanswered for the time being.

She kept herself busy by getting the washing done and sorting out the house. Although she was tired, she felt as though she was finally on top of things for the first time since the baby had been born. This life she'd chosen was going to be tough, but it appeared she could cope after all. All she needed was her ally, her friend, and then she could get through everything—somehow.

Mia was kept busy, Alex made sure of that. By the time Angel arrived just after eight o'clock, Mia was frazzled.

Angel knocked on the door and Mia let her in. She felt a little sheepish after how she'd acted towards her friend, but Angel didn't appear the least bit bothered.

"Hey," she said as she took off her coat. "How's Alex?"

"Oh, just fine, thanks. My mum stayed over last night and said all the crying was due to Colic."

"So how did that go? Did you two play nice?"

Mia felt a shiver worm its way down her spine.

"Er, not exactly. I asked her to leave."

Angel dropped into an armchair and gave a chuckle.

"You're obviously not that choosy who you kick out of your house. For a kitten you seem to have found your claws."

Mia rummaged through the fridge for a beer, tossed it over and then went and sat next to her friend. "You would have too if your mum confessed that who you thought was your uncle was actually your dad."

Angel, who'd just opened the can and taken a swig, spluttered and choked.

"You're kidding me—right?"

"No, it's no joke. She told me last night."

Angel whistled through her teeth.

"Sam clearly got about a bit."

"Hey, I don't think that's fair."

Angel patted her knee and had the decency to look apologetic. "I'm sorry, I didn't mean to offend. But it's kinda crazy, all said and done."

"Tell me about it. I don't even know why she confessed. I mean, what was the point after all these years?"

"I'm guessing it must be because of Alex?"

"What do you mean?"

Angel shrugged. "I dunno. People do the strangest things when under stress. Maybe she told you because you have a child of your own now. Maybe she thought you'd understand?"

Mia bit her lip. It was true, people did do the strangest things when under duress.

"Anyway," Angel added, "you seem to have taken it better than I would have expected."

"Really, and how would you have expected me to take it?"

"Well, you're not crying and none of the ornaments are smashed to smithereens."

Mia laughed out loud. "Oh, I cried alright. Near floated down the Thames last night I sobbed so hard. But today, well, I've decided that what my mum told me doesn't change a thing. I loved my dad and he loved me. He was, and always will be, my dad. However, learning about Sam's come a little too late. Him being my real father doesn't change how I feel. I'll always love him for the person he once was. Plus, he's here in this cottage to protect me, and I'm grateful for that."

"Has there been much activity since you found out he's your dad?"

"No, actually he's been fairly quiet."

"That's a good sign. Maybe now you know the truth, he's ready to move on."

Mia felt a stab of despair. "But I don't want him to leave. I feel safe knowing he's around."

Angel leaned forward and grabbed hold of her hand. "You must understand that the essence of his soul will

153

have to move on eventually. He won't be able to stay here forever, no matter how much he may want to."

"Is that what's happened? Is he a lost soul?"

"Not necessarily. Only those who have passed over recently get to stay for a while. Those with unfinished business sometimes loiter between worlds."

"Is that what Sam's doing? Loitering?"

Angel let go of her hand and stared thoughtfully.

"Who knows? He's clearly here for a reason, and perhaps his desire for you to learn he was your father was enough to keep him here."

Mia nodded. "You're probably right. Maybe he just wants me to learn the truth, before he has to go."

The light above their heads flickered off and on.

"Speak of the devil… I guess he's not so far away, after all," Angel whispered, her eyes glued to the ceiling.

"Is he here?"

Angel nodded. "Oh yeah, he's here alright, and he's trying to get through to you."

Mia reached out and grabbed hold of both of Angel's hands.

"Will you help him speak to me… please?"

Angel dragged her gaze back to Mia. "If I do this, if I allow him to communicate through me, you can't throw me out if he tells you something you don't want to hear. I'll be too weak because he'll zap my energy and drain my strength for a while."

Mia felt a ripple of guilt slither down her spine. "I don't make the same mistakes twice," she promised, "but are you sure you're willing to do this for me?"

"Yes, I'm sure. Besides, for all we know, this may be the only chance he gets to make contact. Now, close your eyes, and whatever you do, don't open them again until you hear me ask you to. Do you understand?"

"Yes."

"Good, then we'll begin."

Mia closed her eyes as Angel clasped her hands. She experienced a thrum of excitement, yet she was slightly petrified at the same time.

"Sam, if you're there… I am ready to be the vessel between our worlds. Come, say what troubles you so much that it keeps you from moving on."

Silence fell around them, heavy like a stone. Mia heard the clock tick on the kitchen wall.

"Hello, sweet pea."

Mia gasped at a familiar male voice, one she hadn't expected to hear, and it brought a swell of sadness to her heart.

"Sam, is that really you?"

"Yes, although I must hurry, I don't have much time…" His voice was filled with a strange vibration, as though he were stuck down some kind of tunnel.

Mia felt tears slide down her cheeks.

"I miss you so much," she whispered. "Since you left me, there's a hole in my heart that just won't heal. I'm so sorry you died, that you had to leave the way you did."

Sam's voice shuddered right through her, as though his soul had touched her own.

"We have no choice but to go when it's our time, but please don't dwell on something you can do nothing about. Death is greater than all of us, but it's also a part of our essence, of who we are. But, Mia, I'm here to warn you… To tell you you're in great danger."

Mia wriggled in her seat, becoming distressed.

"What do you mean? By whom? Who would want to hurt me?"

A rat-a-tat-tat echoed around the room as someone outside hit the brass front door knocker.

Mia's eyes shot open and she saw Angel jerk back, as though something she'd been holding onto had snapped in two. "Who the hell is that?" Mia hissed in exasperation. "And are you okay, Angel?"

"Yes, I think so," she gasped, fighting for breath. "I just wasn't ready for him to leave my body so quickly."

She tried to recover her composure.

"Who can that be at this time of night?" Mia said, annoyed at the unexpected interruption. "Sam was right in the middle of warning me that I'm in some kind of trouble."

Angel looked a tad sheepish. "Yes, that was bad timing, although I hope you don't mind but I wanted you to meet my new man."

"What? Do you mean your boyfriend's been waiting outside the whole time?" Her anger immediately evaporated. "So that's him at the door? Why didn't you say something sooner?"

Angel shrugged, appeared embarrassed. "I was going to; I had it all planned, but then Sam showed up out of the blue."

"Well, let's not leave him on the doorstep any longer. I'll go invite him in." She rushed to the door, a wide grin spread across her lips at the prospect of seeing this new guy of Angel's. She pulled the door wide and... her grin slid from her face.

"Danny! What on earth are you doing here?"

"What? You mean this is your house?" Her unexpected visitor had the grace to appear uncomfortable. "This wasn't my idea, I can assure you. Angel insisted on me coming over, only I didn't realise her pal was you." An unexpected shiver shuddered down her spine. Was this chance meeting more than just coincidence? She stepped outside, pulling the door closed behind her.

"You mean... you're Angel's new boyfriend?" She rolled her eyes. "Seriously? Does she actually know she's dating someone with a criminal record?"

His gaze froze on hers, his mop of thick black hair blowing gently in the breeze.

"Look, Mia, I've never done you any harm. Just give me a break, eh? Don't badmouth me in front of her."

"But Angel's my best—"

"I swear, I would never hurt her. I'm a changed man. She's made me see the error of my ways, brought the best out in me, made me see sense and—"

"Do you honestly expect me to believe your crock of bullshit?"

But before he could reply, the door flew open.

"Hey, what's going on out here?" Angel asked, eyeing them both closely.

Mia swung round to face her, about to speak, to reveal his true identity, and came smack bang against the happiness shining from her friend's eyes. Mia's words died in her throat, afraid of ruining their friendship. She glared back at Daniel, still wondering if his appearance was all just a fluke.

Angel slipped past Mia and to her boyfriend's side. "I suppose I'd better introduce the two of you. Daz, I'd like you to meet my BFF—Mia."

Is that what he calls himself these days? It's not even cute!

He leaned forward and shook her hand.

"Pleased to meet you," he mumbled, staring down at her feet.

She let out a sigh. "Nice to meet you too, *Daz,* and on which note, I guess you'd better come in."

Mia thought it strange how life never seemed to go as planned. Only this morning she'd hoped to share a few secrets with her best friend only to find she now had another one to add to her ever growing list. Danny, or Daz as Angel liked to call him, had turned into this charming young man Mia didn't recognise. She wondered if the change in him was for real and that he had finally outgrown his brother, but she still wasn't yet convinced.

Later that night, once her visitors had left, Mia tucked her baby into the Moses basket and pondered over the day. So much had happened to her in such a short space of time. She thought about Angel and how happy she'd been in Danny's company. She'd seen a side to him she would never have thought existed: attentive, like a puppy at Angel's heels, soaking up every word she uttered, showing himself to be funny, articulate, even making her laugh.

As she drifted off to sleep, her mind floated towards Sam. She would never be able to explain in words how she had felt the moment she'd heard his voice. Elation just didn't come close. She'd never thought it possible, but now realised death wasn't the end, after all; simply the next stage of being a human being.

She was just dozing when she heard her 'phone vibrate. Without opening her eyes, she felt around for it by her bed, grabbed it and forced one reluctant lid open. She read she had one missed call and a text from Ethan.

The message read: "Whether you like it or not, I'm coming round to see you and the baby tomorrow. I'll be there by 12.30 pm".

She bolted upright. "Shit! Shit! Shit!" She lay back down as Alex stirred. Her mind whirled with scheming possibilities. She had no other choice: she would have to take the baby out for a while despite feeling guilty at her health visitor's warning. Alex would be fine, she thought, and she would make sure she wrapped the baby up warm. She relaxed a little, aware that if things didn't get any easier she would have to leave London and move back home. At least she'd be closer to Tegan and her mum, and Jacob was no longer a threat now that he no longer lived there. Perhaps she could even start up her own business when Alex was a little older. Her brain ticked over, working tirelessly to produce reasons for her to run away. There was nothing left for her here, so why stay? Her job? She could get another one… Tick, tick, tick, her brain went into overdrive, and by the time she finally fell asleep, Alex was crying for the next feed.

The following morning, she woke in a flap. Alex had woken every two hours throughout the night but had now decided to have a lie-in. She glanced at the clock: 10.30 am. *Shit!* She dived out of bed in a panic, worried something was wrong with the baby. But as she approached the Moses basket, Alex stirred. She took a deep breath and calmed herself then jumped into the shower. Within twenty minutes she was washed, dressed and ready to face the day. She smiled to herself. If someone had told her, nine months ago, that she could do that, she would have laughed in their face.

Once awake, she got Alex ready too. It was strange, but she'd never fancied breast feeding. Her mother had put her off, telling her tales of cracked nipples and leaky boobs. Although it had been painful when her milk had first arrived, she'd downed a couple of glasses of Andrews liver salts to dry it all up and it had worked a treat.

Once the bottles were prepared and a bag filled with essential baby items, she went out to the shed to get the pram. Angel had said it was bad luck to have it in the house before the baby was born, but the truth was, there wasn't enough room in the cottage. It was quite a snazzy piece of equipment although it's three wheels made it look more like a tricycle. She opened the back door and a flash of black darted past and she jumped back in alarm. "Damn cat," she muttered under her breath, "near gave me a heart attack." She hadn't seen it in a while, but it looked fatter than she remembered. She hoped it wasn't about to have a litter of kittens. She pushed the pram into the kitchen, deciding it would be easier to go out that same way and so avoid the steps at the front of the house. She placed Alex inside, wrapped up warmly, although the weather was still mild for the time of year. She clipped down the fasteners and was ready to leave by eleven thirty.

The backdoor locked, she shoved the key in her pocket and rounded the corner onto the path—thwack! The pram ran straight into a pair of legs.

"Ethan? What are you doing here?" she gasped. "I wasn't expecting you for another hour."

"So I see," he said, placing his hands inside his jacket pockets. "Going somewhere?"

Mia felt her cheeks burn.

"No, er, yes... I was just popping down to the local shop," she lied.

"Oh, I thought you weren't allowed out for a few weeks yet?"

"Really, and who told you that?"

"Angel."

Angel? Wait until I get my bloody hands on her...

"Really? Well, how am I supposed to eat if I can't get any food?"

"Internet shopping?"

"Okay, wise guy, what if I told you my Wi-Fi's down?"

"I know you have 4G."

"Do you have an answer for everything?" she snapped, watching Ethan glance into the pram. There wasn't much point. Alex was so wrapped up it would have been hard to have said there was a baby in there. She turned the pram about face and headed for the backdoor.

Her nerves had already been on edge but she'd certainly not been prepared to see him. He looked so handsome standing there in that black jacket. Its dark shade made his green eyes appear to shimmer like emerald pools.

"Well, I guess I can do my shopping later," she huffed, "and I suppose you want to come in too?" Without waiting for a reply, she unlocked the door and pushed the pram inside, where she unfastened the cover and took out a few of the blankets, leaving Alex asleep.

"Would you like a cup of tea or coffee?" she asked as she rushed over to the sink and turned on the tap, noticing that her hands were shaking.

"No I'm fine, thanks. I'm just here to see my son." The moment the words were out of his mouth Mia saw red.

"How dare you come in here as if everything's fine between us. You left us, said you didn't want to be a part of our lives, and now you stand here as bold as brass and tell me you want to see *your* son."

Ethan turned towards her, wearing the expression of a guilty man. He appeared to grapple for the right words.

"Mia, I know what I said..." and he pushed his fingers through his gelled hair. "I've gone through so much—"

Mia's fury exploded like a hand grenade. "Do my ears deceive me? *You've* gone through so much? How dare you even say that. You abandoned me. You left me pregnant and ran off to Leeds."

"I know, and I'm so sorry; I don't know what to say. We'd only just met. I wasn't sure what I wanted, and I most certainly wasn't ready to be a father."

"And yet you change your mind the minute you hear you have a son?"

Ethan shook his head. "No, of course not, it just made it all...real. When you said I had a child, that's when reality hit me. I know what I did was wrong, but I realise now that I'm lost without you, without *both* of you."

Something inside her snapped. How could he stand there and say all those things now when it was all too late? She dashed over to the pram and grabbed Alex, clinging onto the baby as though her life depended on it.

"Well, you can't always have what you want," she screamed at him, almost hysterical, and Alex began to cry.

Ethan looked shocked, confused. "What are you talking about? He's as much my child as yours."

"You just don't get it, do you? You see, I lied to you. I wanted to hurt you as much as you hurt me, so I came up with a plan."

Mia clutched her weeping child closer to her chest.

Ethan took a step forward, which made Mia take a step back.

"Stay where you are; don't come any closer."

"What's the matter with you, why are you acting all crazy?"

"If I am crazy, you made me this way. You see, I got the idea from a letter Sam once found, one that was supposed to be about Napoleon."

"What the hell are you talking about, Mia?"

"Deception: it can be such a powerful tool."

"Ethan gasped, his eyes growing wide. "Do you mean the baby isn't mine?"

Mia threw back her head and laughed, but the sound that came out of her mouth wasn't at all amusing.

"Trust a man to think like that," she hissed. "No, the child *is* yours."

"Then what?" Ethan asked, throwing his hands into the air. "Stop talking in riddles. What's actually going on here?"

Mia unbuttoned Alex's coat.

"See for yourself," and when she folded back the material, it revealed Alex to be dressed all in pink. "You don't have a son, you have a *daughter*. Alex is a girl, named after my late grandmother Alexandra."

Ethan froze to the spot. "Alex is a girl?" he echoed, his eyes wide in disbelief. "I don't understand. Why would you tell me I had a son when I really have a daughter? Are you insane?"

"Maybe," Mia spat, "but at the time, your rejection was too much for me to bear. I wanted to hurt you as much as you hurt me."

"How could you do that? Tell such a terrible lie?"

"It's simple; I wanted revenge. You abandoned your child and I wanted to punish you."

Through her tears, she couldn't help notice he trembled.

"You thought I deserved that?"

"Yes, and far more."

He was clearly fighting with his emotions, a look of devastation sweeping across his pale face.

"I realised what kind of man you really are," she told him, her voice a quiver.

His jaw tensed and his hands balled into fists.

"And what is that… exactly?"

"Shallow. You're not the man I thought you were. How could you be? A man who loves a woman would die for her, not abandon her at the first sign of trouble."

"I've tried to explain, to make you understand I was frightened. I didn't know what to do."

"So, instead of talking it through, you ran... like a coward."

His eyes grew hard and he lashed out, hitting the kitchen table with his fist. "That doesn't give you the right to lie to me, to make me believe I had a son when really you'd given birth to a girl. That was just plain cruel."

Mia backed away and sat down on one of the wooden kitchen chairs.

"Then we're even," she whispered, the fight in her gone.

Ethan glared down at her, but then, to her surprise, came and grabbed a spare chair, scraped it forward and sat down.

"I should kill you for what you've done to me."

"Then do it, go on, put me out of my misery."

He stared at her as though considering her proposal before placing his head in his hands. "How did we get into such a mess?" he croaked. "Mia, I'm so sorry for all the heartache I've caused you, for being spineless when you needed me most."

Mia let out a sob. His words had struck a chord, and seeing him torn apart was simply adding to her distress. Like rain after a heavy summer storm, her anger evaporated. Much as she hated herself, she couldn't deny she still loved him. She'd wanted to punish him for breaking her heart, but seeing him like this, a broken man, made her feel ten times worse. Now she wanted to reach out and touch him, to comfort him, to heal the wounds her bitterness and immaturity had caused.

Against her better judgement, she let out a long and heavy sigh. "Would you like to hold her?"

Ethan glanced up, his eyes red rimmed with unshed tears, a weak smile playing about his lips.

"Can I?"

Mia bent over and careful laid Alex in his arms. She watched his face glow, felt that spark of hope ignite once again inside her heart.

"She's beautiful," Ethan rasped, and his tentative finger lightly stroked the baby's cheek.

"Let's start over," he said, his eyes wide, pleading. "Let's be a real family."

Mia nodded. "If that's how you feel, then I'm willing to take it one day at a time," she whispered.

"It is," he insisted, pulling the child closer, "and I promise you, my love, I'm here for good this time."

Chapter 14

"You did what?"

Angel stared at Mia, her cup of coffee halfway to her lips. She put it back carefully onto the saucer. "You told him Alex was a boy? Are you out of your tiny frigging mind?"

Mia sniffed, glancing down at the table.

"Possibly; I had just given birth and was under a lot of stress."

"And he forgave you?"

"Er, well, it was touch and go but yeah, eventually."

Angel grabbed her cup and took a gulp of her hot drink. "I'm actually speechless. Of all the dumbass things I've heard people do, you just earned yourself a distinction. I mean, that was a stupid, and above all, crazy thing to do."

Mia shrugged, sheepishly. "Yeah, I know, it could have been a very different story." She took a swig of her diet Coke, still unable to look her friend in the eye. "At least it's behind us now. No more lies, no more hurt. We can just move forward."

Angel was still clearly stunned. "Well, all I can say is you must have a fairy godmother. Lord knows how you got away with that one. Still, I'm relieved it's all worked out. So what's the next step for you both?"

"We're taking it slow, one day at a time, although Ethan stays most weekends. He helps out with the feeds so I can get some sleep." They were sitting inside a coffee shop in the middle of a shopping centre, a bustle of shoppers all around them. Alex was asleep in her pram.

"I can't believe she's over eight weeks old already. It's strange, so much has happened in such a short period of time."

Mia took another swig of Coke and wiped her mouth with a napkin. "You're not kidding, and at least we're both in a steady relationship right now."

"That's true, you're with Ethan and I'm still seeing Daz. I really think he might be the one, you know... He's such a sweet guy, always attentive and *soooo* romantic."

Mia tried not to choke. *Danny, romantic?* That was definitely a first.

"You never did tell me how you two met," Mia said.

"Huh, oh... it was while you were in hospital. I wanted to decorate the cottage with all those helium balloons so I went to Camden Town. I'd been busy, buying all the bits and pieces, and was heading to my favourite shop, The Fairy Gothmother. Oh, it's a great place for corsets... Oops, sorry, I'm digressing. So, anyway, there I was, minding my own business, when I spot this wallet, half hidden behind a green waste bin. So I picked it up and looked around to see if anyone appeared to have lost it. There was no one acting out of the ordinary so I glanced inside and there, in the front, was his driving licence. In the pockets were his credit cards and right at the back a business card with his mobile number on it."

"Wow! That's incredible; so you rang him?"

"Yeah, and it turned out he was also in Camden Town and hadn't even noticed his wallet was missing."

"So how did you eventually get together?"

"He asked if he could buy me dinner in way of a thank-you. Obviously, I said 'Yes'."

"That's such a cool story," Mia said, glancing at her watch. "I'm going to have to love you and leave you soon, as Alex's due a feed, but there's something I wanted to ask you. Do you still have the spare key I gave you when I was pregnant?"

Angel's brows furrowed. "Sure, do you want it back?" She grabbed her bag, undid the zipper and pulled out the key.

"No, that's not why I'm asking," Mia insisted. "I want you to keep it. It's just in case you should ever need a place to stay."

Angel's expression turned from confusion to concern and she shrugged. "Why would I?"

"Oh, I don't know; in case you lock yourself out of your flat or do something equally stupid."

Angel's eyes narrowed but she accepted her explanation.

"Okay, if you're sure." Her hand waivered before she popped the key back inside the bag.

They both stood up and kissed one another on the cheek. "We'll meet again soon," Mia promised and Angel hugged her tight.

"Call me so we can fix a date. I'm off to meet Daz now though; he's taking me Christmas shopping this afternoon and I don't want to be late." She waved as she hurried for the lift that would take her to the lower car parking area.

Mia sat back down and finished the last of her drink. Christmas was almost upon them and she still hadn't come clean about Danny. She'd hoped their whirlwind romance would have fizzled out by now, but judging by the smile on Angel's face, the relationship was far from over.

She placed the empty bottle and Angel's cup onto a tray, walked over to the counter and handed it to the assistant. As she turned, she caught someone learning over the pram. Her heart skipped a beat and she stopped dead in her tracks. A man, his back to her, was bent over Alex.

"Excuse me, don't—" but the stranger turned around, the words dying in her throat. The man... was... Jacob. Mia went weak at the knees. *What the fuck was he doing here?* He stood tall, leering down at her and his smile turned her blood cold.

"This kid yours?" he said, his eyes straying back to the contents of the pram. Mia sensed he already knew the answer.

"Don't you dare touch her," she cried, pushing her way through the few vacant tables between them.

"Hey, easy, tiger, I just wanted to see what all the fuss was about."

"I said, get away from her!" She reached out for her daughter, but Jacob grabbed her arm.

"Be nice," he ordered under his breath, "after all, Danny has let slip where you live." She felt the blood drain from her face. *Danny had told him? Jesus H. Christ!*

She snatched her arm back, clutched the handle of the pram and scurried away as quickly as her legs would carry her, her mind filled with paranoia. Had he been following her, watching her the whole time? Her fear rose a notch. Would he come to the cottage and torment her... hurt Alex? She reached for her mobile, to call Ethan. At least this was a public place; he couldn't do anything malevolent, not here.

"Hi," Ethan's voice said, "have you finished lunch with your pal already?"

Mia burst into tears. "Ethan, he's here, he came over... He tried to touch Alex."

"Hey, calm down, you're not making any sense. Who are you talking about?"

She glanced around, afraid Jacob might be listening to her every word, hidden from view. "Who do you think?" she said, "Jacob of course." Lowering her voice, she told him, "he was here, just now at the Mall; he approached me and said he knew where I lived."

"Did he threaten you?"

"No... but it's... his manner, the way he talks down to me. He knows how to push my buttons."

"So where are you now? Still in the shopping centre?"

"Yes, but I'm scared he'll follow me home."

"Try not to worry, just make your way over to the information desk and I'll meet you there in about fifteen minutes."

"Oh, thank you," she rasped, relief sweeping over her. She wanted to hide away, to find a dark corner where Jacob couldn't find her and Alex. He made her acutely aware of her own helplessness. Who could blame her after what had happened? He made everyone feel small, vulnerable, like a mouse. He knew only too well that he only had to look at her and she would be quaking in her boots. She was pathetic, unable to stop herself from falling to pieces whenever he was nearby. The truth was: he'd stolen her confidence, along with everything else.

As she made her way across the shopping centre, her eyes darted amongst the mishmash of eager shoppers. So many blank faces passed her by, oblivious to her fear, all busy going about their own business. But her eyes never stopped searching, terrified Jacob would appear out of nowhere and strike like a viper once again. She hurried towards the Information Desk and waited nervously for Ethan to arrive.

The minutes dragged by, feeling like hours as she focused her attention on spotting him through the crowd. The moment he came through the automatic doors, her spirits lifted. Since they'd got back together they hadn't been able to share any close intimacy, not so soon after the birth of Alex, but the second he was close enough, she threw herself into his arms.

"I'm so relieved you're here," she gasped, refusing to let go of him.

"Hey, baby, are you okay?"

"Yes, I am now you're here."

"Good; I'm glad; so let's get you both home," and Ethan's arms snaked around her waist and pulled her close. Mia held him tighter. The safety of his embrace made her want to stay in his arms forever.

"He enjoys intimidating me," she whispered in his ear. "He gets a kick out of frightening me."

Ethan took a step back and stared deep into her eyes. "You need to go to the police, to get this stopped once and for all."

Mia shook her head and grabbed a tissue from out of her coat pocket. "We've been through all this once already. I just can't face going through such a gruelling ordeal only to find out his daddy paid off the jury."

"You don't know that will happen for sure. Besides, we have to do something; he can't keep getting away with harassing you like this."

She lowered her head and grabbed hold of the pram. "Just take me home," she begged. "I can't stand being around here any longer."

Mia knew she had no intention of going to the police. She understood it was the right thing to do but she was frightened, terrified of the consequences. First of all, there was her mother and Jack to think about. Much as it pained her, she didn't want them to suffer any embarrassment. Jack seemed to be a good father, even though he was never around much. Then there was the effect it would have on her mother's reputation, her status within the community. Mia couldn't imagine what would happen if it got out that her mother was related to a rapist? Well, she didn't even want to think about the significance of an arrest.

She was well aware Jacob was using mental abuse against her. Then, of course, there were the physical crimes he'd also committed. She couldn't even bring herself to say the word "Rape" let alone stand in front of a court and admit to his unspeakable crime. To have to relive it all over again... No, it was still raw, too painful... that memory etched on her mind forever... one that would never fade however much time went by.

It was all well and good Ethan telling her to be brave and to speak the truth but *she* would be left to suffer all the humiliation and disgrace, and her young shoulders couldn't carry all that. She just wished Jacob would leave her alone, either that or get hit by a double decker bus!

That night Ethan stayed and they talked into the early hours. It didn't matter how much he tried to persuade her, she would not be swayed into going to the police.

"So you're just going to let him get away with it?" he huffed, sounding frustrated. "As far as I can see, you're always going to be his victim unless you report him."

Mia stared at Ethan from her armchair; they were eating Taco's and waiting for Alex to scream for her next feed.

"It's easy for you, you don't have to live with the shame," she said, wishing he'd drop the subject. Ethan jumped up unexpectedly and grabbed her hand. "Listen, love, he's the one who should be ashamed, not you. While you hide behind this wall of guilt, he walks free to do it again to someone else."

Mia heard Alex let out a hungry wail. She reacted by shaking his hand away and making her way to the kitchen. She didn't want to admit it, even to herself, but she was a coward. Grabbing a bottle, she scooped formula into a few ounces of water and shook it hard.

The wind howled outside like a ghoul in the night, and then, out of the corner of her eye, she caught sight of something flapping against the kitchen window. It was dark outside but the moon was full, creating long creepy shadows that swept across the window pane. *What's that blowing outside?*

She put the feeding bottle onto the draining board and headed straight for the backdoor, switching on the outside light as she turned the key in the lock. The bitter wind wailed as she opened the door, forcing her to wrap the short cardigan she wore around herself before dashing outside. There was a piece of cloth tethered to a length of rope that dangled against the window. Her hair blew wildly about her as she reached up, snatched the material and quickly ran back inside. She swiftly locked the door, the baby still crying upstairs. Slowly peeling back her fingers, her heart hammered so hard she could hardly breathe as she stared into her open hand and at a tatty piece of silken underwear, the colour of champagne. She flung her hand to her mouth, stifling a scream. *Oh, my God, how was this possible?* She felt dizzy, nauseous. She heard Ethan call out her name, and in a blind panic, screwed up the underwear and stuffed it inside the nearest drawer. Her heart was racing so fast she thought she might pass out. What should she do? This wasn't just some idiot playing a stupid prank… and these weren't any old pair of knickers stolen from a washing line. She tried to hold herself together, failing miserably as she stared blindly at the drawer that now contained the pair of knickers she's thrown in the bin the night she'd been raped.

Mia didn't sleep a wink that night, telling herself everything would be alright, her head swimming. She was living and breathing a terrifying nightmare, and no matter how hard she tried, she couldn't wake up from it. She had blocked out so much, tried to forget, but an evil, twisted parasite wanted her to remember every indecent moment. Lying in Ethan's arms, she couldn't get the image of the soiled underwear out of her mind. Why would Jacob be so cruel, though? Clearly he was sick in the head. Did he do this for kicks? And how the hell had he got his filthy mitts on those knickers. Her stomach turned: he must have gone back to her hotel room and taken them. She tried to figure out how, then remembered she'd been away, getting the morning-after pill—her stomach heaved; *the sick bastard.* She snuggled closer to Ethan and heard him moan in his sleep, and curled herself around him, spooning.

Her tortured thoughts moved to Danny. Had he really given Jacob her address after promising he wouldn't? Hell, blood was thicker than water and Jacob could be very persuasive. She cursed herself for being a complete idiot for ever having trusted him. He'd always been at his brother's beck and call, his puppet, so why should she expect anything less? She screwed up her eyes, blocked out their faces and prayed for sleep. The night was long, and much to her annoyance, Alex barely stirred.

The next morning, she arose from her bed feeling exhausted. She went to the bathroom, noticing her eyes looked tired, drawn. She showered, cleaned her teeth and prepared herself for the day ahead, forever mindful of what lurked in her kitchen drawer downstairs. Ethan, oblivious to her distress, rose early to get ready for work.

His kiss was tender as he said goodbye. "Are you going to be okay?" he asked, stroking her long silky hair.

She nodded, "Sure, I'll be fine."

"Do you want me to come over later? I mean, I know it's only the beginning of the week, but if you'd like some company…"

She smiled, "Yes, that would be lovely."

He smiled back and relief spread across his face. "That's great… oh, and don't forget: my mum's dropping by later, to go with you to the baby clinic."

"Don't worry, I haven't forgotten, Alex's due her injections today."

She watched him dash off down the hill and bolted the door the minute he was out of sight.

All morning she was distracted. She got Alex ready for the visit to the clinic and then waited for Bell to arrive in the car. Their relationship had been strained since Ethan's return and her terrible lie, but she was always willing to help with the baby.

The clock struck two and it was soon clear Bell was going to be late. Mia grabbed her mobile and sent her a quick text, then her 'phone rang. "Sorry, I've a flat tyre."

Mia felt the hairs on the back of her neck rise. "Have you got it fixed?"

"No, it's a slow puncture; there's a six-inch nail stuck in the rubber. Can you go without me?"

Mia licked her lips. "I guess," she said, not sounding very convincing.

"Great. I'll wait for the AA, and as soon as it's sorted, I'll meet you at the surgery."

Mia was suddenly on edge. She didn't want to go out of the house on her own but tried to pull herself together. *Phone for a taxi, it's only this once.*

"No problem," she heard herself say. "I'll see you there."

She dashed to the kitchen and 'phoned the number on the wall. Minutes later, she stood by the window, waiting for the taxi to arrive. The moment she saw the black cab trundle up the hill, she grabbed Alex and fastened her into the baby carrier, then dashed outside, locked the door behind her and hurried towards the taxi.

"Are you in a rush, love?" the driver asked, the moment she slammed the door shut.

Mia's heart was hammering in her chest; she was convinced Jacob would accost her the moment she stepped foot out of the house.

"Yes, a little," she admitted. "Can you take me to Woodford Medical Centre please?"

"Righty-oh," he replied, doing a three sixty in the middle of the road. "I'll have you there in a jiffy."

They arrived at the clinic just fifteen minutes later, Mia scouring the parked cars along the main road for any sign of Bell's silver BMW, but there was every other make and model but that one. Having paid the driver, she took the baby inside and waited with the other new mums to go through and have the injections.

When her daughter's name was called, she went in to the waiting nurse. She detested being in a clinical environment; it always reminded her of death. When the nurse grabbed Alex's leg and pushed the needle deep into her thigh, Alex became distraught. Mia wanted to cry, unable to bear seeing her child so upset. She wished Ethan was with her, to hold her hand and make her feel better. She put on a brave face and waited until the nurse gave her the nod to say it was all over.

"She may be a little unsettled tonight," she warned as Mia's fingers fastened up her daughter's pink suit. "I've given her a dose of paracetamol, just in case she develops a fever."

Mia simply nodded, wanting to get her baby out of this sadistic woman's clutches as quickly as possible. She grabbed her things and headed for the double doors that led out onto the street and took a deep breath, cleansing her nostrils of the medicinal aroma which loitered in the back of her throat.

There was no sign of Bell anywhere, so, filled with dismay, she walked to the edge of the road and glanced both ways, hoping to spot her private number plate. She heard a loud whistle, then someone shouted her name. A strong wind whipped the words away and she turned quickly, seeing the back of a man as he climbed into a black Audi. She shuddered, instantly afraid. Who was that? She couldn't see his face, but his build reminded her of *Jacob*, and her feet froze to the ground.

An engine roared into life and the Audi turned onto the road, terror exploding inside her heart, for she still couldn't move. She clung onto the baby carrier, subconsciously protecting her child from the approaching car, trying not to fall to pieces, now shaking from head to foot. It was broad daylight; surely no one would try and hurt her out here? As the car slowed, she couldn't see the driver through the windscreen's tinted sun visor, the passenger side window already sliding down.

She gave a huge sigh of relief and cursed under her breath.

"Danny, what are you doing here?"

He grinned, "Just cruising the neighbourhood. Do you need a lift?"

She hesitated. "No, thanks, I'm waiting for someone."

He tilted his head. "You sure?" and she bit her lip.

"Yes, but can I ask...why you broke your promise and told Jacob where I lived?"

He seemed to feign surprise. "I didn't."

"Don't lie. He told me."

"I swear; I didn't utter a word."

"Then how did he know?"

"I have no idea? Perhaps your mum or my dad let it slip?" He glanced into the rear view mirror and pressed his foot onto the accelerator when another car approached from behind, his brows furrowing. "For the record, I wouldn't always believe everything that comes out of my brother's mouth." The passenger window slid closed and the car's tyres screeched as he drove away.

Mia stared after him. Was Danny really telling the truth? She very much doubted it. He appeared rattled, and what was he doing here of all places, anyway? Did he live close by? She remembered him telling her once that he was moving close to Cockmoor, and this place was only a fifteen-minute drive away.

The toot of a car horn caught her attention and Mia glanced up to see a silver BMW glide into view. *Hallelujah, my saviour arrives!*

Bell stopped the car and jumped out. "I hope you haven't been standing there too long?" and Mia shook her head and waited whilst Bell opened the back passenger door for her and Alex.

"So sorry; the AA are a nightmare. They were over half an hour late." She gestured for Mia to get in the car. "How did it go?"

"Awful; the nurse stabbed Alex in the leg with the syringe and the poor wee mite was so upset. I've managed to calm her down and she's asleep now." Mia fastened Alex in and got in beside her, putting on her own seat belt. "She's probably going to be grizzly tonight, so not much sleep for the both of us."

"It's never pleasant but these injections are vital in keeping your baby healthy, and at least it's all over."

"Hmm, for now, and the bad news is: she has another in a month's time."

That night, whilst Ethan was enjoying bath time with his daughter, the 'phone rang. Mia was quite startled. Up until that moment, she hadn't even realised she had a landline. Bell had failed to mention the old BT 'phone was connected, and besides, she'd always used her mobile.

When it rang, a shrill echo vibrated throughout the house, and Mia pretty much overturned everything in the living room in her attempt to discover its whereabouts. It was found behind the TV, hidden by a mountain of Sam's old DVD's and clearly why she'd not noticed it before.

She was breathless by then, and much to her frustration, the caller rang off the moment she picked up the receiver. She slammed it back onto its cradle and cursed out loud. Who would be ringing at this time of night, anyway? Probably just some idiot, cold calling.

She busied herself tiding away Alex's things, amazed at how much mess one new baby could create. The room was littered with bottle tops, soft toys and blankets. She grabbed a handful of clothes and headed into the kitchen. The 'phone rang again. She dropped the pile of clutter to the floor, dashed back into the living room and grabbed the receiver.

"Hello?"

She waited. "Hello, is there anybody there?"

No answer, but she sensed someone was on the line.

She waited a few seconds and was about to put the 'phone down when she heard someone clear their throat. A shiver shot down her spine. It was a man's voice, but the sound was muffled, making it hard to recognise the caller.

"Hello... Can I help you?"

"Slut's like you always get what they deserve," the voice hissed with poisonous emphasis.

Mia caught her breath.

"How dare you! Who is this?"

The line went dead.

Mia stared at the earpiece as though something disgusting had just wriggled its way out of it.

She threw the receiver back onto the cradle, her mind filled with turmoil, causing her heart to lurch. When she glanced down at her hands, they were physically shaking. How much more of Jacob's perverted pleasures could she take?

Ethan came into the room, carrying Alex who was wrapped in a towel edged with yellow ducklings.

"You look as though you've seen a ghost," he teased, but his smile quickly slipped from his lips. "Hey, you okay?"

Mia stared at him, willing herself not to cry, finally admitting to herself how terrified she was. Events were spiralling out of control. First the underwear, then Jacob appearing out of the blue, and now she was getting weird 'phone calls. If she wasn't careful, she might crack.

She tried to smile. "Wrong number," she whispered, taking Alex in her arms and kissing her forehead. "Clearly some guy who gets his kicks out of taunting women."

Ethan looked appalled. "Did you dial one-four-seven-one?" He grabbed the 'phone himself and did just that.

Mia could overhear the automated message: "I'm sorry, but the service you require is no longer available."

Ethan pulled a face and slammed the receiver down. "What a surprise, and there's no caller display, either."

"Let's just forget it ever happened," Mia insisted, even though she was rattled. "If he calls again, I'll either change the number or have the line disconnected." She managed to smile, the idea certainly making her feel better.

"That's a done deal," Ethan agreed, pushing a clean vest and a pink baby grow into her hands. "You don't need a landline anyhow."

Mia concentrated on getting the baby ready for bed. Alex was now sleeping in the nursery and Mia welcomed the opportunity of having her own space once again. She placed Alex down in her cot and covered her with the blanket she used as a comforter. It was strange: Alex was so small yet without it she wouldn't settle. Some babies had a dummy, other's a cuddly toy, but with Alex it was the blanket with the soft silky edging. The tune to 'Twinkle, Twinkle Little Star' chimed out from the cot's mobile above Alex's head, the gentle music lulling her baby to sleep. She found the tune calmed her own nerves, but more so the thought of Ethan staying the night so she wouldn't be alone in the house.

They didn't stay up late, both tired, Ethan falling asleep the moment his head touched the pillow. Mia lay in his arms, her hair fanned out against the pillow as she listened to the calming rhythm of his breathing. She was so grateful to have him back in her life. Since they had got back together she couldn't fault him. He adored Alex and always made time for her, never moaned about lack of sleep and always helped out where he could.

She stroked along his shoulder blade and down his forearm. He stirred and pulled her close and she willingly snuggled into his chest, the scent of his maleness arousing her. She missed his touch, the intimacy they'd once shared. It was a warm night, both naked under the sheets, and in his sleep his lips brushed against her cheek. Mia lifted her face and kissed his neck. His response was immediate. His arms tightened around her waist and his lips searched for hers. She slipped her hand to his thigh, her fingers, like feathers, brushing against his erection. He moaned out loud, turned her onto her back and licked her breast with his warm tongue. In the darkness, she could feel a rosy blush fill her cheeks, then spread down her neck and across her chest. Mia gasped in delight. Already, she could feel the heat of desire between them. Their lovemaking was a frenzy of passion, each devouring the other, their bodies hungry for one another, and she cried out in pleasure.

Not long after dropping off to sleep, her subconscious roused her from her slumber. A frown tugged at her lips as her dreams slipped from her. Her mind had conjured disturbing images of the lake, a piece of torn underwear floating on its surface, a vivid reminder of what lay hidden away from prying eyes. She awoke fully to find she was bathed in sweat and her skin sticking to the sheets. Careful not to wake her lover, she rose from her bed and headed for the bathroom. Switching on the bathroom light, she stared at her refection in the mirror.

Two dark eyes stared back at her. She let out a sigh, aware they looked haunted, then ran the tap and splashed cold water over her face. *I have to just get on with my life... learn to live with what happened that night.* A tear slid silently down her cheek. How much longer could she put on this façade? Pretending to be brave, to be coping? She reached out, grabbed a towel and wiped away the last drops of sweat from her body. She was cooler now, her temperature back to normal. She wanted to jump in the shower so badly but was sure it would disturb Alex. She folded the towel and placed it back on the rail, switched off the light and headed back through the returned darkness towards the bed.

Her eyes had yet to become accustomed to the gloom that now enfolded her like a shroud. Without warning, something touched her, what felt like the ball of a thumb brushing against her cheek. She sighed, feeling guilty that she'd disturbed Ethan, and reached out to touch him, to give him a hug, but embraced nothing but thin air. Confused, she headed back to bed, surprised to find Ethan beneath the sheets. She turned over and switched on the light. Its orange glow suffused the room, vanquishing all shadows, and Mia could see they were alone, no intruder in sight, Ethan clearly asleep by her side. He stirred, and she quickly turned off the light, not wishing to wake him.

She laid her head back on the pillow, still confused, beginning to doubt she'd really felt someone touch her face. But it had been far too real and she knew she hadn't imagined it, therefore she concluded it must have been Sam. Who else could it have been? Then she wondered how he'd managed to make physical contact? She remembered Angel explaining how Sam was still trapped here, loitering between worlds. The thought that he had touched her, though, without her having realised it was him, saddened her. If that was their last moment on Earth together, she wished she'd been able to cherish it. Inside, her stomach knotted. Anyone who has ever lost someone always wants one last chance to say goodbye properly. Could that have been Sam's only opportunity? She fervently prayed not.

Chapter 15

The next morning, Mia woke up to an unexpected surprise.

"I've taken the day off," Ethan announced with a cheeky grin. "I thought we could go to one of the Christmas markets. I believe there's one being held over the Millennium Bridge at Bankside."

Mia threw her arms around his neck and gave a squeal of delight. "Oh, I would love that," she declared, "just getting out of the house is a bonus these days."

Ethan laughed. "Well, there's always that, plus it'll be fun. There's usually a great atmosphere and plenty to see and do."

"You mean plenty to eat," Mia scoffed, aware of all the great food stalls that would be there.

"I confess, I'm quite partial to a tasty bratwurst," he teased, and pulled her close.

He nibbled her ear and Mia let out a giggle. "Yeah, I bet," she chortled.

Ethan leaned closer. "I've got plenty of sausage for you, baby, any time you want it." She threw her head back and laughed and he grabbed her around the waist and tickled her ribs. She yelled in delight as she tried to push him away.

"Shh, that's enough, you'll wake the baby," she scolded, wiping away tears of laughter.

He finally let her go. "Spoilsport," he muttered and pulled puppy dog eyes.

Alex started to cry. "I warned you," Mia declared with a sigh, and headed towards the stairs, but then turned and stared thoughtfully at Ethan. "Thank you," she said unexpectedly.

He frowned and shook his head. "What for?"

"I dunno... For just being you."

She climbed the stairs, saw to her daughter and within the hour they were on the tube, heading into the city. For the beginning of December, the weather was reasonably mild. Alex was snuggled under a few fluffy layers and Mia and Ethan wrapped up in knitted hats and woollen gloves.

They left the tube at Blackfriars and walked the rest of the way to Millennium Bridge. In the background St Paul's Cathedral dominated the sky. With its mesmerising dome and western towers, its architectural beauty was simply breathtaking and indescribable.

Mia found the walk along the Thames exhilarating. There was an exciting buzz in the air. Christmas was on its way and the market had already drawn a large crowd.

Mia and Ethan wandered in between the pretty wooden chalets filled with lots of festive gifts. Mia was captivated by the delicate glittering baubles, the glass angels and the colourful father Christmases. The smell of Gluhwein wafted in the breeze, the delicious aroma almost intoxicating. The spicy cinnamon helped to give the atmosphere a Christmassy feel, along with the smell of citrus fruits which drifted through the air.

Mia bought a couple of handmade wooden toys for Alex, a piece of unique jewellery for her mum and a bright painted Santa for the Christmas tree she had yet to buy. The market was a wonderland of treasures and Mia enjoyed every moment. By three o'clock they had stopped to have something to eat and to feed the baby. They sat on a couple of wooden benches perched close to the water's edge. The market was still extremely busy, many international holidaymakers visiting for the weekend. Mia soaked up the atmosphere and smiled when strangers peeped in the pram to admire her child. She felt safe with Ethan, untouchable, and enjoyed every moment they shared together. When Alex had finished her feed, they decided to head on home. Mia packed up their belongings and tucked the baby back inside the pram. It was then she realised she couldn't find Alex's comforter. She searched in the baby bag, even down the sides of the pram, but the blanket was nowhere to be seen.

"It was right here," she insisted, pointing to the bench. "I put it behind me whilst I was feeding her."

Ethan looked doubtful. "Are you sure? I mean, she has nearly a half dozen in there. Maybe you just didn't bring it?"

Mia glared at him as though he's gone insane. "Of course I brought it. It's the one she has with her pretty much night and day."

Alex began to cry and Mia threw her hands in the air, exasperated. "See, I told you. Now she won't settle without it."

"But you have another, right?"

"Yes, at home…but that's not the point. It can't have just disappeared into thin air."

"Maybe you dropped it when you got Alex out of the pram?"

"No, of course I didn't. I would have noticed."

Ethan tried to calm her. "Okay, so it's gone. There's nothing we can do so let's head on home before she gets too upset."

Mia felt her shoulders sag. Why was she getting herself all worked up over a stupid blanket? She knew she was being ridiculous but couldn't help it. However, she told herself that she mustn't let it spoil what had been a truly lovely day.

As Mia expected, Alex cried the whole way home. It didn't matter whether she was being held or in her pram. It was as if the baby knew the blanket was missing. By the time they all entered the cottage; Alex had worked herself up into a frenzy. Ethan quickly ran a bath in the hope it might calm her.

"She must have been overtired," Mia exclaimed when the warm water finally soothed her. "I guess it's just been a long day for the little mite." Once Alex was in her cot, Mia tucked the spare comforter a little closer to her baby's tiny body and watched her drift off to sleep. Mia sighed, relieved all was well with the world once again.

With Christmas fast approaching, Mia hardly had a moment to herself. Ethan was now practically living at the cottage and Angel was still a frequent visitor.

All too soon it was Christmas Eve and that afternoon Mia sat in her cosy living room, admiring all she surveyed. A quaint little tree sparkled in the window, a pile of presents stacked underneath the small table upon which it stood. A row of Christmas cards hung on coloured string around the room and an array of pretty silver bells decorated the walls. The cottage was too small for her to go mad with decorations but she still had a few bits of tinsel stuck here and there, something that had once been a tradition when her father was alive.

She smiled sadly. Her dad would have loved to have held his granddaughter, to have seen his own daughter happy and in a stable relationship. Why did Christmas always make people melancholic? She yearned for the years when she'd believed her parents had been in love, when her family seemed so content. All too soon she had realised it was all a sham, that neither of her parents truly loved one another. Her thoughts wandered to Sam. Since the night in her bedroom when she believed she'd felt him touch her face she hadn't seen or heard another peep out of him. She thought it strange that he could come and go without warning, that she never knew when he would play his next prank.

She heard a vehicle pull up outside and jumped up, going over to the window to see who it could be. Sure enough, a delivery van was parked out on the street. She watched the driver get out, go into the back and pull out a parcel. Surprised, she headed over to the door and opened it. A guy in a boiler suit held a large brown parcel in his hands.

"Are you Mia Stevens?" he asked, without a smile.

Mia nodded and glanced down at the package. "Yes, I am, but I'm not expecting anything."

The driver shrugged. "It's Christmas and you're my last drop." With that he pushed the parcel into her hands and headed off back to his van.

Mia closed the door and stared down at the parcel. She hadn't ordered any goods, not even from the internet? She pondered for a few seconds, deciding it must be a Christmas present from Mrs Craig, her old boss back home. They'd kept in touch and talked every once in a while on the 'phone.

Hurrying through to the kitchen, she slid the package onto the table, more than a little curious. Her mind buzzed with excitement. She loved receiving presents and the ones you weren't expecting were always the best. She hunted out a pair of scissors and snipped the string holding it all together. Tearing off the brown paper revealed a pretty blue box tied with a sash of gold. The box looked expensive and she couldn't help but grin to herself, eager to see what was inside. *This must be from Ethan*, she pondered. *He's gone out of his way to send me a surprise present.*

With care, she lifted the lid off the box, afraid she would damage what was held inside. Her gift was covered in crepe paper, the deepest, prettiest blue she'd ever seen. Her nimble fingers touched a corner, and slowly, she peeled back the paper.

For a moment she was stunned, unable to comprehend what she saw, then she let out a gasp and pushed the box so hard it nearly fell off the table. Tears swam in her eyes and she grabbed her throat, taking a step back. She yearned to run away but couldn't drag her eyes from the dead and bloodied cat lying there on its blanket bed, a blanket with an all too familiar soft silky edging.

Her mind flew to the day she was at the Christmas market. She had known all along that the blanket had been there. It had been stolen, snatched from right under her nose, and now lay bloody and tattered before her. She thrust her fist inside her mouth to stop the scream that bubbled in the back of her throat. She recognised the cat as the stray she'd been feeding. Why would anyone do this, be so cruel, so sick? She quickly grabbed the lid and slammed it back on the box, then rushed to the back door and flung it open, taking several deep breaths.

Her mind whirled. When would this terror in her life ever end? She tried to steady her nerves, aware she needed to get the monstrosity out of her house. Taking another deep breath, she went back for the parcel. Keeping it as far away from herself as possible, and almost blind with tears, she carried it to the shed, pulled open the door and slid it in, out of sight.

Once back in the house, the door locked behind her, a stream of tears flowed down her face, and no matter how hard she tried, they wouldn't stop. She grabbed her mobile, to ring Ethan, but stopped herself. He would insist she go to the police. In desperation, and bursting into floods of tears, she rang Angel instead.

"Can you come over," she babbled into the mouthpiece.

"I would, but I can't," Angel gasped. "Don't you remember, I'm at my mum's for Christmas and I'm over two hours' away."

Mia felt herself slide down onto the floor. "Please," she begged, "I need you."

"What the hell's happened," Angel rasped, clearly concerned. "Why can't you ring Ethan?"

Mia didn't reply. Instead, she hugged the 'phone to her chest. She simply couldn't cope anymore. With Angel still on the line, she sobbed uncontrollably. It wasn't just the sickening mess that had arrived on her doorstep, it was everything, everything that had happened over the last eighteen months, and the flood gates opened.

"Mia? What the…" Mia was too distressed to recognise Ethan's voice, to feel him take the mobile out of her hand and tell Angel that everything was alright. She only felt strong arms enfold her, recognised his smell as someone safe. She sobbed hysterically into his chest.

"I'm here," he whispered softly in her ear, rocking her to and fro like a child until the tears turned to whimpers. "Shhh, you're safe now. That's it, hold onto me and let it all out."

She clung onto him as though her life depended on it, still unable to speak.

"I don't know who's caused this," he whispered, kissing her tear-stained cheeks, "but whoever it is, they won't get the chance to do it again," he promised.

That night Ethan packed up all their things, rang Bell and asked if she would come and pick them up. It had already been arranged for them to go to his mother's for Christmas dinner but now it was agreed they would stay for a few days more.

Mia lay on the bed in what had once been her room and listened to Ethan and Bell talking about her, unaware she could hear them. They were saying she'd suffered a kind of mental breakdown, and deep inside she knew it was true. How could anyone go through everything she'd suffered and still manage to carry on as if nothing had happened?

Bell had called the doctor who had prescribed rest and plenty of sleep. He'd given her a mild sedative, then offered to call back in a few days to see if she was any better.

Mia soon drifted in and out of consciousness. She was exhausted, but her mind constantly reminded her that she had a daughter to take care of. She couldn't just forget about her, expect Ethan to look after her. She tried to get out of bed but her legs were like lead and her arms just flopped to her side. Her brain wouldn't engage and so she finally fell into a fitful slumber.

She awoke feeling a little refreshed, although her mouth furry and dry. She opened her eyes to see Ethan sitting by her bedside, a cup of tea in his hand.

"Hello, sleepy head," he whispered, offering her the tea. "How are you feeling?"

She rubbed her tired eyes. "Much better," she lied, trying to ease his anxiety. "What time is it, anyway?"

Ethan stared down at his watch. "Well, it's late and you've pretty much missed Christmas Day."

Mia sighed, feeling her chin start to wobble. "How long have I been out of it?"

"On and off, best part of twenty-four hours."

"I have? That's terrible."

Ethan's expression softened.

"Hey, don't worry, we've saved you plenty of turkey and you still have all your presents to open."

"It's not me I'm thinking about, it's Alex. This was her first Christmas. I wanted it to be special, to be there and witness every moment."

"It is special. We're all together, and Alex is surrounded by her family."

Mia was struck by his sincerity. It was the first time she'd heard him class them as a family.

"I guess we are, although today hasn't exactly turned out as I planned. By the way, where is my little girl?"

Ethan reached out and stroked her hair. "Don't panic; she's fine. She's with Nanny Bell."

He chuckled, "Nanny Bell, if that does tickle me every time I hear it."

Mia wiped away a stray tear with the back of her hand.

"I'm sorry," she murmured, "for ruining everyone's Christmas."

Ethan gently squeezed her hand tight. "You haven't spoilt a thing," he insisted. "We're just worried about you, that's all. I don't wish to back you into a corner but are you able to tell me what happened back at the cottage?"

Mia felt a tightening in her chest. She quickly shook her head and turned her face away. "No, please... don't."

"Sorry, I didn't mean to pry. If you don't want to talk about it, then that's your decision, but please remember I'm here if you change your mind."

She lowered her lashes, not wishing to look him in the eye. "I know; thanks," she mumbled, staring blindly into the teacup.

There was a light tap at the door and she glanced up as Bell entered, Alex cradled in her arms. Mia didn't need to force the beam that lit her face. Alex was her life, and the thought of someone hurting her was like a knife twisting in her heart.

She almost threw the cup onto the bedside locker when Bell came over and placed her baby into her arms. She stared down at her child, so beautiful in every way. Her green eyes stared up at Mia, trusting, loving. Mia cooed over her, almost purred with pleasure when her tiny hand reached out and touched her face. Mia kissed each little finger and tried not to cry. She was feeling very emotional and tears were always lurking close to the surface. She hugged her daughter and brushed her cheek with her own, inhaling the scent of her child.

"Why don't you stay here a few more days?" Bell encouraged. "Just until you feel more like your old self."

Mia didn't have the strength to argue. "Yes, I'd really appreciate that, thanks."

"Good, then it's settled. There's plenty of room and I've already bought a travel cot just in case I ever got the chance to babysit." Mia smiled, she was more than grateful. She didn't deserve such genuine support and could see concern written all over Bell's face. They may not have always seen eye to eye over Ethan, but Bell was here for her when she needed her the most. Bell hadn't even reprimanded her when Ethan had told her the truth about her new grandchild being a girl and not a boy. Mia still felt ashamed. A lie she wished she could wipe away from her memory. She was lucky they had both forgiven her stupidity. Plenty of people wouldn't have been so understanding.

Since getting back together, Ethan had been wonderful, more than she truly deserved. There simply wasn't enough words in the English language to praise him enough. They may have suffered a rocky start in their relationship, but didn't a lot of new couples? Especially ones with a baby thrown into the mix only months after meeting. Somehow, against the odds, they'd made it to the other side. All she cared about was that he was here for her and Alex.

If only... If only Jacob would leave her alone and stop torturing her. She pushed all thoughts of him to the back of her mind. She wasn't going to allow him to ruin her life any more.

Mia really enjoyed staying at Bell's over Christmas. The atmosphere was always chilled and relaxed, and both Ethan and Bell made sure she didn't get overtired. She was still a little fragile, but she told herself she was much stronger than she felt. She hadn't realised how much the upset over the last few weeks had taken its toll. It was as though someone had ripped out her heart and then tried to put it back without the right valves being in place, as though there wasn't enough blood pumping around her body. Her brain was sluggish, lethargic. She needed to pull herself together. She couldn't carry on like this, after all, she had a daughter who needed her.

To keep her mind occupied, Mia threw herself into the festive season, enjoying lots of good food and plenty of wine. Mia was grateful to learn that Ethan had popped back to the cottage to retrieve all the presents she'd left behind. She was pleased because she'd wanted them to have the gifts on Christmas Day. For Bell there was the usual surprises: chocolates, a gorgeous smelling candle and a bottle of her favourite perfume. For her present from Alex, Mia had chosen a handcrafted picture frame, bought at the Christmas market. It held a photo of Bell cradling her granddaughter for the very first time. It was a beautiful memory, one she hoped Bell would cherish forever. Now, she was holding Alex in her arms, her face ablaze with pride.

For stocking fillers, she'd bought Ethan a couple of history books and a few CD's. Her most precious gift to him was a silver necklace with the shape of a baby's foot at its centre. Five tiny toes held a small diamond, and inscribed in italics on the back it read: "*To daddy with love, Alex.*"

Mia watched him open the gift, saw his face light up with pleasure. She could tell he was lost for words. It was his first real present as a father and she was positive he would remember this moment for a long time to come. He came over and kissed her, his lips pressing down on hers for several seconds. When he lifted his head, his eyes were warm with affection. "I love it," he whispered in her ear, and inside she melted.

In return, Mia received a beautiful pair of earrings from Bell, in the shape of dragonflies. She cried out in delight, adoring their delicate silver wings and light blue eyes. She was grateful to Bell for so much and was glad to have her as an ally still.

When it was Ethan's turn, he appeared a little edgy when he gave her a large box wrapped in silver paper. She cocked her head to one side, watching him with sudden curiosity. He was always so chilled, so laid back, but he was obviously concerned she wouldn't like his gift.

She ripped the paper and opened the box to find...yet another inside.

"Is this a game, like Russian Dolls?" she joked, intrigued. She pulled off the lid, surprised to find she was right, there was indeed another yet smaller box inside. As the gift boxes grew smaller and smaller, she tried even harder to guess what his present could possibly be, maybe a new charm for the bracelet he'd bought her for her birthday. After persevering, and with lots of shiny wrapping paper and pretty packages strewn across the floor, Mia at last came to a small red velvet covered jewellery box. She stared up at Ethan and saw a light smile touch the corners of his mouth. Excitement flared inside her stomach; whatever waited inside, she was sure she'd love it.

With great care, she slowly lifted the lid, gasping at the beautiful golden ring inside, a solitary diamond sparkled in its centre. Her brain whirled around, confused.

"Ethan... is this what I think it is?" He reached out, gently peeled the box from her fingers and pulled out the engagement ring, getting down on one knee.

"Mia, I understand this may come as a bit of a shock, and I need to finish university first, but would you do me the honour of becoming my wife?"

Stunned into silence, for the first time in her life she didn't know what to say. Never, in a thousand years, had she expected their relationship to move in this direction, certainly not so soon. They were so very young, yet she'd always known he was the only man for her. Over the last couple of months Ethan had changed, become more contented than she'd ever seen him and he adored Alex. Her heart burst with love for him.

"Yes, of course I will," she cried. "And I'm more than happy with a long engagement." She dived into his arms, feeling the sincerity of his warm embrace.

"I love you," he whispered.

"I love you too... always and forever."

Chapter 16

Mia stayed at Bell's a few more days but once she began to feel better the urge to return home became overpowering. Bell had been really supportive and helped her in so many ways but it was time to go back and start her life over.

She didn't mind admitting; she was a little scared. Unsure whether Jacob might have left her another unwanted gift during her short absence. Dread tugged at her heart but despite everything she'd gone through, she vowed she wouldn't let him win.

They arrived home after supper on New Year's Eve. They'd spent the whole day with Bell but now Alex was worn out and ready for bed. It was Mia's turn to bath her, and give her a last bottle before settling her down. They both took it in turns and Mia loved the time she shared with her daughter.

As soon as she was tucked up in her cot, Alex drifted off to sleep, her tiny cupid bow lips sucking something that wasn't there. Mia bent over and kissed her forehead. Her daughter never stirred, already in a deep slumber. She crept out of the bedroom, left the door ajar and descended the stairs. Ethan was waiting for her in the kitchen with a glass of wine.

He kissed the tip of her nose, then held her close. She was unaware how her cheeks glowed pink, or how beautiful she looked in the soft glow of evening light.

"Our first New Year's Eve together," he whispered softly. "Who would have believed we'd be sharing it together after the fiasco I put you through?"

Mia let out a sigh, sipped her drink. "I guess it was a test of love which you almost failed. But, thankfully, you realised sex with me was the best you'd ever had so you came back with your tail between your legs."

Ethan grinned and the warmth of his smile reached his eyes. "Oh, is that how you see it? More like, I finally allowed you to get those sharp kitty cat claws into me."

Mia drew her pencilled eyebrows together. "Oh, I get it, you let me ... huh? As I recall, you did all the running."

"Pfffff, excuse me ... I did nothing of the sort and I'll have you know, I'm quite a catch."

Mia's laugh mocked him. "Seriously? Why I never realised you were so deluded."

Ethan, chuckled and pulled her close, nuzzling her neck. "Well, the way I see it, we should celebrate. A New Year is about to begin and we have made the first step to being a married couple." He turned, his brow furrowed. "Don't you have any Champagne?"

Mia clicked her tongue in the roof of her mouth. "No, sorry, I guess I haven't had much to celebrate lately. Won't a bottle of wine do?"

Ethan shook his head fiercely. "It most certainly will not. We must start off as we mean to go on – in style." Mia shrugged her shoulders. "I guess the local shop might still be open, you can perhaps grab a bottle there?" Ethan dived over to the other side of the kitchen, snatched his coat off the back of a chair, headed for the front door.

"I'll be back in two ticks," he announced, "because only the best will do for my fiancée." Mia beamed, it was the first time she's heard him use the word fiancée and it sounded good, made everything between them real.

"Okay, I'll go and run a bath, see you when you get back."

As soon as he was gone, Mia headed upstairs. She checked on Alex and then went into the bathroom, turned on the tap, sprinkled expensive bath salts into the water, a Christmas gift from Bell. The bath soon filled turning the water a luxurious turquoise.

She turned off the taps, nipped into the bedroom and closed the curtains. As she undressed, she heard a noise, someone was coming up the stairs. *Wow! That was quick, Ethan's back already.*

194

She headed towards the doorway in her bra and panties, a light smile dancing across her lips.

"Hey, do you have superpowers, only you got back in record time." She reached the top of the landing and a gasp left her lips. It wasn't Ethan, it was a stranger, a man, wearing a balaclava. She opened her mouth to scream but the intruder lunged, pressed his gloved hand over her mouth. She fell to the floor and he landed on top of her, winding her. She was petrified, her brain unable to piece everything together, to think clearly.

She tried to get up but he forced her back onto the floor, grabbing both her hands. He sat on her legs and the next thing she knew he pulled something out from underneath his jumper. She recognised it at once, a roll of duct tape. *No,* she tried to scream out, but his hand was crushing her face. She started to cry, terrified, watched him tie both her hands together, bound them so tight it hurt. His heavy weight pinned her light frame to the ground. She was finding it difficult to breath but she daren't lose consciousness. Before she realised what was happening, he slapped her hard across the face, almost knocking her senseless. Immediately she felt a pressure against her mouth and realised he had covered her lips with the duct tape too. She started shivering with fear. This was not a common burglar; this was someone who'd planned his every move and intended to hurt her.

Although she couldn't scream, she still tried to make a noise, desperate someone might hear. Her tongue pushed at the duct tape but it never moved, it was stuck fast. She watched him climb off her body and immediately kicked out. He laughed at her, his voice muffled by the mask. His laughter freaked her out and she shuffled on her back, trying to get away from him, but he bent down, picked her up with his huge hands as though she was just a bag of feathers.

He crossed the bedroom floor, then threw her onto the bed. Mia's eyes grew wide. There was something about him, the way he moved which seemed familiar. Her mind filled with thoughts of Jacob and she began to whimper. Tears of terror poured down her cheeks, a sob catching in her throat when she saw him unzip the flies on his trousers. Her body shook violently as he pulled her legs apart. She tried to fight him, to get away, but he was far too strong. Her eyes searched blindly for a weapon, or a way of escape, but all her attempts were futile.

A flash of bright light made her turn her head and from off the dressing table, she saw one of the large glass perfume bottles rise into the air. It hovered barely a second before it was flung clear across the bedroom. It flew with such force that Mia heard a loud crack as it hit her assailant on the back of the head. He howled in pain, turned sharply, fists clenched.

Mia saw her chance to escape. She lashed out with her feet and kicked him hard, just behind the knee. He went down like a sack of potatoes and she wriggled to the edge of the bed, jumped to her feet. She rushed past him, but his hand shot out like a viper and grabbed her ankle. He yanked her so hard she fell onto the floor, her hands still bound, unable to save her. She rolled onto her back, adrenalin pumping through her veins and with her free leg, used the flat of her foot to kick him in the face. She heard the crunch of bone, saw blood splatter all over the carpet. For a second her attacker appeared disorientated and he let go. As soon as she was free, she bolted for the door.

Her breath was ragged as she ran down the stairs two at a time. She kept glancing back praying he would stay down long enough for her to get out of the house. She was frightened for herself and for her daughter. She needed to get him away from Alex, to keep her safe. Panic stricken she headed straight for the kitchen door. She dived over, her hands grabbing the handle and shaking the door violently. Her heart skipped a beat, the key was gone. She heard footsteps behind her and before she could run, strong arms came out of nowhere and grabbed her from behind, jolting her neck and spine. She gasped, her fingers flying to her throat. Although her hands were still bound she tried without success to free herself from his clutches.

There was a noise, a familiar sound and Mia realised Ethan must be home. Desperate to warn him, she jabbed her attacker hard in the ribs. He wheezed, bent over double but his fingers remained around her throat. Like a startled deer, she watched Ethan step into the kitchen. Their eyes locked and in that moment she saw her terror mirrored in his own.

In a split second, Ethan lunged. He tried to grab hold of the intruder, but the man was much stronger. He turned sharply, punched Ethan straight on the jaw. He stumbled, crashed into the table and chairs. He appeared dazed but when the intruder dragged Mia into the living room, Ethan threw himself at her attacker. He knocked him sideways and in the confusion Mia broke free. She fell onto the floor, turned to see Ethan grab hold of the mask, tearing the balaclava off the intruder's face.

Mia was frozen to the spot, unable to believe her eyes. Her attacker wasn't Jacob or Danny for that matter, it was … Jack, her mum's husband. She stared opened mouth as he tried to punch Ethan once again. She glanced at the small table which they'd almost knocked over, saw the bottle of Champagne Ethan must have put down when he got in, slide to the floor.

Like lightening, she dived over, snatched hold of the bottle. She jumped to her feet and without hesitation, brought it down on the back of Jack's head. Smash! The glass shattered, Champagne and a stream of bubbles exploded high into the air. Jack dropped to the floor, blood pouring from a large gash in the back of his skull.

Mia dropped the jagged neck of the bottle onto the hearth as Ethan dashed to her side. He gently dragged the tape from her mouth before untying her hands.

"Are you hurt?" he asked breathlessly, he hugged her when she shook her head, placed his jacket around her trembling shoulders.

"Thank God you came back when you did," she sobbed. She glanced down at the body lying on the carpet. She couldn't tell if Jack was breathing. "Oh, no, I think I've killed him."

Ethan cupped her face inside his large hands, forced her to look at him.

"Don't worry, he's still alive. You've simply knocked him unconscious."

Mia didn't believe him. He was so still, almost lifeless. There was a tiny movement then she heard a murmur escape his lips. She tried to let out a sigh of relief but already a part of her wished he was dead. She turned on her heels, dashed upstairs and came back seconds later with the duct tape. With Ethan's help, she rolled Jack onto his back, tied his hands and then bound his legs together.

"I'm calling the police," Ethan said flatly. He reached inside the jacket she wore for his mobile. She watched him dial the number. Aware the animal lying before them needed to be put behind bars as quickly as possible. To think … she'd believed it had been Jacob doing all these cruel things to her and all along it was … Jack. She still couldn't believe what had just happened, unable to comprehend why he wanted to do such terrible things to another human being. Her mind came up with its own conclusion. Jacob had told his father what he'd done to her at the lake. It made perfect sense. Jack had come here to take a piece of what his son already had. She shivered uncontrollably, her nerves in tatters. Bile filled her mouth and without warning she vomited all over the carpet.

Ethan held onto her until she'd finished, then he quickly went into the kitchen and came back with a bowl of hot soapy water and a cloth. He mopped up the mess, all the while his eyes never left her face.

"Just take deep breaths," he soothed, trying to ease her distress. "Just stay with me baby, we'll soon have him out of here."

Her tormentor finally came round, with difficulty he sat up. He was no longer the nice guy she once remembered.

Instead he'd turned into Jekyll and Hyde. He stared at her, his eyes feasting on her bare flesh and then he started to laugh, the sound was that of a madman.

"You're nothing but a filthy whore," he spat, "doing your best to entice my boys. I saw the way you wiggled your arse at them and then tried to play the innocent."

Mia simply couldn't believe her ears.

"Are you mad? I've never done anything of the sort. Don't blame me for your sick mind. You're vile, a predator, and I promise you will pay for what you've done."

Jack continued to stare at her, his dark eyes filled with disdain. "Don't give me that crap. I could see you were a tramp, a prick tease, the moment I laid eyes on you. Jacob said you thought you were a cut above the rest. Always trying to play hard to get. Then at the wedding you humiliated Danny, so I made it my business to teach you a lesson you wouldn't forget."

Mia found she couldn't breathe. Suddenly she saw everything with complete clarity.

"Do you mean it was you, not Jacob who followed me down to the lake?"

His eyes turned to slits and his breath hissed between his teeth.

"You seem surprised? But it was your mother who insisted that I make sure you were alright. I'd seen you taunt my boys, watched you play the maiden in distress. You made it easy for me, going out there … *alone*. I followed you down to the water's edge, crept behind a few bushes so you couldn't see me. There was no one around, everyone else enjoying the party and you were like a cherry … so easy to … pick." He puckered his lips, blew her a kiss, his eyes mocking her.

"You sick bastard, you were in a position of trust."

Without warning, Ethan punched him straight in the face.

Mia gasped but Jack simply chuckled, wiped away a trickle of blood from the side of his mouth with his tongue.

His eyes switched back to Mia. "How do you think people like me get close to their victims? Without trust we'd always be on the outside looking in."

Mia could feel anger bubbling in her belly. He was almost boastful and showed no signs of remorse. "So it was you all along? You're the one who hung my tattered underwear across my kitchen window? And it was you who sent the dead cat wrapped in Alex's blanket?"

Mia caught Ethan's stare, she'd have to explain about the cat which was still in her shed later.

Jack simply laughed out loud. "Who else would have the balls to pull a stunt like that? You were so easy to manipulate and I enjoyed the game of cat and mouse. I had my eye on you from the first day I met you." His gaze dropped to her breasts. "I just wanted your body all for myself and once I'd had a taste..."

"Your mother paved my way every time. She'd already confessed to me about her affair with Sam and still had his telephone number in her address book, even after all these years. Then when Alex was born and she arranged for us to stay, before I left, I simply helped myself to a spare key. It was that easy and it was as though I'd hit the jackpot."

Mia flicked her gaze to the piece of broken glass lying in the hearth. For a second she contemplated thrusting it into his jugular. So many emotions rose up inside her like a giant wave. He deserved to die and killing him would give her closure.

A siren wailed outside, and she instantly felt guilty for having contemplated murder.

"The Police are here," Ethan stated, heading over to the window. "I think you'd better check on Alex and then go and put some clothes on before they come inside."

It was at that moment Mia realised the seriousness of the situation. That Ethan had probably saved her life— along with Sam, of course. If Ethan hadn't come back when he did, though, and tackled Jack, she would probably be dead. There were no words of thanks she could say. She could only love him even more.

Chapter 17

The next few days were like confession time for Mia. She had to explain herself to so many people that in the end her head hurt like crazy. With Jack's arrest, it appeared an influx of women came forward to give statements, their own experiences spanning some thirty years. Many had been abused during his time in the music industry, whilst others had been at his mercy simply through his wealth and affluent connections.

Mia had been given no choice but to provide a statement to the police. It had been the hardest thing she'd ever endured in her entire life. Reliving her ordeal took its toll, but with the support of her family and Ethan, she made it through the darkest days. Although she'd washed away the evidence of what Jack had done to her that fateful night, the underwear she'd hidden in the drawer of her home was given to forensics. This solitary item not only held his DNA but enough evidence to prove he was guilty of his crimes against her. Against such an abundance of mitigating evidence, he was charged with multiple counts of rape and faced a lifetime behind bars.

It is also said that the apple doesn't fall far from the tree. Mia hadn't told the police about the sexual harassment she'd suffered at the hands of Jacob. Somehow, compared to what his father had done, it seemed she could forget if not forgive. It wasn't that she didn't want to let him get away Scott free, it was more she couldn't deal with yet another brutal round of intense questioning. Now that she knew the truth, that Jacob wasn't the one who'd raped her that dreadful night, she could bury the memory once and for all.

However, the day Jack's arrest became public, Jacob simply disappeared. He took his passport, cleared out his bank account—Danny's too—and was never seen or heard of again.

With no money of his own, Daniel didn't have time to sit on his laurels. Instead, he got himself a job as a bouncer at a prestigious London nightclub. The money wasn't bad, either. The flat he owned was in joint names with his brother, so at least he would always have a roof over his head. With Jack facing a life of imprisonment, the press soon became involved. It meant that Mia had to come clean with Angel about Daz and tell her the truth about him being her stepbrother. Angel had been furious at first, but given that she loved Danny and that he was the light of her life, it finally made it easier for her to forgive her best friend.

Now it was time for Mia to do some forgiving of her own. Her mum was due to come and stay with her for a few days whilst Jack waited for his trial. Sandra had blamed herself for what had happened to Mia, and within twenty-four hours of his arrest, had filed for divorce.

She arrived at the cottage driving a brand new Mercedes convertible. Ethan, who'd been warned of her imminent arrival, quickly made himself scarce and stayed over at Bell's.

It was the first time Mia had seen her mother since her confession about Sam, and what Mia believed to be her darkest secret. She'd had time to think things through and had decided to let the past stay exactly that, and learn to live with the truth.

Mia had also invited Tegan to come and stay, but it seemed impossible for her to get away, with her never-ending work commitments. She'd recently moved out of her flat and in with Jonas. They'd talked about making a life together, especially now Tegan had been promoted to deputy ward manager. She deserved a good fellow and Mia believed Jonas was certainly the man for the job.

Sandra arrived at the cottage, immaculately dressed as always. The two-piece she wore was made by Chanel, her shoes from the same designer. She parked the car, then dragged out a large suitcase.

"How long are you planning on staying?" Mia cried.

Sandra waved her hand dismissively. "It's not all mine, most of it's what I've bought for Alex. I've been to New York on a shopping spree. I thought I'd spend as much of Jack's money as possible before the lawyers get involved." She made her way over to her youngest daughter and pecked her lightly on both cheeks. "It's been such a long drive and I'm parched; any chance you have a bottle of Chateau Du Cedre lurking around the house?"

Mia grinned; she'd got two in specially. "By the way, mum, we've got company tonight. I've invited Angel over for dinner, to give you both the chance to meet one another."

Sandra gave a thoughtful tut. "Is that the girl who's dating Daniel?"

Mia raised her eyebrows. "Don't be like that, she's nice, you'll like her, and I want you to get to know her."

Sandra grabbed her hands, so they were facing one another.

"Of course, darling. From what I hear she's been more of a mother to you than I have of late."

Mia tried not to let her jaw drop. Was her mother actually being nice?

Sandra gave a sudden pout. "Where *is* my granddaughter? Surely she isn't in bed already?"

"Yes, she is. She's such a great little sleeper, always in bed by six o'clock."

"And she sleeps right through?" her mother asked, astonished.

"Pretty much, although she usually has me up by seven most mornings."

"Well, at least she'll be as bright as a button. I was just hoping for a quick cuddle, but it appears I'm far too late."

"Don't worry, you've got all day with her tomorrow, and believe me, by the time six o'clock comes around, you'll be glad of the break."

Sandra took her suitcase to her room with the help of her daughter and then changed into something more comfortable. When she came downstairs, Mia offered her a large glass of wine.

"Mmm, delicious, and just what the doctor ordered," her mother cooed. "Mia, about Jack… I'm so—"

"Mum, please don't talk about him. It wasn't your fault and I don't want him spoiling out time together. It's over so let's just get on with our lives."

Mia put her arm around her mother and they headed into the living room. They both made themselves comfortable and waited for Angel to arrive. Mia had already prepared the food for dinner so there was nothing else to do but sit and relax. She'd lit several large candles to create a mellow mood and the room basked in yellow light. Sandra made herself comfortable in one of the large armchairs whilst Mia curled herself on the floor at her feet, like a languid cat.

"What time's Angel due to arrive?" Sandra asked, taking a sip of wine.

"I told her eight. Thought it would give you time to settle in before she gets here."

Sure enough, just as the kitchen clock struck the hour, there was a knock at the door. Mia jumped up to answer it.

"Hey, you made it. Come on in."

Angel crossed the threshold, took off her leather jacket and hung it up on a hook in the vestibule, along with her bag. She was wearing a dazzling pink and black corset finished off with a frill of white lace. Mia felt completely underdressed. For sure, Angel certainly knew how to make an entrance. Her legs were encased in fancy fishnet tights and she wore heavy black boots. Mia thought she looked amazing.

"Is that one of the creations from the Fairy Gothmother?" she whispered in her ear.

Angel grinned, showing a row of perfect white teeth, her new shade of black lipstick just as dark as the last.

"Yes, Daz bought it me for Christmas. I haven't had the chance to wear it yet so I thought tonight would give me the perfect opportunity."

"You look divine," Mia purred, "although I'm not too sure what my mum will make of you."

Angel walked straight into the living room where Sandra was waiting. Mia watched her mother carefully. She was always so cool, so aloof, but there appeared to be genuine warmth in her smile.

What had got into her? This genteel creature must be an imposter?

After they'd been informally introduced, Mia guided her guests into the kitchen, the table already set for dinner. She'd made a tasty beef stew in a crockpot, using a recipe taken from the Hairy Bikers cookbook.

"So you work alongside Mia at the auction house?" Sandra asked, helping herself to a small dollop of mash potato.

Angel nodded as she offered up the mixed veg. "Yes, I've been there a couple of years. My mum used to go to university with Ethan's dad; that's how I got the job."

"And what about Daniel, how did you meet him?"

Mia rolled her eyes. Her mother was giving Angel the third degree.

"Mum… please… don't be so damn nosey."

Sandra frowned. "Don't be silly, darling, I'm just showing an interest in your friend."

Angel chuckled. "It's fine, honestly. It was the day I bought the helium balloons to decorate the cottage for Alex's homecoming. I'd been to the spiritualist church in the morning and was heading to my favourite Goth shop when I found Daniel's wallet wedged behind a wheelie bin."

"And that was the start of a beautiful relationship?"

"Yes, I guess so. He's a great guy and the only man I've ever met who didn't freak out when he heard I talk to the dead."

Sandra shook her head, clearly confused. "Sorry, you've lost me. Do you mean you're a medium?"

Angel paused, her fork halfway to her mouth.

"Yes, that's right. I sometimes go to the spiritualist church so I can join in with the sittings, to ensure my gift doesn't go rusty."

Out of the corner of her eye Mia saw her mother squirm.

Clearly Angel had seen it too.

"Does it make you feel uncomfortable that I can communicate with those in the afterlife?"

Sandra shook her head. "No, quite the opposite. I find the whole subject fascinating." She took a large gulp of wine.

Mia felt a shiver of concern. Why was her mother acting so weird?

Angel placed her knife and fork onto the table.

"I sense you've lost someone whom you loved deeply?"

Sandra nodded and wiped her misty eyes with a linen napkin.

"Yes, and I've been trying to find someone to help me connect with them, but so far they've all been fakes."

Mia stared open-mouthed at her mum. This was the first she'd heard of it. She tried to catch Angel's eye but she was staring straight at her mother.

"Would you like me to try and help you? I can't promise anything, but I'll give it my best shot."

Mia thought it best to interrupt. "You don't need to do that," she insisted, trying to give a signal with her eyes that said it wasn't such a good idea.

Angel ignored her and continued to focus her attention on Sandra. "Really, I don't mind. I can see it's important to you, and besides, that's what my gift is meant to be used for."

Sandra came alive with excitement, so much so, she almost knocked the wine glass out of her own hand.

"Really? That would be wonderful, but I do hope I haven't put you on the spot. That was never my intention."

"No you haven't and it would be a pleasure. So, let's finish our meal, clear away the dishes and then we can get down to business."

As soon as dinner was over, Mia pulled Angel to one side. "What do you think you're doing?" she whispered. "Don't you think one ghost in this house is quite enough?"

Angel smiled. "Chill out, your mum clearly needs closure with someone she loved and I'm going to try and help her."

"It's apparent to me who that is. She wants to talk to Robert, my dad, and if you don't get through she'll be devastated."

Angel let out a sigh and then reached out and gave her a hug. "Relax, and stop getting so worked up. It's what your mum wants…needs. I can see she's holding onto a lot of grief, and if I can help release some of that sorrow, then she'll be able to move on." Before Mia could argue, Angel headed into the living room where Sandra was waiting. Mia felt exasperated. Angel was such a strong personality and had clearly made her mind up.

Mia followed on her heels, the living room aglow with the candles she'd lit earlier. To her surprise, they appeared to flare, burn brighter as Angel entered. Mia felt a shiver run down her spine. She really didn't want her friend accidently making a connection with any wayward spirits. She was afraid one of them might latch onto her and stay here indefinitely. Angel headed for the vestibule and seconds later she came out carrying her bag.

"Can we all sit on the floor and hold hands," she asked, sitting down, cross-legged. She rummaged inside the bag and pulled out a wooden bowl and an object that appeared to be made of dried hay, resembling a scarecrow's hand. The fingers had been woven together and then tied with a piece of hessian.

Sandra came and sat beside Mia, making a small circle. Angel glanced up and held their gazes.

"I can see by your faces that you've never seen one of these before. Although I'm not a witch, I often use incense when I hold a séance. These magical objects are known as a suffumigation and are filled with frankincense and sandalwood. When burned, they attract spirits and helps them materialise."

Mia was blown away. Did Angel always come prepared? Her mother was clearly in awe of her too, Mia could see that by her expression. Already, Mia noticed excitement dancing in her eyes. She had never seen her mother appear so full of hope and it gave her a youthful appearance.

Angel borrowed a lighter to set fire to the suffumigation. A dry woody aroma of pine mixed with lemon filled the air, followed by an earthy aroma. Angel inhaled deeply, the air already filled with a light spiral of smoke, the scent rich and powerful.

"I must start with a prayer of protection," Angel explained, staring straight at Mia. "I wouldn't wish any unwanted ghost or negative spirits getting through. Please close your eyes and hold hands. Once I say the prayer I will invite Sandra to call upon the person who she wishes to communicate with. No one must open their eyes unless I ask you to do so, and whatever you might feel, do not break the link that will bind us together by letting go. Do you both understand?"

Mia and her mother both nodded and obediently closed their eyes.

"Very well, then we'll begin... Dear spirits, like the candles that surround us, let the light from the flames radiate love and protection to all four corners of this room. I ask at this time that all negative energies be banished from this space. Bathe us in your purity and love, turning this dwelling into a sanctuary. We are here to listen to your gentle guidance; please join the circle and honour us with your presence."

The room went cold and Mia felt a shiver worm down her back. Although she was a little frightened, she kept her eyes firmly closed.

Angel spoke again: "Sandra, who in the spirit world will you call upon this night?"

Mia felt her mother's grip tighten around her fingers and her voice was shaky when she spoke.

"I wish to speak to the only man I ever truly loved. I call upon Sam Stevens." Inside, Mia's stomach flipped, not expecting this. It hurt that it wasn't her father and she felt confused, but tried hard to be understanding and to respect her mother's wishes.

From out of nowhere a gentle breeze lifted and blew against Mia's face. Her mother gasped out loud.

"He's here," Angel announced softly, "and he says he's ready to answer any of your questions."

Her mother's grip of Mia's hand tightened.

"Sam... is it really you? I... I... just wanted to say I'm sorry. Sorry for not believing you when you said you loved me. You'd always played the field, had scores of women falling at your feet, and I just thought you were being nice, trying to do the right thing by me when I told you I was pregnant.

"I never wanted it to turn out the way it did, yet over the years I watched your love for me turn to hate. You were filled with such bitterness it made it hard for me to tell you that I still loved you. I would have left Robert, you know, if only we'd both been a little stronger. Please believe me when I say I will never forget the time we shared together. I still treasure your love and I'm thankful for our daughter. Please, can you find it in your heart to ever forgive me?"

Mia felt a lump grow in her throat. She hadn't realised just how much her mum loved Sam. She heard a strange sound, as though Angel was exhaling all the air from her lungs. Then a voice she recognised filled the air—Sam's, and it came in waves, rolling inside her head like breakers hitting a sandy bay. Inside, Mia's own spirits soared. Sam was really here, in this room, with them.

Her mother's hand trembled in Mia's.

"Sam is that really you?"

"Yes, Sandra, it's really me, and I'm touched that you've asked to speak with me. You're right, I was filled with bitterness, but there is no place for such empty emotions here. I have already forgiven you. There is no point in dwelling on the past. Since crossing over, I have learned that holding onto such sentiments only brings heartache. I am truly sorry that I didn't fight harder for you. I should have, I realise that now.

"Instead, you gave me a beautiful daughter, one I am so very proud of. She's grown into a fine woman and I can now rest easy knowing she's at last safe from harm. Let go of the past, Sandra. Live your life to the full each and every day; simply never look back. Love will bring harmony into your world and then you won't have to wait until you die to find inner peace."

Mia felt a single tear slide down her cheek. Her mother sounded heartbroken, and Sam's words made everything seem so final. She didn't want him to leave; he would always remain a huge a part of her life.

"Don't go," she whimpered, her voice pleading. "Can't you stay here with us, just for a little while longer?" A coldness touched her skin, and to her complete surprise, she felt a gentle kiss upon her lips.

"Goodbye, sweet pea," Sam whispered in her ear. "It's time for me to go; I am no longer earthbound and cannot stay, but remember, I will always watch over you." She gently pushed herself forward, trying to hold onto his caress for as long as she could. There was a loud sigh and then she felt Angel pull away, breaking the connection.

Mia's eyes shot open and she saw Sam's energy disperse into the air. It was like watching tiny orbs fly upwards, towards the ceiling, before disappearing. Her eyes flickered for just a second before she glanced down to see Angel slumped on her side on the floor. She hurried to her, and the second she touched her, Angel let out a moan.

"Are you hurt?" She gently pulled her up into a sitting position.

"No, I'm fine, just a little zapped, that's all."

Mia glanced over at her mother. Her face wore a shadow of sadness, and so she reached out and grabbed her hand. "At least you got to talk to him one last time," she said encouragingly.

Sandra gave her a weak smile and wiped a stray tear from her eye. "You're right, and we made our own peace, which is all I ever wanted."

Mia sighed. "I wonder if we'll ever get the chance to speak to him again?" Angel shook her head, frowning. "I'm afraid not; he's moved on to an astral plain we can never reach. Take comfort knowing he's in a better place."

Mia pulled her mum and Angel close, wrapping her arms around them, forcing a group hug. "We still have each other, though," she whispered, kissing them both on the cheek; "a bond that will last, always and forever."

Epilogue

After that day, Mia did exactly what her uncle had said: she never looked back. Once Jack was imprisoned, ordered to serve no less than two life sentences, life for her went back to normal. Although she would never forget the harrowing experiences she'd suffered at his hands, she promised herself she would not let him ruin her life.

Indeed, things had changed for the better. Her mother was no longer the bitter, twisted woman she once remembered. Since the séance, she radiated warmth and had a lighter step wherever she trod. She had kept so much pain hidden deep inside that she had lost the ability to love. Receiving Sam's forgiveness was all she had ever wanted. It was also a wakeup call, now realising what a truly wonderful family she had, wishing to cherish them always.

Mia was extremely content, surrounded by those she loved. Her mother had moved house, to be closer to her, and Tegan and Jonas were thinking of relocating so they wouldn't be quite so far away. Finally, those threads of happiness were woven together to make her life complete.

Angel and Danny were still going steady and were now living together. Danny had the sense to rent out the flat for a substantial amount of money, and after just a few months had raised enough collateral to invest in the night club. He turned out to have quite a head for business and within two years owned a night club of his own. Mia couldn't be happier. To see Angel settled in a loving, stable relationship, and Danny content at being his own man, no longer in his brother's shadow, meant more than words could say.

Today, Mia is sitting in the garden, drinking iced tea. The summer has been hot and sticky but she's enjoyed being outdoors, nonetheless. She hears the back door open and turns quickly on the lounger to look. She relaxes and smiles brightly when she sees it's Ethan.

"I thought I'd find you out here, lazing about with your feet up." He comes over and gives her a lingering kiss.

"Isn't that what summer days are all about?" she says when he finally pulls away.

She stares into his beautiful green eyes. It doesn't matter how often she sees them, they still melt her heart. The rocky road she'd embarked upon is now smooth and paved with gold. She understands what real contentment is made of: to be with the man she adores, the one who loves her unconditionally, the father of her child—her hero.

"I have a surprise for you."

"You do? What is it?"

"Well, it wouldn't be a surprise if I told you," and he throws his head back and lightly laughs as she watches him, amused.

"I love you."

"I love you too."

Mia picks up Alex from the bright red tartan blanket she's spread across the lawn. She holds her close, cuddling her.

"Okay, I'm ready; so what's the surprise?" Placing his arm around her, he guides her to the house and into the kitchen, where he points to something lying on the table.

"So what's that?"

"Have a look."

She hesitates, unsure. Why does he seem so excited?

"Go on," he urges, "it won't bite."

Mia takes a hesitant step forward. It appears to be a document, filled with lots of legal jargon.

"What's all this about?" and she turns towards him, brows furrowed. "It has this address on it?"

He shakes his head. "You really know how to deflate a moment, don't you?" he teases, dashing over to join her. "Can't you see it's the deeds to this cottage?"

"So?"

"So, it has our names printed on it?" He points close to the bottom, where their names are etched in black ink.

"Yes, I see, but what does it all mean?"

He reaches out, gently turning her towards him, and she can see excitement dancing in his sea green eyes.

"It means, my darling, that this house belongs to us," and he grins as her jaw drops.

"You mean…"

"Yes, mum has signed the house over to us."

"No way!"

"Yes way. All that's needed is our signatures and then the lawyer can seal the deal."

Mia is truly stunned. "But why?"

"Because she wants to give us as an early wedding present."

"But this house… It was Sam's…and he left it to Bell."

"And now it's ours. It's what mum wants. She said it should have been yours in the first place."

"Really? Did she say that?"

He nods. "Yep, and naturally I agreed."

She throws herself into his arms, almost squashing Alex between them who lets out a loud squeal of protest.

"Sorry, sweet pea," she whispers, kissing her cheek, turning an admiring look at her lover, marvelling at his handsome features and how much she adores him.

"So this is now *our* own home?"

He bends forward and kisses her passionately on the lips.

"Always and forever."

Biography of Lynette Creswell

Lynette was born in London but moved to Burnley, Lancashire, when she was a small child. From the tender age of five, she was raised by her grandmother and given books to help keep her quiet. Lynette found she had a passion for reading and subsequently started writing once she began school.

Years later, Lynette's husband encouraged her love of writing by buying her a laptop. Within days she had created memorable characters and exciting realms such as *The Kingdom of Nine Winters*, in readiness of a fantasy trilogy.

Her first novel, *Sinners of Magic* was published in 2012 and was soon followed by *Betrayers of Magic* and *Defenders of Magic*.

Winner of the 2014 'Write On' Competition, affiliated by East Coast Pictures, saw one of her acclaimed short stories adapted for TV. Lynette's success as a writer continued to flourish when she published a romantic short story through Solstice Publishing. *The Witching Hour* is only available via Amazon Kindle.

Lynette now lives in North East Lincolnshire and is looking forward to writing more women's fiction.

You can find out more about Lynette on her website: www.Lynetteecreswell.wordpress.com
You can also follow her on Twitter: @Creswelllyn

Printed in Great Britain
by Amazon